A RIGHTEOUS KILLING

A RIGHTEOUS KILLING

BARBARIAN PRINCESS™ SERIES BOOK 02

MICHAEL ANDERLE

DISRUPTIVE IMAGINATION

THE A RIGHTEOUS KILLING TEAM

Thanks to our JIT Team:

Rachel Beckford
Zacc Pelter
Peter Manis
Dave Hicks
Jackey Hankard-Brodie
Diane L. Smith
Dorothy Lloyd
Jeff Goode
Paul Westman

If I've missed anyone, please let me know!

Editor
SkyHunter Editing Team

*To Family, Friends and
Those Who Love
To Read.
May We All Enjoy Grace
To Live The Life We Are
Called.*

— Michael

CHAPTER ONE

"Get to it before it can go underground again!"

Cassandra felt like her warnings fell on deaf ears. The twins had a habit of getting into trouble, more obsessed with plunging into a fight than ensuring they were in a position to win. It was the story of their lives, she felt, and they would have been dead or behind bars months before if she hadn't stepped in to protect them from themselves.

There was the fact that they had a tendency to protect her from herself on the rare occasion when she needed it, but there had to be a reason why she had stuck with them for as long as she had.

The ground shuddered again and she flicked her spear around and tried to judge where their quarry would emerge since they had allowed it to go under again. She had begun to get a feel for how the creature moved. All three of them had been surprised by how fast it was given the fact that it was larger than the average draft horse and covered in hard stone armor.

She'd never seen anything like it, which meant they had to learn about it while they fought it. Probably the most important part of dealing with the creature was surviving it, which meant

1

they had to stay away from the tail. It was weighted and bone spikes protruded. With the speed at which it could move, they had to be aware of it constantly since it could crush or impale them at any moment.

And then there were the claws and the teeth, although neither were quite as fast-moving as the tail. Still, one wrong move from any of the three of them, and they would have to dig the massive claws out of their chests.

Or the teeth. Both were used to dig into the earth with annoying speed and enabled it to move through the tunnels it created. Cassandra assumed the whole area was crisscrossed with the damn things, which made it impossible to find out where it was going and where it would come from once it was out of sight.

A hint of a tremor in the ground gave her something resembling an idea. She jumped up on one of the rocks and drove her spear into the dirt, looking for the beast.

She missed. The magic of the spear allowed it to cut deep, almost halfway up the haft, before she decided it hadn't struck her intended target.

"Over there!"

Tandir's warning made her yank her spear out as rocks burst up and spewed in all directions from where the beast emerged. The heavy claws grasped a nearby boulder and threw it smoothly at where she stood. She was forced to dive out of the way to avoid being crushed.

"I hate this bastard," she whispered as it pulled itself completely free of the earth. The powerful jaws dug into another handful of boulders, which crumbled. "I seriously, truly hate it."

Aside from how its body was plated with rocks to protect it, the fact that the damned beast almost looked like a dragon didn't help matters either. She couldn't tell if the rocks were growing out of it or if it had somehow managed to find a way to make them stick.

They were probably in the damn nest too. It couldn't dig tunnels that quickly, not without showing some sign of it on the surface. It likely merely laid in wait for something to wander past and when it did, the beast barreled from underground, ate it, and retreated.

And that was precisely what would have happened to the traveling group of—she assumed—bards and performers and it would happen to them if they didn't kill the fucking monster. They had no idea how far its nest went, and the group had concluded that they were safer around the three who fought the creature and so far, she and the DrakeHunter twins did the job of keeping it away from the band well.

The only question was how long they would last. The damn aberration dove underground the moment they came close and continued to try to catch them off-guard, by surprise, and generally from behind.

She grasped her spear a little tighter and her eyes widened as she watched the creature move.

"Oy, you big rocky bastard!"

A javelin hammered into its shoulder and barely dented the armor, but it did provide the time Cassandra needed to position herself to attack. Another javelin struck it in the head but bounced off. It was almost impossible to land a clean hit on the creature's head with its short neck that shifted it too quickly. Its eyes twisted independently of each other, which made it impossible to catch unawares.

"I've never heard of this kind of creature before," Bandir shouted and hefted another javelin as the creature dove into the dirt again. "I don't suppose that if we killed it, we could find some pompous academic who could name it after us?"

"The pompous academic would name it after himself and say it's our name in some dead language." Tandir shook his head. "There's no time for that. We'll make some sketches and name it after ourselves."

"That all happens after we've killed it," Cassandra called and again tried to determine where it would emerge. "Anytime the two of you decide to do so, let me know and I'll start to take this fight seriously."

"You take everything seriously." Bandir pointed his javelin at her. "That is your problem. Every time you're out in the glory of battle and swing your spear or sword into the face of some man or beast, you have to understand the absurdity of the situation and laugh at it. Enjoy and savor it."

"The alternative is that you are miserable while doing what you end up doing the most and the best," Tandir added.

It was odd that they would have something resembling a point on the matter, but she would be dead before she admitted it.

"Yes, and you recall that your standard of fun was what almost killed you two when we met?" She inched to the right and narrowed her eyes until she thought she had a good idea of where the monster would push through next. "And I had to introduce both of you to the ground before you came to your senses. Or did I hit you too hard and you lost all memory of the event? Because I would be more than happy to relive it for the benefits that the reminder will have for you."

She jumped to the left and growled with effort as she drove the spear down as far as it would go. This time, there was considerably more resistance and more importantly, it felt like the whole earth bucked under her in reaction.

It was a result she should have anticipated along with what followed. The rock and boulder-covered ground kicked and suddenly, the tail was out again and the spikes and weight of it hammered into her shoulder. It was not an accurate strike, but even a glancing blow made it feel like her shoulder was on fire.

The amulet she wore was enough of a defense to prevent her arm from ripping off, but it heated against her chest after the strike. It had begun to do so ever since her battle with Belladonna and she did not want to consider precisely what was happening to it. Perhaps the damage done had affected the amulet itself and it was about time she found a replacement or a repair for it.

But that was a matter for later. For now, while her shoulder was painful, she was able to regain her feet as the creature pushed above ground. The spear had gone in through its back and punched through its armor and into what she assumed were the ribs. It wasn't enough to kill it, unfortunately, but it was enough to wound it and prevent it from burying itself again.

The twins realized this and threw the last of their javelins to ensure that it would not attack Cassandra while she was recovering. It uttered a roar and fixed its swivel eyes on the brothers as they rushed forward and shouted battle cries. A mace hammered into the creature's jaw and an ax swung toward its neck.

It was easy to see that the former did more damage than the latter. The beast was stunned by the mace and showed absolutely no reaction as the ax buried less than an inch into its neck.

The jaw snapped viciously and both twins were forced to stumble back. It was more than capable of killing them even though it was wounded and jarred, but its attention and both its eyes were locked on the pair, which left her the opening she needed.

She pushed to her feet and drew her sword before she surged forward and hoped that the tail, which flicked this way and that, would not accidentally hit her.

Luck intervened and created an open path for her to leap onto the boulder formed on the monster's shoulder to drive her blade into the gap between the rocks on its spine.

It was not enough to kill it but this time, she felt bone snap and with a pitiable cry, the beast collapsed, all use of its legs suddenly removed.

There was still a danger, and she drew her sword out and yanked the spear free as well before she inched closer to the neck.

With a deep breath, she drove the spear through until it came out the other side and buried itself in the dirt below.

That was enough to finish it, although she checked quickly for any signs of life before she pulled the weapon out.

"I think we have no need to revisit old glories," Tandir muttered and brushed the dust from his shoulder. "Just because you enjoyed that fight doesn't mean we need to hear about it."

"I assumed you would feel that way." Cassandra pulled a cloth from her pocket and ran it over the length of the spear's copper-shod haft and the head to wipe the blood away. It never ceased to amaze her how easy it was to clean the weapon. It must have had something magical about it, but it seemed to repel any blood, dirt, or grime that might have clung to more ordinary weapons.

"Besides, many folk around these parts are more than willing to inflict violence upon us," Bandir pointed out as he began to collect the javelins they had flung at the beast. After the way it buried itself, all that was left were the heads with the hafts snapped off. It was cheaper to replace a haft, though. "I am sure they would adore it if we were to turn on each other."

"And here I was, thinking the two of you didn't mind some friendly battling."

The twins darted her a glare that told her they knew that she knew what they were talking about but she was being intentionally difficult. All she had to offer them was a cheeky grin as she checked the beast again to ensure that it was dead. She remembered Skharr talking a great deal about how mages and alchemists put a great amount of stock in certain beasts and were willing to pay coin for certain elements of the monsters that were slain in battle.

He was told that there were standing contracts on the bits and pieces, and there were always those interested to find out about how certain creatures worked and didn't work. It was likely another source of revenue that could be tapped if they knew where and how to do so.

Cassandra did not know where or how, and from the twins' lack of interest in the body, they likely didn't know either. Either that or there wasn't enough coin in the process to make it viable since they were as far away from civilization as they could get.

Although she supposed that depended on how one defined civilization. She had higher standards than most. For the rest of them, there were handfuls of hamlets in the region with inns, taverns, and other dens that catered to all the different vices that were called for.

It was better than nothing but fell well short of what she considered civilization. Even their little hamlet that had begun to form on Draug's Hill fell short of that lofty standard. Still, there was much to fight to defend in this region of the world.

And much to defend them from. Finding a small band of performers on the same road they were traveling was merely the latest in a series of situations that needed their attention.

Bandits, brigands, treacherous sellswords, and the occasional monster were the sum of what they had dealt with since she'd killed Belladonna. They took in the meager rewards and tried to determine whether they would be able to survive on what could be gathered this way.

The riches looted from the dead Herald's army had disappeared quickly and soon. They were looking at weapons and armor that needed the time and coin required to repair or replace them.

"I always thought that returning to Edge's Rest was a mistake," Cassandra muttered as they left the dead monster and moved to where the group was still waiting for them, allowing their horses to remain where they were.

Strider in particular looked about as bored as a horse could be, and she found she was better able to tell what the horse thought simply from the subtle signs of its body language.

Or it was merely a case of wishful thinking. She liked to think she was in tune with the animal she had chosen for a companion, and perhaps her mind made it seem so without any real reasoning to it.

At some point, she would try to find a way to determine if the horse could understand her.

"Do you have any idea how long we have been without real drink, food, and other amenities?" Bandir asked and raised an eyebrow. "I would say we were due a visit to the place."

He made a good point. Then again, they all needed a little time away from the constant fighting for their lives. There were no promises that would happen when they reached Edge's Rest, but at least there was the guarantee that if they did need to kill someone, that person was likely to be laden with coin that they hadn't had the chance to spend yet.

Nomads, bards, minstrels, and the like were the types they hadn't thought to encounter in the region, but if they were to find such a group, it made sense that they would be in danger and that they had to step in to do the saving.

"Do you think they'll be willing to offer us some kind of reward for helping them?" Bandir asked as they approached.

"Look at them," Cassandra answered. "Threadbare clothes, flea-bitten horses and mules, and barely enough food and supplies to take them to Edge's Rest. I am not sure what they could afford at this point."

Still, it was always a good idea to check and see if there was anything that could be earned from their efforts. There was no point in letting word get out that they were willing to work for free, or folk would start to think they could be called in to solve any and all local disputes that needed intervention.

As they approached the group, she could see the reason why they had not started to move yet. One of their number had been injured—by the beast's claws judging by the state of his mangled shoulder—and was in desperate need of help. A few had gathered around him and spared a few drops of healing potion, but it wouldn't do him much good.

"He needs real care," she muttered and nudged a handful of the bards and folk aside as they approached where the man lay on the dirt, groaned softly, and writhed in pain.

She dropped to her knees beside him, inspected the wound, and after a moment, placed a piece of cloth on it to stem the bleeding. There were things she could do and preventing a man from bleeding to death was easily one of them.

Once she was sure he would not pass away while she applied her ministrations, she laid her hands on the man, closed her eyes, and let her power seep into him.

It had been a long day and there was no certainty as to how her body would be impacted when she started the healing process. To stop in the middle of it would only make his condition worse.

Still, as she started, it was clear that the wounds looked gory but were shallower than they appeared at first glance. The only real danger was that an artery had been nicked by the claws, which explained the blood. Once the nick was sealed, it was a simple matter to see to it that the rest of the superficial wounds were tended to.

The fact that she had saved them all and then magically healed one of their number was likely the reason why none of them spoke as she pushed to her feet again. Her knees wobbled slightly at first, but nothing to suggest that she would not be able to continue on her journey.

As she stood again, Cassandra realized that the twins were no longer at her side and had decided instead that they would make an attempt to pry a few claws and teeth from the dead monster.

And it looked like they were about to fight each other over it.

"You take from the left, I take from the right." Bandir growled in annoyance. "That has always been the way."

"It has not. You only want me to take the claws that are the most worn from the fighting and the digging."

"Consider it an even trade since the shit is missing four teeth on my side."

Cassandra narrowed her eyes and approached them. "Have you faced a creature like this before?"

"No," both answered quickly.

"Then how are you able to establish who gets which side?"

"Well…" Tandir let his voice trail off as he motioned to the creature. "We might never have seen a beast like this before, but if you look at the skin and the jaws, it's clearly a drake of some kind. A sand drake, I think we'll call it. Or a stone drake."

"You have no imagination," Bandir interjected. "What happened to us naming it after ourselves?"

"Batandir is no proper name for a beast like this. It needs to describe it and prepare anyone else who might choose to fight it for what they will face."

"Batandir is an odd name. Tabandir is not."

"You're an idiot."

"Wrong," Cassandra cut in. "You're both idiots. Why are you taking the teeth and claws?"

The twins exchanged a glance before they both looked at her.

"Well, it's a kind of drake, right?" Bandir reminded her.

"And your point is?"

"That we are DrakeHunters. The name is not merely a name taken by our clan. It means something. Most of the drakes were driven away from our homeland, but we are still honor-bound to kill those we find and collect some form of proof to show all those who might question our courage or that we killed it."

"And you are arguing about which side you think is the most valuable?"

"It'll appear as though he took on a more fearsome beast while I waited in the back to handle the smaller creature like a weakling."

"Neither of you is a weakling but both of you are dumbasses." Cassandra snorted and shook her head. The group of pilgrims appeared to show a few signs that they were ready, willing, and able to continue. "I wonder if it comes from your father's side or your mother's. Or maybe the two of you lay claim to it all on your own."

"Fuck that, it's the both of them," Tandir retorted as they approached the man who appeared to be the leader of the group.

He was a tall, gangly-looking man whose beard was sculpted into an odd cone shape and his hair flowed down his back. As they appeared to be a group of traveling artists, she assumed he put on a show of being a master magician.

She had seen men and women who had no skill in magic perform feats that even she had no explanations for. Despite many mages turning their nose up at such acts, she found it fascinating.

Still, when away from the act, he appeared less of a commanding presence. Cassandra assumed it had to do with the realization that there was little he could do with his arsenal of tricks to beat back the monster that had tormented them.

"Your arrival was fortuitous," he stated with a nervous chuckle. "I fear that the monster would have killed all of us in minutes had you not appeared."

His accent sounded well-bred and straight out of the empire capital, but when she listened closely to it, subtle inconsistencies told her it was an affectation. She guessed that he felt a great deal more comfortable speaking in common intonations.

"There was no trouble," she answered. "You were in need and we helped, although if your thanks were to come in the form of coin, we would not turn our noses up at it."

"We would like nothing better than to pay you for your help," he said and his voice told her that she would not like what came next. "But you'll find us equally desperate. We have been traveling toward greener pastures and the locals pay little for entertainment. I assume it has something to do with how desperate folk are to survive here. Our riches are few and made even less given that the damned sand drake killed a few of our horses and drove more off in the scuffle."

Cassandra sighed and glanced at the twins, who were still arguing as to who got which parts of the drake. Neither had heard what the leader had called the beast, although sand drake did seem like a fairly obvious name. She would consider that to be it until it was proven otherwise.

"You're on this road so can I safely assume that you'll make your way to Edge's Rest?"

"For a stop to resupply and hopefully earn a few coppers to see us on our way again."

"The road there is fraught with dangers." She shook her head. "And even more so for those who are slowed by the lack of horses. I think we should probably see to it that you are behind some walls before we part ways, although I cannot guarantee that you will be any safer inside Edge's Rest."

"Why would you do that?" His tone was almost suspicious like he couldn't understand why someone in her position would volunteer to do more work when it was clear that they could not pay for what had already been performed.

"I put myself through a great deal of personal injury and more than a little annoyance to ensure that you survived the attack of the…sand drake, was it? I intend to see to it that my time and effort were not spent in vain. You will survive, at least until we reach Edge's Rest."

"They will?" Tandir asked. The twins must have come to some kind of understanding over who would take what, which enabled them to join the conversation.

"They won't pay us so why should we care?" Bandir added and made Cassandra roll her eyes.

"I just fucking explained it. Do you need me to go through it again?"

"You might have explained it in a way that made sense to you, but I didn't understand a word of what you said."

"And how is that my problem?"

"It isn't until you volunteered my and my brother's services."

"You said you would follow me through thick and thin and find battles and glory in it for yourselves. If you had told me it would involve this much whining and complaining about the paths I happen to choose, I would have left you to your own devices. We put in the work to ensure that these people survive their trip, at least until they reach Edge's Rest. Or would you see all the effort you put into killing the damn drake go to waste at the hands of the odd desperate bandit or deserter?"

The twins thought about that for a moment and finally, both nodded in agreement.

"It would be a damn shame to see such glorious efforts wasted."

"And the loss of life as well, wouldn't you say? The deaths of so many fine folk would be a terrible thing as well."

After another shared glance between the two, they nodded again.

"Yes, I suppose so."

They were a work in progress, she was willing to admit, but so far, they seemed very willing to learn. Or at least failed to put up much of a fight when she presented them with morality that might not have been quite what they were brought up to believe but was perhaps closer to what she was coming to think of as the ideal barbarian.

Maybe she was a naive idiot, but Cassandra couldn't think of a better concept for a former paladin who called herself a barbarian princess to bring into the world. Perhaps it was time for her to make some kind of change in the world, even if it was only to the minds of a couple of barbarians who needed a little purpose in life.

More than a few would call her mad for the attempt, but it didn't matter. She would do what she needed to do, no matter what kind of ideals others forced on her.

"Right, then," she muttered and motioned the pair forward as they mounted again and checked their weapons to make sure all was prepared. Her attention returned to the leader. "I hope you don't mind but since we are heading in the same direction, I would say it would be best for us to travel together. You know, to ensure there is no possibility that any of the other dangerous locals take advantage of your current state. I wouldn't want to see all our work dealing with the creature to go to waste."

"I know. You have told me this and I heard you say the same to your comrades. Are you sure it would be no trouble?"

"It means that we would travel a little longer than we would have otherwise but aside from that, I can see no issues presenting themselves. Most of the bandit groups that travel these lands tend to not fight with each other since they would prefer to avoid losing too many of their members even should they win. They know better than to commit to battles against troops who look a little too well-defended."

"And…how would you know this?"

"Experience and common sense. The kind that would have told you to avoid traveling these roads without an escort."

"Well, I'll be sure our bards put some time aside to sing of your glories. The Barbarian Princess and the DrakeSlayer Twins."

"DrakeHunter, as I recall."

"Truly?"

"As far as I can remember it."

"Well then, the DrakeHunter twins and their Barbarian Princess. I think there is the kind of ring to it that would see your fame spread."

"I'll have to take your word for it." Cassandra attached her spear to the saddle before she mounted Strider and settled as the leader appeared to spread the word that they would move out soon.

"It's not that far to travel," she said, almost justifying her decision to the twins as they approached her. "We planned to reach

Edge's Rest in the middle of the afternoon and now, we'll reach it by nightfall. There's nothing more to it than that."

Tandir grinned. "You notice how we're not arguing with her and she still feels like she needs to make her point to us."

"I am merely anticipating your complaints and providing you with a proper explanation before you ask. Or better, before you stop yourselves asking and allow bitterness to enter your souls."

"As you say."

CHAPTER TWO

Edge's Rest was much as she remembered it. There was the little port at the river through which most of the town's business was transacted. The rest came by the roads heading to the top of the little cliff overlooking the river, where walls had been erected to keep out any of those who might have reason to invade.

Unless, of course, they came in large enough numbers. Then again, there were more reasons to prevent anyone from invading Edge's Rest than only the walls. For one thing, most of the town's inhabitants were armed to the teeth and each one was ready to give their lives to ensure that their little center of vice and depravity was waiting for them when they had coin to spend.

Cassandra wondered what exactly would happen to any army that tried to take it, only to find the entirety of the town was populated by bloodthirsty, ruthless, and experienced sellswords. It would be an interesting day, that much was certain.

"Night has fallen," the leader of the group lamented. "We'll have to find a place outside the walls to make our camp."

"I think you'll find the gates are open well into the night around these parts," she told him and nudged Strider forward. "Most of those who ply their trades inside the walls are those who prefer to do so absent the light of the sun to reveal them. It would be poor business for the guards to close off all entry to those who would pay for those wares."

"Have you been here before?"

"Once, in passing. I would say the little town has its appeal to those who have a mind for distraction from a bleak existence. The types who come here are those who prey on anyone they can in the world, never knowing how or when their death might come, only that there is the very real possibility that it might be the next day. It makes any coin they have on their person wasted if it is not spent as quickly as possible."

The man watched her for a moment, narrowed his eyes, and tried to decide if she was telling the truth, why, and where the rant had come from in the first place. She decided she didn't owe him anything in the way of an explanation and clicked her tongue to push Strider forward again. It would take them some time to decide where they would spend the night and as far as she was concerned, the merry group could find their own merry way.

Something about their incessant music and positivity wore on her nerves, even if she didn't want to break it to them like that precisely. There was enough time and space for them to go their separate ways.

Cassandra still wasn't sure why she'd agreed to have the sand drake's head strapped to Strider's back, but that was the concession the brothers had agreed to. She had no idea why her horse had to carry it. Taking trophies had never been something she had cared about, but perhaps some kind of power could be gained from displaying kills in such a fashion.

Although she wasn't sure how long the skull would remain intact. After a few more days, there would be nothing but a rotting mass of flesh and bones behind her. She hoped they had a plan for what they intended to do with it. Otherwise, she would simply drop it and let it rot elsewhere.

The guards appeared to grasp their weapons a little tighter as the group approached. She wondered if it was because they recognized her, the twins, or both, or they weren't sure how to handle the group of bards and entertainers who would soon fill the town with their music. Music, she realized, that would tell stories about her and the twins. Perhaps that was how they thought they would pay them for saving their lives. It was an interestingly annoying experience.

It might explain why Skharr hated it so much. Bards detested sticking to the truth of events and would talk about how the Barbarian Princess struck a real dragon from the sky with her magic spear or something. It wouldn't be so bad if folk didn't suddenly decide that they would expect such feats from her everywhere she went.

Still, the guards gave them no trouble as they slipped in, and she noticed that they were not the only ones looking at the approaching group. It seemed that all eyes were on her and the twins. Perhaps they were looking at the sand drake head, but it seemed like they stared directly at her. Cassandra wasn't sure how to explain it and wasn't sure that she wanted to.

They would find a way through this, especially since it seemed the groups weren't hostile toward them. A few even saluted them on the way in. There was no telling what prompted that, but it was an interesting development. She'd assumed that they would have made a few enemies in the town given that they had thinned the numbers of those who caused trouble in the region.

She couldn't help inching her hand to her sword despite the salutes. A part of her couldn't help the feeling that they would attack at their first opportunity.

No attack came, however, and they parted ways with the small band of merry travelers, although she had a feeling they would run into each other again before too long. She had her hand on her sword anyway as they dropped from the saddle, handed their horses into the care of the gate stables, and began to approach the closest inn.

In the oddest of oddities, it appeared as though they were popular somehow. When folk saw them enter, they raised their mugs and glasses.

"Barbarian Princess!"

"The DrakeSlayer Twins!"

"DrakeHunter twins!" someone else corrected as she walked through the crowd.

"I was about to say," Bandir muttered. "How is it that the folk around here know about us?"

"We have sent a good many of the local bandits, sellswords, and misfits to their graves over the past few months," Tandir answered as they reached the bar. "I would have assumed that it would have made them hate us instead of greeting us with salutes and raised drinks."

"I had the same feeling," Cassandra said and sat. "I thought we would have to fight through throngs of wronged shits who lost brothers, sons, and friends to our exploits."

She raised her hand to engage the interest of the nearest tender who would be able to deliver a few drinks to them. By now, she was in the mood for something rich and red that would immediately suffuse her body with a little relaxation. Since her battle with Belladonna, she'd had a difficult time of it and she needed to find ways to settle her spirits.

"You won't pay for a drink here," a man said behind her.

Cassandra turned quickly, ready to start a fight, and expected to see a group of men who had their weapons drawn.

She was half right. A group of men stood ready but with their coin purses, not their weapons.

"What?"

"There's much to be said about the Barbarian Princess and the Twin DrakeHunters who follow her," the man closest to her said and inched away when he saw her hand on her sword.

"We would be more than willing to ensure that you do not pay for a single drink this night if you were to share a few of the stories. Not much in the world we live in isn't about killing, raiding, and raping everything and anything that comes across their path. I would say something a little more heroic is in order."

She narrowed her eyes, released her blade, and looked around the group to notice something she hadn't seen before. It was odd, but it almost seemed like this rag-tag group of errant mercenaries, sellswords, and other evil-doers genuinely looked up to her— or at least a concept of her that had been told to them through a variety of stories.

"How can I say no?" Cassandra asked and gestured for the man to take a seat. He was quickly followed by a woman and a dwarf, who immediately surrounded them. "Although I would draw the line in the sand at paying for my food. It's been a long day and I am starved, as are my two companions."

"Hear, hear," Bandir grunted as the tender poured ales for them.

She pointed to a small cask from which she could smell red wine.

"You'll hear no complaints," the dwarf said and chuckled. "Barbarians are known for being hearty eaters, and I doubt even all the coin of the folk in this inn would be enough to properly sate them."

"Then you haven't heard about how much we can drink," Tandir shouted and raised his mug to the room. "Although I assume you will be introduced to the details shortly."

She grinned when the twins lifted their mugs to their lips, gulped quickly, and didn't put them down until they were both empty. They slammed them on the bar top and the rest of the crowd cheered. She took only a sip from the glass of wine that was poured for her.

It was not the best but she had a feeling they would not find the finer vintages in this area of the world. But it was red, it was dry, and it was strong. It would do for the moment.

"A meal as well for myself and my friends." Cassandra motioned to the brothers and put three silver coins on the counter to cover their food. She still had some of the treasure from the dragon's hoard, but most of it had gone into helping the villagers complete their home on Draug's Hill. It had been a little more rundown than previously suggested.

Perhaps it was time to start taking work that paid real coin for their efforts.

"What stories would you like us to tell?" she asked and looked around the room.

"There was one story about how you managed to spear a griffon out of the sky," the woman next to her stated and raised an eyebrow. "Although no one has been able to confirm it as yet."

"That was an interesting one." Tandir growled a chuckle. "That pride of lions attacked over a larger region than anticipated."

"As it turned out," Bandir continued, "the pride was being led by a griffon. It had killed the last male that ruled the group and took over, and it had begun to breed with the lionesses. Extremely dangerous, I would think. Besides, I didn't know that it could...you know, happen at all."

"It's an oddity and a rarity, but it does happen." Cassandra laughed and shook her head. "Griffons are generally the creation of magic, hybrids between lions and eagles. They tend to not be able to breed with either, only between themselves. Given that most of the griffons are created by mages looking to use them, that rarely happens. When it does—which usually involves the mage who created them killed and the griffons left to their own devices—it results in what is known as a royal griffon."

She realized that the rest of the room was watching her as she'd gone on about the creatures a little longer than was strictly necessary.

"What?" She shrugged and took another sip of her wine. "I've been taught and trained to deal with most of these fuckers. Anyway, one of these damn things found itself a small pride of lions and was intent on spreading its seed and growing a small army. It was intelligent and flew into the clouds to guide the beasts to find prey of all kinds. It was all rather…ingenious."

"You're forgetting the good part." Tandir's mug was filled again, and it appeared to go down about as quickly as the last one had. "Most of the baby griffons were already up and flying, which meant that as we rode into them, they squawked and attacked us from above. Bandir and I must have killed…about a dozen of the bastards before the rest of the lions even showed up."

"I didn't forget. I was getting to it." Cassandra rolled her eyes. "But yes, the twins managed to toss their spears in and kill the monsters. They are rather skilled with their javelins, these two. I would love to see what you would be able to do with a proper bow, though."

"Fuck off."

She stuck her tongue out at the two of them. "As I rode in to drive the lionesses off, the griffon appeared. It was a massive creature—twice the size of my horse, at least. Its beak was hooked and long and its wings were tipped with gold and silver. The talons appeared to have been forged from steel.

"It tried to catch me, but my armor held it off. Still, it knocked me from my saddle and left me nothing but my spear to hold it at bay with as it began to circle and return for another attempt. I was the only one fool enough to be stuck under it as it dove as the other two jumped out of the way. I planted my spear into the ground. The next thing I knew, I was hit by a creature the size of two of my horses. It knocked me over and impaled itself in the process."

Tandir groaned. "Eight hells. You could tell the whole history of the empire in the span of a drink and make it as drab, boring, and—"

"Precise?"

"Whatever you'd like to call it. You need to make the statement with more power, force, and the ability to make the whole world tremble with awe." The barbarian stood from his seat and she could tell he had most of the people in the room enraptured by the sound of his voice. "Who is next? Which stories do you want to hear this time?"

"There was that one where it was said you killed three men with one strike?" the dwarf asked and motioned for the twins' flagons to be refilled as he placed another silver on the bar top while the others moved a little closer.

"Now that is a tale." Tandir paused when their food arrived. Platters were piled high with sausages, mutton, and steaming rice, although it was odd that the locals appeared to be more comfortable eating it all with a pair of sticks instead of the traditional forks, knives, and spoons.

Still, they at least offered the utensils to those who were unable to manage the damn mystery devices.

She was glad that someone else would take the work of telling the stories. It at least meant she could have time to eat and drink and possibly even hear a good tale while she was at it.

And some of it might even be true.

"But they weren't men that we fought, no." Tandir shook his head and took another swig of his drink. "There we were, camped for the night with a fire lit to keep the rabid monsters at bay. We had finished our evening meal and were preparing for the night when our horses began to paw the ground. Barbarians have learned to communicate with horses, you see, and we knew something was amiss. Their senses are keener than ours."

So far, it was fairly factual, although the man was right about one thing. He knew how to give the story a little more flair than she did.

"We knew something was coming, but they were intelligent creatures, intent on attacking us once we had fallen asleep and not a moment sooner. We pulled our blankets over our bodies and waited for something to happen. As our fire died into embers and the full moon filled the night sky, the sounds of footsteps drifted to us. Before long, they reached our encampment, ready to attack. Three orcs led a group of hobgoblins. Now hobgoblins have no stomach for fighting during the day but are fierce warriors when the night falls. They proved it that night to be sure."

It was still more or less accurate, although Cassandra would not correct the barbarian about the fact that both he and his brother hadn't noticed a thing and were quick to fall asleep before she managed to wake them carefully a few minutes before the attack came.

"They were armored and carried wickedly curved sabers, as sharp as you'd ever believe and able to cut clean through my gambeson before my brother stepped in, his ax at the ready, and waited for them to come a little too close. They fell to his ax, four in a single blow, and dropped like saplings."

"And my brother was not one to be bested," Bandir interrupted quickly. "When the rest of the creatures attacked, his spear was ready and he stepped in to throw it with enough power to skewer three of them in a row. One was cut through the neck, but the other two were stacked like meat on a skewer."

It had been an impressive sight. Cassandra would give them that. And an impressive throw as well.

"With half their number felled in two strokes, I'll tell you, the orcs and the hobgoblins began to realize that they had attacked the wrong camp." Tandir growled and took control of the narrative again. "Our princess stepped in, leapt down from a rock, and punched her magical spear through the head of one of the orcs. She left it there, drew her sword, and disemboweled the other.

"We thought it would be enough to tear the fight out of the creatures, but we knew that if we allowed them to run, they would only attack another group of travelers so we fell on them. My mace crushed the skull of a couple, my brother's ax claimed the heads of three more, and the princess's blade and spear took the lives of all but the last orc, who managed to slink away into the night. I would assume he was able to reach another group and spread word of our exploits. I would imagine as a warning to prevent any from attacking the camp of the Barbarian Princess and the DrakeHunter twins!"

He raised his mug at the last sentence and it prompted a roar from the patrons, who downed their drinks quickly in response.

It was a good story and had mostly stuck to the facts as well.

"They should tell you about how they killed a massive sand drake as well!" a voice from the back shouted, and Cassandra realized it was one of the merry band they had saved, who made his entrance carrying a lute. "Although I suppose I should tell you myself. A new song composed this night—gather round and hear the exploits!"

Another cheer was offered, which gave the three a little time to focus on their drinks and the food that was still hot and steaming.

The song was a good one too, with a jaunty, pleasant tune that she knew would be stuck in her head for days after she'd heard it.

The food was a little bland but it was warm and filling and was complemented by the drinks on offer. It was the kind of issue that would arise in their work, she supposed. It was difficult to not compare their equipment, falling to pieces as it was, to that carried by the other mercenaries.

The simple fact was that they used theirs more often, but it also meant they needed to spend their coin to ensure repairs and replacements were effected.

Otherwise, all three would charge out dressed like the barbarian princess, although the twins didn't have an amulet that protected them from harm.

Having their tales told and sung around these parts would help, not only with the free drinks but also to have folk search for them and be willing to pay for the work. Then again, if the tales spread, it meant they would reach unwelcome ears as well.

She had expected to hear more from Grimm the Cruel since his Herald was killed, but it had been a few months now and not a peep had been heard. She doubted that word of his sound defeat hadn't reached him, which meant he had either abandoned all plans for invasion or was laying down plots and plans even now.

The former wasn't a consideration by her reasoning. The lack of any word from him nagged at the back of her mind. They should have seen some sign of the man's armies coming to wreak vengeance on those who had wronged him. None had come forward, yet—no armies, no attacks, nothing.

It was suspicious. Something was wrong and she felt the need to correct it before it was too late.

As the song came to an end and another was taken up, Cassandra finished her meal and her third cup of wine and pushed slowly from her seat.

It hadn't been enough for her knees to be left shaking like a newborn lamb's but there was a hint of unsteadiness. The wine was heady and she intended to have a little more before the night was finished.

"And where are you off to?" Bandir asked.

The two had already far outpaced her when it came to their drinks, and she had a feeling that it would take them a while before the effects were even felt.

Drinking like a barbarian was a skill she would have to master eventually.

"The night is long and I need to take a piss," she muttered. "Although I'm sure no one wants to hear any more drab and dry tales from me."

"It is not fitting for a princess to aggrandize herself," Bandir told her. "That is why most have those who tell their tales for them. Well, not princesses. I don't know of any princesses who have tales worth speaking of, but the point is that it is better for you to let someone else spread word of your greatness. It will only serve to help you along."

She shrugged. "I'll have to take your word for it. In the meantime, it might not be princess-like but my body functions like even the commonest of folk and it needs to be relieved from time to time."

That was a lie. A few more drinks would be needed before she felt that particular need, and yet the one that touched her at the moment was the need to be away from so many people crowded around her.

They had to find work. There was no Guild Hall in Edge's Rest, but that didn't mean there wouldn't be paying work for the likes of them and that was what they needed. Assuming they had any intention to eat in the near future or at least pay for their food.

If Grimm the Cruel decided to make an appearance in her lifetime, she wanted them to be as well equipped and prepared for the fight as they could be.

"There might be some way that we can make some coin from the damned drake head," Cassandra muttered as she approached the well in the tavern's courtyard and drew a bucket of water up slowly. She still wasn't sure about how strong the wine was and it was better to be safe than having to do all the work again.

Not much could be made from a drake's head that was missing its larger teeth, but if there was a mage in town, they might make some coin from the creature's innards before it all turned into a seething mess of rotting flesh and maggots.

Strider was in his stable a short distance away, which meant she couldn't talk to him about her problems. She still wasn't convinced that the horse could understand the words, but he did understand the tone. Horses communicated through intonation and body language instead of words anyway.

Cassandra steadied the bucket from the well on the stone ring around it and scooped some water out carefully with a nearby cup. She took a moment to ensure that it was clean and not brackish or spoiled in any way before she sipped to confirm it and let her gaze scan the area around her.

Edge's Rest was an odd town. It had been established as a trade settlement to the outer reaches of the empire and then left to its own devices as it was immediately apparent that the empire wanted little or nothing to do with it. No one came there who didn't need to, but they had made it their home in their own way.

No children mucked about in the streets and there were no casual conversations and the exchange of gossip between the local women. Everything was about the businesses in the area, and she could understand why those who wanted to have a family would find somewhere else to do it.

And yet folk remained there. She couldn't understand that. Thousands of towns like Edge's Rest had been quickly abandoned once trade routes dried up to leave nothing for people to stay for, but this settlement had endured. It had the potential to become a true city over the next few years, provided that it was not destroyed by some invading army or another.

It had been a mistake to think about that. Cassandra shook her head and let the bucket drop into the well once she'd had her fill of water and began to crave something with a little more kick. She would have to ask the innkeeper whether he served some of the more potent spirits since she had every intention of making the night both memorable and hard to remember at the same time.

They were still on the subject of the sand drake when she returned and the attention was drawn to the bards who performed a piece that involved one coming up with a line and another creating a rhyming line to compliment it. They were rather good at it and kept to the beat with nary a pause. It appeared as though it was something of a game, where the singer who took too long to answer lost. The patrons cheered increasingly louder as more verses were produced.

She took her seat again and motioned for her wine cup to be filled as the twins joined her.

"What do you suppose we'll do here?" Bandir asked. "I assume there won't be anyone paying for our food and drinks for our whole stay, and we need to repair our fucking weapons and armor. It irks me that most of the mercenaries in this damn place are better outfitted than we are."

"I feel the same way," Tandir added and took a swig from his flagon. "You'd think we would have better weapons than all of them."

"It simply means that we use ours more," she reminded them. "Although they might make more coin from less work than we have, which brings me to your point. Langven is in Edge's Rest—him and his Ebon Pack. We might be able to find work from him or he might at least be able to direct us toward those who might need our services and do not have a habit of being slow to pay their dues. If we can find such work, the coin we have now will be enough to have us supplied and equipped for real work."

"Real work?"

"Not generally the kind that sees us being sung about, mind." She raised an eyebrow. "I think the two of you are enjoying the attention a little too much."

"For our part, this is a pleasant change from the generalized loathing we usually face," Tandir pointed out. "Enjoyment is merited, especially if the tides will turn again quickly and see us out of favor."

"Well, we had better see you outfitted and supplied quickly. Merchants are more likely to drop prices if they know they are helping those who have a reputation for protecting their caravan. They won't want to fuck over someone who might hold their life in their hands later on."

"You are a devious one," Bandir muttered from around a

mouthful of bread and sausage, and she could see that he had no difficulty with the pair of sticks the locals used to bring the food from their platters to their mouths.

She would have to talk to him about how he accomplished that, but there would be time for that later.

"I'll see about contacting Langven in the morning," she said and turned as the verse battle between the two bards appeared to heat up considerably. "For tonight, we enjoy what little fame we have in these parts."

CHAPTER THREE

The night had been long. It had also been memorable but for the life of her, Cassandra couldn't remember much of it. She vaguely recalled a blur of drinking and eating and a few scattered images of her swinging her fist into someone's face, but she wasn't quite sure whose.

All she knew was that when she woke, her head pounded, her mouth tasted like a cat had shat in it, and every inch of her wanted to lay down and stay there for a few weeks.

It was a feeling that would pass, but she found it was oddly the kind of reminder she needed. There was always a price to pay for having fun like this, and healing it immediately would take that lesson away and prompt her to get back to drinking the next night too.

As honorable as the thought was, she paused, winced and covered her head, and felt like someone was physically beating on it with a hammer. She whispered a few words of power and focused her abilities into the fingertips that rubbed her temples. The pain receded slowly and the need to throw up passed.

Maybe a bit of healing, she compromised. She would be

miserable for the whole day and she might as well be able to function.

"I'm getting too old for this," she whispered and pushed slowly from the bed she'd occupied—alone, thankfully. There were no other signs that trysts had been engaged in the night before, which left her little else to worry about but pushing out of the room.

That decision was a mistake as it turned out.

"Agh...fuck!" She raised her hand to stop the blazing sun from cooking her eyes and almost stumbled on a small rock that was in front of the door to her room. It was one of the rooms that encircled the courtyard of the tavern where they'd spent the night before, but it appeared more mundane than it had under the light of the moon and torches.

The inn was a squat, two-story building that branched into a handful of rooms that closed around the courtyard—one, as it turned out, that was littered with corpses, although of the kind she had a feeling would rise soon enough and without the intervention of a necromancer.

Signs of the party were everywhere as it had extended well beyond the tavern as well. They were less pleasant the longer the party continued, and she remembered why remaining in the midst of it all could be entertaining in that moment. Seeing it again from the outside was merely a terrifyingly accurate mirror of the idiot she had been the night before.

It had been worth it, though.

She stretched and felt a hint of her headache creep in as she left the inn behind. There would be no real reason to return since all her possessions were either on her or being guarded in the stables at the gate alongside Strider. It was oddly liberating. All she needed to consider were the clothes on her back, her amulets, her coin purse, and her sword.

The coin purse was more or less as heavy as it had been when the night began, which meant that the folks at the inn had lived up to their promise that neither she nor the twins would pay for drinks for the whole night.

The sun was still a little too bright, and Cassandra wandered through the streets for a while until she found a well that provided a quick drink. She splashed some of the water on her face as well. The chill shocked her body to consciousness with no further help needed.

If someone had offered her a little koffe, she wouldn't have turned her nose up at it, of course, but it was time to stop looking for excuses to sit and enjoy the day.

Langven was somewhere in the town. He had left Draug's Hill after a few weeks, claiming that his men needed work. She wondered if there wasn't more to it than that, but there wouldn't be time to discuss it, especially if she intended to ask them for a favor. That was certainly the most important thing since they had to find more coin to work with.

"Oy, you," she snapped when a halfling passed pushing a cart of apples that was clearly meant for a human. She was putting a fair amount of work into it, which Cassandra could respect. "Can you point me to where Langven is? I need to share words with the man."

"What's in it for me?"

It was the anthem of this town. Everyone asked how they could turn a profit for themselves. It was something quite unique in Edge's Rest. There was no spirit of comradery or togetherness in the town, which had its own way to keep itself together.

"A silver coin." Cassandra pulled one from her pouch and held it up for the halfling to see the gleam it had when it caught the sunlight. "Although if you press my patience, it'll be a copper and then nothing at all."

"Coin first."

She shook her head, tucked the silver into her pouch, and withdrew a copper. "Do you want to try that again?"

The halfling rolled her eyes. "You'll find the quarters of

Commander Langven over at the edge of the cliff. You can't miss it. The Ebon Pack make no attempt to conceal themselves."

"Quarters?" she asked. "Commander Langven?"

"I answered your question. Do you have a copper for me or not?"

She tossed the coin and the halfling caught it and palmed it without so much as missing a beat. Once she had her pay, she pushed her cart again and whistled a tune that Cassandra recognized from the night before. That seemed to trigger all the songs to come together in her head and she couldn't tell them apart.

Exactly like the twins. She had taken to referring to them without names and letting them respond with the proper names. And just when she thought she had it all right, they surprised her. She needed to break a nose again.

And the halfling was right. There was no way to miss where Langven had situated himself, although she had thought the man would at least have the good sense to give himself and his pack a low profile. But it appeared as though subtlety was not one of his stronger suits. One of the larger buildings close to the edge had a banner and a shield up, displaying the black fang that represented his pack.

A deep sigh was all she could muster. It appeared as though the pack had stumbled on better fortunes than they'd had before she'd fought with them and in fairness, they had put in the work to earn the coin they'd made helping the folk of Torsburch drive their enemies away. It hadn't quite been as much gold as Langven wanted, but it appeared to have done a great deal to raise their standing in the eyes of the locals.

Cassandra wasn't sure what to expect from what waited inside but as she approached the door, a young man stepped out in front of her, dressed in the kind of garb she'd seen squires wear in the past. This one had the crest of the pack sewn into his shirt.

"Do you have business with the pack?" he asked in a polite yet firm voice, clearly meant to stop her from advancing into the building until she'd told him what her business with them was.

"That would be one word for it," she answered.

"Have you made an appointment?"

"An—what?"

"Commander Langven is a busy man. If you made an appointment with him, I am sure he is in to speak to you. If not, I can make no promises that he will be present."

She narrowed her eyes and wondered for a moment if this was all a grand joke that Langven was pulling on her. The closer she scrutinized the youth, however, the more she realized that she was speaking to someone paid by the man to keep the riff-raff away.

Langven had become rather choosy with the people he did business with. It was what one generally did when one could afford it and not a moment sooner.

"I am a friend and a former comrade," Cassandra stated. "I am Cassandra, the Barbarian Princess. Announce me if you wish, but I am sure he'll see me. Because if he doesn't come out himself, I'll have to tear through this ridiculous façade and drag him out myself!"

She raised her voice with the last sentence to ensure that the rest of the serving staff present could hear her, as well as a few members of the pack who were closer to the door. A few of them reached for their weapons, but those who remembered her chuckled and shook their heads.

The young squire cleared his throat.

"I will see if he can spare the time to meet you but I cannot make any promises, especially to one so...hostile."

"A mercenary avoiding hostile guests. Now that is a sight I never thought I would see."

He had nothing to say to that and immediately backed away. She didn't doubt that he would hope that some among the pack would help if she made good on her threats, but he would have to ensure that she was telling the truth first. Cassandra wondered if there was something to the tales that had been told about them that made him even consider believing her about being friends.

Before a full minute had passed, the young man rushed out again with a grim smile on his lips.

"Princess Cassandra, of course." He motioned her through. "If you would follow me, the commander will be with you shortly. I was instructed to offer you any refreshments you desire while you wait."

"Water," she answered almost before he could finish his sentence. "As cold as you can find it."

"Right away."

He rushed off to find her some water and she took a seat. It was time to seriously consider using a little more power of healing on herself as the heat and the walking had begun to make her head throb again. And perhaps she was a little annoyed that she had stumbled onto Langven in the middle of turning himself into a titan of industry in the little town called Edge's Rest.

"What did he do right that we've done so wrong?" she muttered as the squire rushed back with a jug of water that was sweating as a result of the cool liquid inside.

"Pardon?" he asked, poured the contents quickly into a glass, and handed it to her.

"I was talking to myself. Carry on. I'm sure you have better things to do than hover around me."

"Of course, Princess."

He bowed. She hadn't expected that but before she could comment on it, he had already returned to his post at the front of the building, likely to turn the rest of the folk away.

Cassandra knew the answer to her question, of course. Langven and his Ebon Pack took work that made them money after they survived the Herald's forces. It had made a name for them and seen their fortunes rise over the few months since. He certainly hadn't taken any of the charity cases she and the twins had spent their time on over the past few months.

Although she assumed that the man was starting to go soft. Needing servants and having a squire to ensure that those who were not the right kind were allowed in. It was all very formal.

And yet, as the door opened to reveal him, there was nothing of the softness she expected. Yes, he was dressed in robes fit for a lesser lord in a smaller town in the empire, but she couldn't help the feeling that it was like draping a pig in the finest jewelry in the land.

Not to say that Langven was a pig. Far from it, but he looked uncomfortable in the rich robes. Or maybe they didn't quite fit him as a person. She wasn't sure which was accurate or why, but it was an unsettling thought. He was not a lord, no matter how much he wanted to appear as one to the rest of the town.

He saw her almost immediately and a broad grin settled on his features.

"If it isn't the Barbarian Princess," he said and raised his arms. "I do believe you had certain words for me when we last parted ways. As I recall, you told me that I would be cursed with a useless cock and the inability to eat my favorite meal until we saw each other again."

"And that curse did wonders for you. I am basking in the glow of your newfound fortunes. Or maybe it is that bright red silk shirt you are wearing. I can't tell one from the other."

Langven laughed as she extended her hand. He took it at the wrist and grasped it firmly.

"It is good to see you alive and well, my friend. Tales of your exploits have reached even my ears."

"I didn't think that a busy commander would have time to listen to what the bards have to sing about."

"I was referring to your exploits last night. From what is told, you drank half the fucking town under their seats and then got into a fight with those who were still standing. A friendly brawl, but still one that you won."

Cassandra narrowed her eyes. "I...vaguely recall something of the sort. Something about them deciding I would not pay for a single drink all night, and myself and the twins taking advantage of that promise. How about you? I've heard no songs to tell of your exploits but from the looks of things, there have been enough of them to fill your coffers."

"It is interesting, but the kind of contracts that pay well are rarely those that have the bards scrambling for their pens. But we have been swimming in them. Given that your reputation was somehow linked to ours, many wanted the services of those who were responsible for the death of the Herald, no matter how large or small their role was."

"Interesting. I don't suppose you have enough of those contracts you're swimming in to share?" She poured herself another glass of the impossibly cool water and felt it wash over her in a perfect wave that was almost as good as a healing potion. "I and the twins are in need of the kind of work that pays of late."

Langven scratched his jawline, nodded, and gestured for her to follow him.

"There is no real branch of the guilds in this corner of the world, and between the two of us, no real reason for there to be one. But there is still work they want done and they've sent me what they can pay for and the coin to see it completed. We pick and choose which we take for ourselves and hand out the rest to those we are confident can perform their duties, as long as a percentage of the coin owed to them comes to the pack as a means to provide for us in providing for them. I'll withdraw such considerations for the work we hand to you and the twins, of course. You three are practically members of the pack."

"How noble of you." Cassandra followed him into the office he had set up for himself and sat where he directed her to. "Although I guess that does explain your rise in fortunes."

"There is coin to be made both in the work and passing it to others. We collect from both ventures and in turn, see to it that the other mercenaries in this fucking town have more to do than prey on hapless travelers. I feel like I am doing my part to ensure that this is a safer place for the average citizen."

"Although there were many shites who showed up and tried to rob the innocent passersby that I happened on."

"It's a work in progress."

She couldn't blame him for making a name for himself, of course. And the fact that he had made a decent amount of coin in doing so was not something to be scoffed at either. She wondered if the feeling she had was one of jealousy. Maybe she should have thought of the concept first.

"Ah, here we go." Langven pulled a few sheaves of paper from the stack he had been looking through. "Numerous offers for contracts requesting mercenary work of one kind or another. These are the ones that pay the best and ask for a half-dozen or fewer members to help."

"Smaller-scale work, then?"

"Well, there are only the three of you. Some ask for armies, quite literally. I told the guilds that it was unlikely we would find anything of the kind in this region, but they asked that I post the contracts anyway."

Cassandra nodded, looked through the contracts he offered her, and tilted her head. "Well, these aren't terrible, I would say, but I know you have something a little more lucrative. I think you might consider it as something for myself and the twins to work up to and something you won't want to commit your men to for some reason or another."

He scowled. "I hate it when you do that. Act like you're smarter than everyone else."

"You hate it because I am smarter than everyone else. What's the contract you so secretly pushed to the bottom of the pile, hoping I wouldn't notice?"

Langven grinned, pulled out the document she'd seen, and pushed it across his oak desk toward her as he leaned back in his seat.

"Some petty lord at the border of the empire has had his lands infested with ghouls after the emperor's armies passed through. He's been tasked with clearing them out but lacks the means and willingness to commit his men. He is willing to pay a hefty sum to those who would take the work on in their stead, however. A handful of cannibal scavengers might not be worth your time, but I assume the amount would be more than what you need at the moment."

She raised an eyebrow. Her time as a paladin and experience fighting undead creatures told her that ghouls were a little more than scavenging cannibals looking for their next meal. While one of them was not usually much of a problem, an infestation was difficult to root out and required the work of mages and a small army if it was not handled quickly enough.

And worse, an infestation of the beasts spread quickly if left unchecked or improperly checked. Every new body was another addition to the swarm.

Besides, the creatures were far wilier than the average animated skeleton or revenant.

Even so, the coin offered was enough to make her pause. It was the kind of coin that would make almost anyone a little greedy, and she was no exception. The impulse needed to be fought down before she looked at Langven.

She realized that he was studying her, trying to gauge her reaction, and she felt her pride prickle her a little harder.

"This sounds a little more like it. We'll take the work." She smiled. "I do appreciate your help in this, Langven. Are you sure you don't want to take your usual commission at the end of the job?"

"Not at all." He chuckled as one of the servants arrived with a small tray containing a handful of refreshments. "As long as you make mention of our relationship should you be successful and avoid any mention of it should you fail. I have a feeling that a good word from the barbarian princess will be worth more than any percentage I could take out of what is owed in coin."

"You might not have seen the amount offered so I'll take your kind offer and thank you for your generosity before you happen to change your mind."

"Ghouls?"

Cassandra nodded and sat next to the twins. They looked about as bad as she felt, although they hadn't benefited from any healing magic. She assumed they were the ones who drank half the town under their seats and her participation was merely noted as being close to theirs.

There was no real shame in that. The larger barbarians likely had a higher tolerance.

If they asked, she could probably offer them a little healing but otherwise, it was probably best to leave them with the consequences of the night before.

"I've never fought ghouls before," Tandir muttered and sipped from a tankard that held only water. "Are they anything like the revenants?"

"Nothing like them," she answered. "Well, they are undead but that is where the similarities end. Ghouls aren't shambling animated corpses, at least. They are cannibals, always hungry and about as clever as some animals. There are a few that are even capable of speaking, although it is generally only used to scream, mock, or lie.

"They have dirty claws and teeth that may or may not be laced with poison but either way, you will want to avoid being struck by one. If they break the skin, the chances of infection are high, the kind that even I would have trouble healing you from. They tend to burrow underground and strike from their warrens. While they are not destroyed by sunlight, they hate it and avoid it as much as they can manage."

"One might consider thinking twice before taking work like that on," Bandir muttered under his breath. "No matter what is being paid for our services."

"Does that mean you're not up for it?" she asked. "I am sure I can find some easier work with Langven."

"Up for it?" Tandir snorted. "Do you think they can entrust this kind of work to anyone else? They would be murdered and eaten on the spot without so much as the chance to raise their swords."

"Like it or not, they need us," his brother agreed. "And far be it from us to turn away those in need. Wipe out the fucking horde is what we'll do."

"I'll kill more than both of you." Tandir raised an eyebrow and took a sip from his glass. "There's nothing more to it than that."

"A tall order and one I look forward to seeing you fulfill," Cassandra answered with a slight shake of her head. "It won't be that far to ride. We can gather what supplies we need for the trip and be on our way as the sun rises tomorrow."

"Tomorrow?"

The three turned around to where the leader of the entertainers stood with a few of his bards.

"What?" she asked.

"Heading off tomorrow to fight through a horde of undead monsters should prove to be a story worthy of the telling," he stated firmly. "We would very much like to be present to witness a few more displays of your fighting prowess. Last night, the Slaying of the Sand Drake was some of the best work we've done in a long time, and it showed in the coin that was paid to us for it. It would help to relieve us of our misfortunes if we were able to witness and sing more about Cassandra the Princess most Barbaric and Glorious."

The line did sound familiar, she had to admit. It was likely something that one of the bards had come up with the night before when she was deep in her cups. It would explain why she was having a difficult time remembering precisely when it had been said.

She sighed, shook her head, and tried to think of any reason that could come to mind that would allow her to turn them down, but none presented itself.

"I cannot keep free folk from traveling and if you happen to be on the same road we are, I cannot stop you," she mumbled finally. They were only making their living, after all. "But let it be known that those who travel with us will be responsible for themselves, and I am under no obligation to feed, shelter, clothe, or protect any who follow. As long as that is understood, you are free to come and make songs of whatever you wish."

"You will not regret this, Princess."

"I already do, but there was no way to avoid that. We'll leave the city as light breaks and we will not wait for any of you."

"Of course."

They seemed overjoyed by the prospect, and she had a feeling they were somewhat lacking in subjects to write about if they were so excited to write about her.

Still, it was likely that they would change their minds when they saw where they were going. And she would be there to remind them that she had been against them joining the travels in the first place.

CHAPTER FOUR

An odd paradox existed in the landscape they were looking at. They were barely a day's ride from Edge's Rest, moving away from the desert that was so close to it, and things were supposed to be fuller, more interesting, and more colorful.

All they had seen were the browns replaced by drab greens and grays. Going across the river and approaching the edges of the land controlled by the emperor was supposed to be a sign of life returning to the area.

Her jaded senses saw only something that felt like depression made into a living, breathing landscape, intent on spreading the same feeling to anyone who somehow came into contact with it.

"There aren't many places I would want to be free of quickly," Cassandra muttered as she guided Strider ahead of their group. "But I would be glad to see this place behind me."

"Indeed," one of the bards agreed and shook the mud from his boots as he tried to guide his donkey through the muck on the road. "I would say that the land itself is warning us by somehow attempting to appear haunted."

They did have a way with words, these bards. She supposed that was what came from writing them for a living.

It had rained recently, but instead of the water soaking into the ground that needed it desperately, it settled in puddles and grew moss and all manner of unsightly, unpleasant things.

"What person would want to be lord over this kind of land?" Tandir asked. His lips curled downward and his nostrils flared in disgust as his horse picked carefully through the puddles ahead of them.

If there were places in the world that she hated more than the desert, it was the swamps, and this region was covered by them. Cassandra hated every inch. The smell and the muggy heat made it impossible to think about anything other than the way it seeped through her clothes.

And the fact that the only real distraction was the sheer number of insects that also tried to get under her armor didn't help matters, amazingly.

She steadied herself in her saddle and drew a deep breath. The one way to track ghouls was the scent of rot that followed them, which would make things difficult given that the whole area reeked of some kind of rot. The bard was right. Something about it wanted the word spread that it was haunted. She could only imagine the misery that came from being a foot soldier fighting a long campaign in this region.

"I would say the kind of lordling who doesn't much care about where he is lord of as long as he has a claim to some land," she answered and nudged Strider forward again once she was more or less sure they weren't stumbling into a ghoul warren. "He likely thought he could hand off the care of the area to an adviser and had every intention of spending most of his time in a mansion at the capital, letting the local peasantry sponsor his lavish lifestyle."

None of the traveling group had much to say about that, although she wondered if that was mostly because they wondered what it would be like to live under the rule of that particular kind of ass.

"Either that or he had no choice," she continued and Strider took her to the front as they approached what appeared to be a village. "Maybe he was sent here as some kind of exile to be away from the rest of his family, which ironically enough leaves the lordling less than interested in the welfare of his people."

She knew that did not inspire much confidence in what they were doing, but the fact that they had sent a contract out for someone to at least deal with the ghouls told her that someone was interested in the welfare of the region. Even if it was because the emperor himself had demanded that the lord take some fucking action before the ghouls spread to the rest of the empire.

The town somehow didn't look much better than the rest of the landscape. There was no wall around it, although there was a modicum of protection in the form of a moat. The only means to cross were two bridges that could be lifted to deny passage to any who might attempt to attack or pass through without paying the toll.

She assumed that was a business practice in the town. It generally meant the bridges were lifted as a rule and there was a guard on the other side, but for the moment, they were down and there were no guards. The houses were mostly wattle and daub, with thatch roofs that appeared to be in need of repair. Still, as they approached, it looked as though most of the work had gone into securing the doors and windows of the houses instead. All the windows were boarded up and the doors appeared to have been reinforced as well.

The whole area looked like it had been falling into disrepair. Gates were coming down, fence posts were rotting, and even the road was riddled with potholes. Little to no work had gone into maintaining the settlement, and she knew it was one of the signs that the people living in the region had all but given up.

They were not the kind who would need to deal with regular thieves and the like, which led Cassandra to assume that they were preparing themselves for attacks from the ghouls. It was an unsettling thought. All the villagers stared at them as they passed, averted their gazes quickly when their looks were caught, and shuffled away without saying a word.

"You'd find more cheer in a graveyard," Tandir muttered and shook his head as they rode past a small group of children being ushered forward by their mother and told to not look at the strangers.

"I would imagine they don't like outsiders," his brother added.

"It would be more accurately stated that outsiders don't like us."

The group came to a halt and everyone turned to an older man who stood on the side of the muddy road and leaned heavily on a cane. It took her a moment of suspicion to decide that this likely was not Theros in some type of human guise. She blamed the god himself for making her so suspicious.

But no, this one was rail-thin and looked like he hadn't had a full meal a day in his life. He sported a scraggly beard and thinning hair, and he shook his fist at them as they passed.

"I would imagine not, especially with the wars that came through this region," Cassandra answered and brought Strider to a halt. "But we are here to help you. Or at least rid you of the infestation that plagues these lands."

"You would do better to rid us of the empire and let us defend ourselves, but no. We aren't even allowed to carry weapons 'cept for hunting. They don't want the possibility of a rebellion."

"We're no army to drive the empire out."

"Clearly." His eyes, heavy with cataracts, narrowed as he studied the group that had ridden in. "Still, it's good of the bastard to finally send for some help. His men have been as terrified of the beasts as we are and lock themselves in their castle whenever word goes out that an attack is coming. Cowardly shits."

He spat on the ground but to the side to ensure that the spittle did not strike the newcomers.

"I see."

"There's not much you can do against the monsters that fill our lands, though. But any help is welcome here. Although if you truly wanted to help, you would drive out that miserable excuse for a lord along with the ghouls."

The old man turned away and walked shakily to one of the huts Cassandra assumed was his home without another word. The group continued to the other side of the town. As they trotted across the second bridge, they caught sight of where the lord of the region most likely made his home. A small rocky hill elevated above the swamps that appeared to be taking over the rest of the landscape overlooked most of the region. This made it a tactically sound location to build a fortress. Even better, it looked traditional, carved and made from stone instead of wood.

It was likely that the town they passed had a wall to it that had been ripped down. She imagined they would have been against the villagers putting a moat in and only allowed it because it was likely the only way they could stop the warrens from spreading into the village. Ghouls dug because they had to, not because they loved digging, and they disliked water almost as much as they did the sunlight.

Based on what she knew of them, it was odd for the creatures to infest a region that was practically all swamp, but she imagined they had grown used to it by this point.

"I would say the rest of the townsfolk agree with the old man," the bard leader muttered under his breath as they started up the winding road that led to the fortress. "And I cannot say I blame them, especially if what he has to say about the lordling in his castle is true. A lord is meant to protect his people from attacks. Even if it isn't out of the kindness of his heart, folk who are too afraid of the undead to do any work can't pay any taxes."

The man had a point, and Cassandra wondered what would drive the lordling to hide away while still sending word for mercenaries to be hired at an exorbitant rate to deal with the monsters plaguing his people.

It didn't make much sense, but she didn't care much about sense. They would find a way to end the damn infestation. The fact that they were there meant that something had changed or someone had forced the shite to get off his ass and do something.

They followed the road as it skirted a lake at the base of the hill and the relatively flat and open area made it easy for anyone in the fortress to see them approach. She assumed that the large body of water was the starting point for irrigating the fields in the area, but the mechanisms in place to feed it to the rest of the landscape were rusted, rotting, and falling to pieces. A few had come away altogether and added to the quagmire the region had become.

Even the walls on the fortress looked pockmarked and like a gust of wind could blow them down. The portcullis was heavily rusted and the gates showed signs of disrepair. It was clear that the keep was not immune to whatever monsters haunted the land.

The guards who watched them enter through the open gates were armed and armored, but a gaunt, haunted look to them made an odd, annoying feeling touch the back of her neck. They did not appear to be hostile, only tired. She assumed that the continuous threat of the ghouls attacking anything that appeared to be a target was enough to put them on edge.

She assumed that the situation had gone on for years. That was a long time to live on the edge. It had a way of draining the life from the people who had to endure it.

They came to a halt in the courtyard in front of the keep. It had another gate and portcullis. This one was in better shape than the last, and she was certain she knew why. The people within certainly did not want any possibility that the ghouls could get inside the safety of their fortress.

She could understand the appeal of that, even if there was an issue with leaving everyone else out to die.

One of the guards had already rushed in to alert their master that they had arrived, and the others were willing to leave the newcomers unchallenged and even allowed the servants to help with their horses.

A few minutes passed before a small kerfuffle announced that the local lord was coming out to meet his guests.

He was not an impressive man. While he couldn't quite be considered old, his belly bulged over his belt and his hair had begun to recede, although there was an attempt to sweep the remaining hair over the top to hide it.

A vain man by the looks of it. Cassandra knew spells existed that could help those men who suffered with such problems. Some mages were willing to perform them, although none of those capable of it would take the trip to this backwater edge of the world for any amount of coin.

Still, he was well-off judging by his clothes, but being far away from what she assumed was his home, the change was likely a recent one and it had not been one he agreed with.

"My saviors have arrived," the man declared and scratched the scraggly beard that had sprouted after what appeared to be a week or so without seeing the edge of a shaving knife. "Or, at least, those desperate enough for the coin to come and take the work offered. There have not been many."

"I assume that is why the price is so high," she answered and climbed the steps to greet the lordling. Her gaze immediately shifted to two young women who remained in the shadow of the doors like they were ashamed to be seen.

She could understand that impulse, at least.

"The price is high because the emperor demanded that I deal with the problem and gave me the coin to hire those who would be needed. If I had known that only three of you would arrive, I might have gone off to find a small army on my own instead of entrusting the matter to the guilds."

"My experience with ghouls is that no army would be enough to push them back. You need a small motivated and experienced unit. And fortunately for you, we happen to be here. Tell us where the problem areas are, and some food and water would not go amiss while we rest and prepare to resolve your issues."

His smile was unpleasant. "And who are you to command me?"

"I am Cassandra, the Barbarian Princess. These are Bandir and Tandir, twins and the mightiest warriors of the DrakeHunter clan. And who are you to question my commands?"

A hint of doubt slid into his eyes as if he wondered if he was addressing someone who was his superior. It was an odd thought and one she wouldn't correct him on.

Finally, he decided there was no need to antagonize those who had come to help no matter what his mood, and he gestured toward the door.

"I am Lord Selby Severan, regent of Massar by the grace of His Majesty the Emperor. If you will follow me? I will have food and drink prepared for you in the hall."

The keep felt almost deserted when they entered it. The strange sensation had weight to it, regardless of the reality of the situation. Footsteps echoed through halls that had been designed to house many more than the current inhabitants.

Perhaps it was truly haunted, she mused.

They were already preparing the food that would be served. The wine was somehow inferior to what could be found in Edge's Rest, and the food was certainly worse. Rice, potatoes, mutton, and beef all tasted of questionable quality as though they had been forced to pay for the cheapest food that was imported.

"I know what you're thinking," Selby said, sipped his wine, and made a face as he tasted it. None of them had shown any sign of complaint about the food or drink since it was provided in good quantity. Despite the quality, it was infinitely better than the food they had prepared on the road.

"What are we thinking?" Cassandra asked and took a mouthful of the beef stew and a bite of the dark bread.

"Massar used to be the breadbasket for the region. What you saw all around were not swamps but once were paddies where the locals grew rice. There were ducks, pigs, and massive cows that had no problem trudging through the mire. I never found any appeal in it, but they did. The locals are deeply passionate about the work they do. Given that there is a desert not two weeks from this region, I would say they have reason to be. But over the year since the empire took control, problems festered."

"And they sent you to deal with them?"

He laughed. "Heavens no. I had a torrid and passionate affair with another lord's wife. As it turned out, she wanted to leave him for me and I couldn't do that, so I told him about it. The complications were such that my family sent me here in some kind of exile. I suppose they thought they would teach me a lesson through it. Massar needed a lord and I needed to be sent away from the capital."

Cassandra narrowed her eyes. At least one of her guesses was right, then. She couldn't decide what a woman would see in the specimen of masculinity who lounged on the little wooden throne before them. Skharr she could understand, at least. A barbarian the size of a small house would be a new and titillating experience in the cushy, contained lives ladies lived.

There was no way to understand why a woman would fall for the spoiled lords who must surely be a copper a dozen in the capital. Truly, there was no accounting for taste.

"When did you discover there was a ghoul infestation?" Tandir asked and broke the silence that had fallen over the room.

"When we arrived." Selby sipped from his goblet again and made another face. "My party was traveling up the road to the fortress when the ghouls leapt out of the ground. There is a crypt on this hill, you see. With the marshlands all over, there is not much space for the dead to be buried properly. This is the only place for miles.

"In fact, the locals think this little hill holds some religious significance. They have explained it to me a few times but for the life of me, I cannot understand. It has something to do with how the gods raised the land so it would protect their dead from the monsters. Although it didn't do them much good, but that does raise the question of how ghouls arrived in the first place."

"Ghouls are clever enough to follow armies as they march," Cassandra informed him. "And intelligent enough to stay away from the army and feast on the corpses left behind. Especially the larger ones that have folk dying of disease and injuries even when they aren't on the battlefield. The chances are that the imperial armies crossed an area infested with the creatures and they followed them here. There was likely a battle in this region and they remained to devour the bodies."

"Well, I know that now," he snapped and extended his empty goblet to be filled again. "Or at least I found it out after the fighting. A bloody battle occurred here—the last of the war that was being fought—and when it was over, the army dispersed and returned home while the ghouls remained.

"They had an entire battlefield of bodies because no one could be bothered to collect them from the paddies, swamps, and mires. The locals simply sectioned off the areas with heavier infestation and continued to farm. By all accounts, these ghouls don't have much of a taste for the living, so they would simply attack those who approached, content with the bodies left behind for them."

"And that is what your men did. Approached. They likely saw them feeding on some corpses and decided to intervene?"

"Not merely feeding on some corpses!" Selby rose to his feet, his face contorted. "No, by the time we arrived, the dead from the battle had long since been consumed and they were tearing into the crypt beneath this fucking place. I might not have many beliefs left in me, but I do believe that desecrating the dead is not something any man or beast should be allowed to do. I commanded my men to drive them out."

"And they were massacred."

"In a word, yes. I traveled with forty men and a dozen returned. Three more died from their wounds and we were instructed by the locals to burn the bodies. They assumed that the wounds would turn them into ghouls as well, and we could not risk it."

Cassandra tilted her head. "That is…not accurate. The ghouls procreate like most other humanoid creatures do and even faster when they have a reliable source of food. There is a certain magic that raises the dead to create them in the first place but after that, they are oddly similar to humans in many respects."

Selby dropped into his seat, his face red, and he appeared to be a little out of breath. "I didn't know that. How do you know that? I was under the impression that barbarians did not have any interest in magic or the learning of it."

"Your impressions are mistaken," she replied firmly and shook her head. "Besides, my knowledge of the beasts has come from killing them. Any doubts you might have regarding our ability to deal with the nightmares you face should end there."

The lord raised his hands in surrender. "I've heard too many tales of the Barbarian Princess and her twin companions to question your abilities. But I think you fail to understand the issues we face here. If you did, your attitudes would be a little more somber."

"Aye," Tandir agreed. "Do you remember how somber we were when we faced…what was it? Almost two thousand men the Herald sent against us? I farted and my brother did not even try to take responsibility for it."

"In fairness, I did try to pass the responsibility to one of

Langven's men, the poor bastard. I stood my ground and insisted that he had shat his trousers while staring at the fucking army."

Cassandra couldn't help chuckling at that. She hadn't been present for it but she didn't doubt it for a second.

"Or what about the time I caught that half-orc through the chest with my spear and did not even make a joke about him being split in half with my shaft?" Bandir laughed.

"There was also the time we faced the troll, and you pulled our trap down on its head and made no mention about how his brains were made of stone at that point."

"I don't think I was there for that one," she commented.

Bandir tilted his head and nodded. "Yes, you are correct. That was when we were still dealing with our troubles in the mountains. My mistake."

"As you can see, we have no intention of taking your situation lightly," she continued and turned her gaze to the lord on his throne. "But the sheer number of dangers we face on a daily basis does have the tendency to dull the effects that such dangers would have on our minds."

He did not seem pleased with the explanation but realized that there was little he could do. It seemed like even his guards leaned forward to hear more. Folk starved of hope and any kind of happiness found what they heard from the twins almost contagious.

"What happened next?" Cassandra asked. "I assume there is more to the story."

Selby nodded slowly, sipped his wine, and no longer winced at the taste. "The dead had to be respected. I sent my men at arms to seal the crypt, hoping it would drive the creatures away. Instead, they began to prey on the living. Beasts that have no other food source tend to grow in desperation and these fuckers are cunning. It started with them imitating the cries of children from the woods. When folk went in to investigate, they were set upon. A few dozen died that way and they began to learn even more. They imitated human voices calling for help.

"People learned quickly to avoid the woods after that. They started to attack the town, break into houses at night, and steal the sick and the elderly from their beds. My men managed to build a moat around the settlement that held the attacks at bay, but it had an unexpected downside. The villagers do not want to leave the safety of the town without a group of guards to accompany them. Any group leaving the area in numbers will attract the beasts and lead to more battles, more fear, and more of my men lost."

"I suppose this is when the emperor made his wishes clear."

She knew that if she didn't interrupt him, the man would wallow in the misery of his life and depress all those in earshot within the hour.

"He sent a letter with stern words for me to get my lands under control. I replied that the situation required a great deal more effort and soldiers to eradicate the undead, and all he did was send coin and tell me to deal with it. Seriously, deal with it? How the fuck was I supposed to do anything? A year ago, I managed my father's estate while he found whores to fuck and boars to hunt. I enjoyed it. Now I'm here in the ass-end of civilization, trying to find the solution to a magical problem I had no part in creating, far from my family, my friends, and everyone I ever cared for."

Cassandra tried to not make her eyes rolling too obvious. Folk tended to take offense at that, but there was only so much whining she could take from a pompous shit like him.

"I'm sorry." She growled in annoyance and pushed from her seat. "But when you were born with that silver spoon shoved up your ass, did you think there would be no challenges? Did you think life would always be what you enjoyed? All this time, you had every single man, woman, and child who have entrusted their lives to you, and you simply sit around and mope because you weren't prepared for the responsibility?"

She could see a hint of anger in his eyes. As dangerous as it was to challenge him so, it was better than the apathy that hung over him.

"You enjoy all the privileges provided to you by the luck of having been born to the right parents, but you neglect the responsibility, allow it all to go to ruin, and do nothing but complain when work is expected of you to make things better. You will be the death of all those who entrust their lives to you because you cannot pull your head from your ass to acknowledge the pain faced by all of them. Is it too much of an inconvenience for you to deal with?"

The anger that coursed through her body made her voice rise until it rang through the hall. It had appeared before she even realized it and grew from annoyance to pure rage as she looked at the man who refused to work to save the lives of the people.

She could see that her anger had affected him as well.

"You will not speak to me like that!" he snapped. "I am the lord of this castle."

"Then act like it! Until then, I'll treat you with all the respect you deserve. At least you had the good sense to find those competent enough to resolve the troubles that you lack the ability to manage on your own, even if it meant waiting for the emperor to hand you the coin to fucking do it."

Cassandra pushed away from her seat and strode to the doors of the chamber through which they had entered. She half-expected the lordling to shout for his men to stop her, but once she reached the doors, she realized it was unlikely that he would try to retaliate.

For one thing, he still needed her and the twins to take care of their ghoul problem. For another, she had probably told him what he had told himself for months already, and it was the truth. Everything about him spoke of a pampered lifestyle in which all those he interacted with treated him with the respect his position gave him. He hadn't earned any of that respect himself but after years and decades of folk saying that being born into the right family was all he needed, he would begin to believe it to be true.

In the end, having someone shout his mistakes at him had disabused him of the notion that no one would challenge him for his failings.

She didn't pause to look back but heard the sounds of the twins' boots following her and paused for them to catch up while she focused on the gates of the keep. At least they hadn't abandoned her for her tirade.

"It's about time someone put that fat ponce in his place," Tandir muttered as they descended the steps to the courtyard. "Not that I'd make a habit of publicly scolding every lord who crosses my path, but damned if it wasn't satisfying to see someone do it."

"He needed that," Cassandra retorted. The heat still rushed through her veins with every beat of her heart. "As much as he might hate me for saying it, that needed to be said. Folk are dying and all he can do is drink and complain about how he is not the man for the task."

"And we all enjoyed it, mind," Bandir added as they walked toward the stables. "But don't you think it might have been a little…uh, unwise to make an enemy of the man we expect to pay us once the work is done?"

She shook her head, pushed the doors to the stables open, and looked around for where their horses had been stalled as evening began to fall.

"For one thing, if making an enemy of the lord of this land means he will start to save the lives of his people, I would say it was worth it, even if we do not get paid. But secondly—and most important—that is not how the guilds work. They take the coin first and keep it for as long as the contract is active and pay those who fulfilled it without the involvement of those who paid. It prevents mercenaries from being fucked over by those of means who suddenly decide they do not like how certain work was done or that they did not like who did it."

"So, you did your yelling with the full knowledge that he couldn't take our pay away for it, even if we did the work?"

"Indeed."

Bandir narrowed his eyes as they reached their horses. "Would you have still shouted if there was the possibility that he would withhold payment for that reason?"

"It might have given me pause, but I like to think that scolding lords into making the correct decisions for their people is enough of a reward for me to have done it anyway."

She stepped into the stall with Strider, ran her fingers through the beast's mane, and let the familiar gesture calm her mind and her body.

It would be some time before the heat had dissipated fully and by that time, night was likely to have fallen and they would have to wait until morning to make any plans to attack.

The stable hands had already put in the work to provide their horses with fresh hay and a good brushing, which was nice to see as it was needed after a long, hot day of travel. They had even placed the saddles and reins on stands to ensure that it would take little work and even less time to ready their horses for travel again when they needed it.

And it was possible that they would have to make a hasty getaway if Selby decided to send his men out to kill her and the twins for the affront to his honor. The real challenge would be to find soldiers who were willing to take the task on without a thought for their own lives.

He could not have made it more obvious that he was an unpopular ruler over these lands, and these soldiers would not have been ordered to kill those whose task it was to ensure that the monsters plaguing them were killed and done away with.

They would at least wait until the ghouls were dead. Once

that was finished, they would make their move, if moves would be made.

One of the hands stepped into the stables and looked a little contrite and in awe of the three of them. She assumed word had spread quickly about her confrontation with their master.

"I have been instructed to show you to your rooms for the evening," the young girl said and wrung her hands nervously.

"We won't attack the ghouls now?" Tandir asked and hefted his mace.

"Attacking them in the dark will see us all dead," the barbarian princess answered with a smile. "We'll rest, recover from our journey, and set our minds to the task with clear heads."

CHAPTER FIVE

There was no sign of any attempt to murder them in the night. Cassandra doubted that they would be greeted warmly by anyone, but it at least meant they would not have to worry about anyone trying to kill them before the ghouls were dealt with.

And if all did not go to plan, they wouldn't even need to do any of the work themselves. As much as they enjoyed playing the fools in the middle of a storm, that possibility always hung over their heads. The fact that they put their lives in danger so regularly should simply be laughed at or madness would set in.

Sometimes, it set in while the laughing happened, and it made everything that much easier.

"Are you sure you do not want us to come with you?"

Cassandra looked at the leader of the bards as he descended the steps after her. He looked like he had groomed his beard and was in the perfect mood to write more music that would be stuck in her head for the rest of eternity.

"We have traveled together for a few days now, and I haven't asked your name yet," she answered and raised an eyebrow. "It was rude of me since you know mine, of course."

"Julian."

"A very imperial name."

"Aye. I had another but it has been struck from memory. Besides, when the stories are outlandish, you need a simple name for people to remember their source. Julian has a certain ring to it so I have used it ever since."

"I agree. And I think I've heard it before. Did you and your merry troupe ever perform in Verenvan?"

"That is where we hail from. Remaining in one town for too long invites unwanted attention for rovers like us so we chose to travel the world again. We do hope to return one day, however."

"As do I, honestly. Now, why on earth would you want to invade a crypt full of troglodytic man-eaters with me? I know it is not because you think you can help."

"I...might be a distraction."

"And a welcome one for the fifteen seconds it would take for them to pin you down and use their claws to remove your heart, liver, and kidneys while you are still screaming. And if you are very, very fortunate, they will remove them in that order."

Julian cleared his throat and nodded. "Well, point taken. I think. What was your point again? Or were you merely informing me of the dangers we would face in the crypt?"

"We won't face any dangers in the crypt."

"Are you not—"

"I will face dangers in the crypt. Tandir and Bandir, daft idiots that they are, will face dangers in the crypt. You will not. You will stay here and relate your tales based on whatever the damn twins tell you on the journey back. Why would you want to head in with us anyway? Do you want me to tell you about the ghouls that eat nothing but male genitalia?"

That description appeared to do a little better as the man took a step back and his hands instinctively covered his groin.

"No...that won't be necessary. But we watched you fight and honestly, seeing it all happen before our eyes was rather inspiring. I would say it resulted in some of our finest work yet so I was hoping to tap that vein again."

Cassandra smiled and patted the man on the shoulder. "I wish I could say that I fully support you engaging your muse for music by watching me inflict violence, but I cannot have you dying over it."

"You allowed us to watch your battle with the sand drake."

"I was relieved of the choice in the matter. It was either herd you and your people like sheep and leave the twins to deal with the drake or help them in the battle and hope it would turn out the way we hoped it would before it turned its attention on your group."

"We do appreciate what you did to save us."

"Since you put so much effort in to make our actions be for naught, I will have to wait and see it to believe it."

Julian nodded and lowered his head. "Very well. I shall do as instructed and remain here, and content myself with tales from those who saw the fight firsthand."

She grinned and patted him on the cheek. "There's a good lad."

The fact that he was probably around her age or perhaps even older was entirely irrelevant. Her point was made and she didn't have to worry about having to watch over those who could not defend themselves while in the crypts below.

Bandir and Tandir waited for her at the base of the steps, the horses ready and eager to proceed as the sun began to peek over the edge of the walls. A few hours after sunrise was a little late to start their work in her opinion but in the end, there was no rush to venture underground.

"Why are we heading into the crypts?" Bandir asked. "I thought Lord Incompetence had already sealed them to stop the monsters from entering. Should we not scour the countryside for any sign of the bastards?"

"Do you recall how we weren't attacked while we approached?" Cassandra asked as she checked Strider's saddle.

"Aye."

"And do you recall how the lord of this place was attacked as he rode up?"

"Yes, because they intruded on the beasts' feasting."

"And yet, with a group as large as ours, they never once gave us any trouble. We heard no sounds of crying from the forests or anything like that. They must be hungry if they are deprived of the crypts, yes?"

"Because the crypt is sealed."

"Listen, moron," Tandir interrupted his brother. "The monsters will have found another way into them and we wouldn't be able to track them in their warrens anyways. They'll feast on their own, mindless eaters as they are, and once we start to kill those that are in the crypts, we'll draw the rest of them to us. It might take a fair amount of killing for that to happen, but a feeding frenzy would be the quickest way to rid this whole fucking place of the monsters."

She studied the barbarian carefully as he mounted up.

"I might have found a few books on the topic. Even the guards were trying to find ways to kill the ghouls and the library was surprisingly well-stocked."

Bandir narrowed his eyes. "I didn't know you could read."

"Can you?" she asked.

"A little but not very well. My mind doesn't take to it. All the letters become a jumble after a few minutes and I cannot make any sense of it."

"Huh. Interesting."

It wasn't something she had ever considered and she likely should have asked them about it before, but it never came up.

Skharr could read, as far as she was aware, but there was no telling how common that was among the barbarian clans as a whole.

There would be time for those kinds of considerations later, of course. Cassandra pulled herself up on the saddle once she was sure they had all the weapons they would need.

As it turned out, killing ghouls was not that difficult. They were humans, more or less, and cutting the head or the abdomen had the same effect it did when it happened to humans. Although, oddly enough, whatever transformed them into ghouls immediately turned on them as they died. Gangrene set in almost immediately and dozens of their fellows would devour them.

As intelligent as they were, ghouls were mindless in their hunger. Cassandra had seen the like before, although vampires did not appreciate the comparison. They thought themselves higher and loftier somehow but there was nothing that different in her eyes.

Not that she had ever spent much time with a true vampire. It would have been interesting, but all she knew about them was what had been written about the creatures. They had been extinct for centuries according to the histories, and the magic needed to create them was erased from all memory.

That was intentional, she assumed. An infestation of ghouls was nothing compared to what a single vampire could do to an entire city in a matter of hours. Or so the books told them.

She brought Strider around and followed a narrow path that led away from the one they had followed to the keep and took them to the back. The hill the fortress was built on extended for a few miles and allowed no intersection between it and the crypt to ensure that an enemy would not be able to undermine the defenses.

The road was about as reliable as the others in the region, although it became more perilous as the hill grew steeper around them. It wasn't the highest of drops but still enough to kill them if they fell. She steadied herself on her saddle and tried to not look down as they turned a corner and the opening to the crypt came into view.

Cassandra could see why the locals believed it was sacred.

Trees grew around the entrance and entwined with the stone arch like they incorporated it into themselves. She was willing to guess that seeing it at night would feel even worse.

As they approached, it was clear that the young lord had not lied about ordering his men to seal the entrance. Stone and mortar had been used to wall it off, although she could see a handful of places where it appeared that the ghouls had attempted to break through given the way the rocks had been clawed away.

"Why did you tell the bards that they could not join us?" Tandir asked, dismounted, and approached the walled-off entrance.

"They would have been killed in seconds if I hadn't."

"But they would have been a distraction and the smell of their bodies would have attracted more of the creatures. The books were right about them having a strong sense of smell, yes?"

She nodded. "My books told me that as well. This was shoddy work. I should be able to get through it."

Something was wrong but not physically. All three appeared ready for a fight, but the twins sounded like they needed to bicker a little more. They should be talking, farting, and laughing about the latter a little too much.

Instead, they stared at the wall like they were half afraid that she would rip it down and they would be stuck with the consequences.

"I would like to think that I know the two of you rather well," she said and placed her hand on the wall. "And yet, as I stand here, all I see are strangers. Will you fight with me or should I send for the bards?"

Calling their courage into question wasn't quite her intention, but anger flashed in both their eyes.

"We are with you," Tandir snapped and stepped forward. "And yet...there are things we have been taught to fear. Magic, for one thing, but we've grown used to that. The undead are another."

This revelation was interesting, although she supposed she should have realized it sooner. Barbarians were famous for their hatred of magic, but there was a reason behind it. Generally speaking, it was a very good reason although there were exceptions. She knew most of those, yet the concept of dealing with the undead seemed rather logical when he pointed it out.

Skharr had always been rather disparaging of the monsters—alive, dead, and undead—that he killed, but that probably came from experience. The kind of experience that these two sorely lacked.

"Well, if you have any questions, doubts, or fears, be sure to address them to me," she said and placed both her hands on the unstable wall blocking their way. "I'll try to assuage them as best I can."

He would never truly be comfortable seeing magic performed. Tandir had come to terms with the fact that folk beyond their home were more than happy to use it without much fear of the consequences. Soon, he and his brother allowed themselves to trust it a little more and even started to wear a few of the talismans and amulets that helped to protect them from the dangers they faced.

But he would still never get used to seeing Cassandra whisper a few words of power and thrust her hands out. The air twisted between her palms and the wall and as she pushed, the structure began to crack. Another push caused it to crumble. The way the air warped at her whim and will sent chills down his spine.

Once upon a time, he'd thought it was a bad feeling but these days, it was more fascination—morbid, perhaps, but still.

The wall was not very strong in the first place, even if it was enough to keep the ghouls out for the moment. Bandir already had his javelins on his back, hefted his ax, and carried a shield for good measure. He'd collected one of those from the lordling's armory. One could never be too safe when dealing with monsters that had to come in close to attack them.

"Well?" Cassandra asked, gathered her weapons, and stepped through the doorway she'd created. "What fears plague the minds of the otherwise fearless DrakeHunter twins?"

"What?"

"You two said you fear the undead. In my experience, fear has two sources. One comes from healthy knowledge and the other from unhealthy ignorance. Allow me to cure you of the latter. What did your barbarian leaders tell you about the undead that makes you feel uneasy?"

He wasn't sure why, but her confidence was rather infectious and he pressed through behind her as her voice echoed through the tunnel.

After a deep breath, he continued. That was easy to do as the crypt had only one path. The walls were lined with pockmarks, dug in deep so the dead could be laid to rest in the stonework. A few—the wealthier ones—had coffins provided for them. The poor had to make do with simply letting their bodies lie.

The coffins had been dug into as well. The smell of rotting flesh was not new and it clung to the walls. He had a feeling it would never go away.

"So…we know the bite or a scratch from a ghoul does not turn folk into ghouls, yes?" Bandir stated and lit their torches so that they did not wander in complete darkness.

"Well, they eat the bodies of the people they find," Cassandra answered and lifted her torch to follow the path that curled slowly and headed deeper into the earth. "Right down to cracking the bones open and sucking the marrow out. There wouldn't be enough left of the bodies for monsters to be made."

"Right," Tandir interjected when he saw where his brother's mind was going. "Yet one would think this part of the legend would have to come from somewhere or start somewhere. Are there undead creatures that can turn you with a single bite or scratch?"

She tilted her head and her golden hair dropped over her shoulder. With a grimace, she tried to tie it back with one hand while the other held her torch.

"From what I read, it was originally assumed that a vampire's bite could turn one into a vampire as well. It was later discovered that the truth of the matter was that a vampire needed to drain the victim of their blood and provide some of its own to turn them into a spawn. I think folk confused ghouls with the revenants at one point, and the legends of both were mixed. The revenants—or the dead that walk—transmit their curse through a bite and any who suffer the bite will be transformed into mindless husks when they die. It was suggested that all those who ever fought the revenants be marked in case they were bitten so their bodies could be burned to ash just in case."

"What is the difference between revenants and ghouls?" Bandir asked. "Both are undead, yes? Raised by the power of necromancers and the like."

"They are different curses, I think. It was said that the revenants are the spirits of men who were wronged in their death and show the resolve to take their bodies back—or any others that lack a soul—so they might take vengeance before they find peace. This myth was dispelled quickly as a necromancer was able to take control of the shambler easily and force it to do his will. Of course, necromancy is banned except under the proviso that it is studied. A lot of magic has been banned by this point."

"Have these bans stopped those who have a mind to perform these magics?"

"Well, it has kept the incompetent from unleashing dangers on the world accidentally. But I doubt they do much to stop those who have a mind to unleash the dangers on the world intentionally."

Bandir chuckled and shook his head. "And folk wonder why barbarians have such an aversion to magic while trying to ban everything they encounter that could have the potential of ending the world as we know it."

That made the former paladin pause, or maybe it was simply her trying to determine where the tunnel was leading. The stench of rot grew stronger as they pushed forward, and a sting to it began to make Tandir's eyes water.

"I don't think anyone wonders why barbarians hate magic," she whispered, placed her hand on the wall, and smelled her fingers immediately after. "They have been around magic so long that they have come to accept the good as well as the bad, the possibilities and the risks all in one. They don't understand folk who would not bother to risk it at all."

"Like I said, folk wonder. What are you doing?" Bandir asked.

She continued to touch the walls and sniff them. "I am trying to determine if the smell is merely sticking to the walls from what might have happened here in the past, or if there's a constant source of it coming from deeper in the tunnels."

"And?"

"It's coming from deeper in the tunnels," Tandir insisted. "The air is fresh and cool down here and moving. The smell will follow us."

Cassandra nodded. "I think that when people called this an infestation, they might not have considered how right they were. It means the monsters have found something to feed on. Come. We need to continue."

"Ah, yes," he muttered and followed closely as she drew her spear and held her torch in her other hand. "Let us move deeper into these tunnels lined with corpses and into the depths of a ghoul warren."

"Don't be ridiculous," she snapped although she turned to face them with a small smile. "All the bodies in this section are long gone. We'll have to go deeper to find those the ghouls haven't devoured yet."

"You're very cheerful about all this."

"Don't misunderstand the situation. The bodies this close to the doors were laid to rest hundreds of years ago and would have since turned to dust. As time passed, they needed to push in and dig deeper to accommodate more bodies. The originals were never disturbed. See here." She held her torch up to the section above one of the holes in the wall. "A name and a number. And then below, a series of numbers that follow. Parents above, siblings on either side, and children below."

"No grandchildren?"

"I would assume the children have markers for their children, their children, and so on. The numeral markers are to direct families. They help them to remember somehow."

Tandir approached one of the walls. From the size of the holes and the depths, folk were pushed in feet-first with their heads closer to the entrance. There were three to each row on both sides of the tunnel, each one marked with the name of the dead and the numbers.

"I would assume the living have stone markers for their relatives to make them easier to visit," Cassandra continued. "And they go on and on and on...winding around the hill and digging deeper until even the swamps are not a threat to the dead."

He didn't want to know more. Holding so much to the dead was a foreign concept to him. While he could understand folk wanting to know where they came from and remember their ancestors, this had been elevated beyond it—had fetishized it almost. People were so obsessed with the dead that they somehow forgot to live.

"No wonder this whole fucking place feels haunted," Bandir whispered, his mind on the same topic as he shook his head. "They spend so much time thinking about the dead, it's bound to show in the landscape."

She looked at them and tilted her head.

"Is there any truth to the myth that twins can feel what their twin is feeling? Or know what they're thinking?"

They exchanged a look and tried to think it through before they answered.

"There might be," Bandir stated finally. "Although I would think it has more to do with the two of us simply…uh, knowing each other better than others might."

"That sounds about right." Tandir shook his head. Maybe that was her tactic while leading them through the tunnels. She tried to keep them talking about whatever came to mind so their fear of the undead was left behind.

The fact that it was working was the oddest part.

Cassandra raised her hand and pointed ahead to where the tunnel appeared to widen. The stench was stronger there than it had been at any other point, and when their route opened into a vast chamber, he could see why. More of the holes in the wall were visible, and these showed signs of the monsters attacking. Claw and tooth marks were gouged directly into the rock from where the beasts had rooted through the corpses of the recently deceased. Even worse, he could hear the slow drip of water filling a pool in the center of the room.

Thousands must have been laid to rest in this chamber alone, but the dripping water was a new development. There was no sign of stalagmites or stalactites, which meant that it had not been dripping for very long.

If he had to guess, it might have had something to do with the monsters that dug holes all through the area.

"I would say we are directly under the lake," Cassandra surmised and narrowed her eyes.

Bandir paused and studied the ceiling. "Do you think we should leave? Before the ceiling caves in?"

"It's a slow drip. If it was enough to cause a cave-in, it would have happened by now."

"And those are words spoken by every man and woman ever caught in a cave-in, I should imagine."

She smiled and shook her head as they moved deeper into the chamber.

All three came to a halt when they heard movement somewhere ahead of them. It was an unpleasant feeling, knowing something was out there. They had no idea how many of the ghouls were present, but they were likely about to find out.

Tandir took a step forward, grasped his shield with one hand, and held his torch with the other. He would willingly drop the torch and reach for a weapon, but he wanted to be able to see as far as possible for as long as possible.

It wasn't long before they saw movement in the blackness ahead. Vague forms shifted and shuffled in the darkness for the most part, like the beasts intentionally stayed away from the light.

Finally, one of them moved closer and its eyes gleamed in the torchlight. It remained low and its long, slim limbs glided over the ground while its claws scraped the rock they stepped on, the sound only too easy to hear.

It was bigger than the others that approached—perhaps a leader of the pack—and a half-dozen or so appeared behind it. Their eyes reflected the light of the three torches eerily as well. Their teeth clattered like they were communicating with each other and this was followed quickly by low growls and groans.

They were curious about the invaders, although he knew the curiosity would give way to hunger shortly.

The stench was somehow worse, and Tandir had to actively fight the urge to throw up as more of the creatures began to shift in the darkness. A dozen more sets of eyes appeared and their eyes glowed with unnatural interest.

"Fuck." Cassandra growled and hefted her spear into a firm grasp.

CHAPTER SIX

There was no telling how this many of the ghouls were able to procreate, spread, and feed without turning on each other.

That was the fate of most ghoul packs. They were hungry, vicious animals that would eat one another as happily as any other food source.

A few would be left after the in-feeding, which generally kept the roving packs smaller until they found an army to follow, but this was unprecedented, at least in her experience.

Not that it mattered much. This was what they had been called in to deal with and now that the wait was over, she was more than willing to dive into the thick of it, come what may.

This was also a part of being a barbarian and one of its most appealing features.

Bandir already had a javelin in hand. He dropped his torch and threw the weapon at the largest of the creatures that they could make out in the shadows cast by the torchlight. Whatever curiosity the ghouls had over the intruders quickly turned to bloodlust as three or four immediately began to devour the one he had killed.

The others were not so easily distracted, and Cassandra held her spear at the ready as the creatures swarmed forward. They had no sense of tactics and made no attempt to outmaneuver or kill their enemies at minimal cost to themselves.

Perhaps that was what came from being part of a group that ate their dead.

She jumped forward as two more javelins cut through the beasts to leave only one at the front of the initial charge to take her spear through its chest.

It was a smaller creature and would likely only reach her neck if it stood to its full height. None of them did, however, and they walked on all fours, their backs hunched with bones visible beneath their pale gray skin.

Her spear sliced cleanly through the first one, and she heard a hiss when the head of the spear made contact with the undead creature. It lurched back with a howl and clutched its wound while others immediately dragged it back.

They were building to a frenzy much faster than she had expected them to, and she could hear them almost immediately howl and screech from the corners of the cave. Others were coming and likely wouldn't be satisfied to only consume their fallen.

More of the javelins punched through, and one was even thrown with enough force to fell two of the beasts that were a little close together before the twins ran out of projectiles to throw. Instead, they took their weapons and their shields up and joined Cassandra at the front. They had dropped their torches and left them on the ground where they could cast a little light, at least.

It wasn't much, however, and she had to hold hers aloft and high enough to be of some use to them. She grasped her spear firmly and drove it forward and through another of the ghouls. Like the previous one, it hissed, jumped away, and clutched the injury like the blade had somehow burned it.

She grinned at a sudden surge of bloodlust and took a step

back. Tandir used his shield to hammer a couple aside when they tried to lunge at her. She swept smoothly around him, swung her spear low, and severed the arms and legs off three of them in a single strike as the twins rushed in to finish the wounded.

It was a little unnecessary given that the ghouls were more than willing to kill their wounded, but it seemed like they had been touched by the bloodlust as well.

Cassandra heard them laughing, almost as proof that she was correct, and she pushed forward and swung her torch like a mace. It connected with the jaw of one of the ghouls and she almost retched at the stench that resulted as it howled in pain.

The cry was cut off when she thrust her spear through its throat and yanked it out again to impale one of the beasts that had climbed the wall and tried to launch onto the twins from above.

She would never tire of watching them in action. The two barbarians had fought together for so long that it was like they knew what the other would do before it even happened. They covered and attacked in almost perfect harmony. All she could do was try to stay out of their way so she didn't interrupt their rhythm and use the range of her spear to help as best she should.

Before long, the corpses began to pile around them and made it impossible to draw more of the creatures to the group.

Without hesitation or conscious thought, Cassandra raised her torch to about eye level, looked over the fight, and whispered a word of power. It was one of the first she'd ever learned in an ancient and forgotten elf tongue.

It translated simply to fire, and it was one of the easiest spells to learn since all it did was take the flames already present and spread them.

Although simple to execute, the result was efficient. The fire streaked through the darkness, immediately caught the stinking bodies of the dead ghouls, and set them aflame. The conflagration illuminated the chamber better than any torch could. The only downside was that her torch was now unlit. She used it to smack another of the beasts across the mouth before she tossed it aside and let the burning bodies do its work instead.

She held her spear with both hands and stepped to the left to catch a few of the ghouls that had attempted to encircle the twins. Stinking blood spattered from the wounds.

"Fuck me," Tandir shouted over the screeches and cries that filled the chamber. "You would think these creatures would at least smell better on the inside than on the outside."

"Why would you think that?" Bandir asked. "Humans smell rather terrible on the inside."

"I couldn't imagine anything that smells worse."

"You're right," Cassandra muttered and tried to not breathe through her nose. "I have a feeling I'll need to burn these clothes."

A long bath likely wouldn't do much to help either. It would be a while before she finally left that particular characteristic of this place behind them.

It was good to see the twins in their regular spirits again. She'd had a feeling that their reticence had been borne of fear of the unknown. Now that they had seen, stabbed, chopped, and crushed the unknown, it held little fear for them.

"These kinds of things never make it into the stories, do they?" Bandir muttered.

She looked up and noticed another attempt to scale the walls. Fewer monsters appeared through the tunnels that branched out, although the enthusiasm of those that did told her it wasn't because the survivors had lost their nerve for battle.

A few dozen of them had been killed already, and the others either gorged on the corpses or threw themselves at the team in search of fresher meat.

"What doesn't make it into the stories?" she asked as she speared one of the beasts that tried to drag the body of another ghoul away.

"The smells. Battlefields have a particular stench to them but no one ever talks about it. In all those songs of glory and the like, no one mentions the foul stench of it all."

"It's not surprising," Bandir answered, cut the head from the shoulders of one ghoul, and used his shield to guide another into the path of his brother's mace. "If they told the truth about what battlefields are truly like, they wouldn't have nearly as many young idiots willing to sign their lives away in conscription offices. They have to make a grand gesture about how glorious it all is to bring the crowds in."

"True," Cassandra conceded since he was not wrong about that. "But there is also the fact that no one wants to hear a song about what it looks like to see your friend shitting himself when he's pushed into the front lines of a shield wall for the first time."

"Because they want to hear the glory of it all," Bandir acknowledged. "That's what they think war is all about. Personally, I'd like to hear more songs of counts and lords getting themselves into scandalous trysts and the like. It's always good fun to learn of the high and mighty putting themselves in a vulnerable situation."

She paused, drew a deep breath, and regretted it instantly as she could almost taste the foul smells that filled the chamber. Still, it appeared that the monsters were dead for the most part. She couldn't see any of them running away or even trying to drag any of the bodies back. The fires spread almost unnaturally and ignited the corpses as though they were dry firewood.

The smoke was acrid and oily, but burning the bodies was the best way to ensure that there would be no return of the stragglers to eat them.

They would either die of hunger or move on to areas where there was more food to be had.

It seemed like there should have been something a little bigger—a leader of the ghouls or a larger creature inhabiting these tunnels for them to deal with. By the looks of things, however, their work was done and all they had to do was ensure that the fire consumed the rest of the corpses before it was extinguished.

"I honestly thought they would put up a little more of a fight than that," Bandir commented, breathed deeply, and shook his head with a grimace. "It makes you wonder why the locals had so much trouble killing the bastards."

"Not everyone can be the mighty DrakeHunters," Cassandra countered. "And most of them don't have our experience in dealing with monsters. Most would be able to kill one or two, but the moment they saw their comrades felled by the dozen by a swarm, they would turn and run and become easy prey for the beasts. Folk tend to underestimate the benefits of having experienced fighters in tight spaces. There was one time when I saw one step into a room with two or three dozen enemies, kill two of them, and sit to enjoy a drink, telling the rest to make their way out. And they did."

"That wasn't you, was it?"

She looked at Tandir as the barbarian nudged one of the corpses closer to the fire.

"I'm not that mad."

"Well, it is a possibility. You wander into a fortress in nothing but undergarments with the intention of distracting all the soldiers inside. I suppose you could have done the same to convince others to abandon their fortress."

"I never told you it was a fortress he was taking."

She helped them collect the last of the corpses and push them into the flames to ensure that there would be none for any possible stragglers to feast on.

"The story might have been spread about. I heard it when we were in Edge's Rest." Bandir tilted his head. "Late in the night when the bards ran out of songs about us and started singing about another famed barbarian from Verenvan. Or... fighting out of Verenvan, by the sound of it. Either way, it was an interesting and humorous song about how he took a fortress of bandits by killing two of the men and letting the rest leave before he did the same to the rest of them."

"That's interesting." Cassandra shook her head.

She knew Skharr wasn't one to brag about his exploits, and she knew she hadn't told anyone about it, which meant a certain halfling had put the work in to spread the news. There was no telling why. Maybe she wanted a little clout for herself.

"What's interesting?"

"Nothing. I merely didn't know that the story had reached the ears of bards."

That was all she was willing to say on the matter. There was no real point in delving deeper until she knew a little more about it.

"Come on," Cassandra muttered when she was satisfied that the bodies would be nothing but ash over the next few hours. They had to hope that none of the monsters would try to put the fires out.

They had no fear of being killed but ghouls tended to avoid fire and especially if it had a magical origin.

Somehow, the walk through the winding tunnels was shorter than the walk down, even with the light of only one torch to show them the way. They had retrieved one of those that the twins had dropped before the fight started. The other had been caught in the blaze. Fortunately, the smoke had somewhere to escape, which meant they did not need to struggle through it.

She knew a handful of spells that would allow them to breathe through smoke and even one that would enable them to breathe underwater, although she wasn't sure if that would ever be useful. There was no telling if she would be able to even perform the spell if she was underwater. Or maybe it was meant for her to perform when she was above water for the benefit of those who would go below.

If she could spare the time, she would have to put a little more study into the matter.

When they reached the door again, Cassandra paused and drew a deep breath of the fresh air. If she had to bet on it, they would need to put considerable work into cleaning the smell from their clothes and bodies and in the end, she was prepared for the possibility of simply having to burn the clothes and start with fresh ones.

But for now, all she could do was enjoy the fresh air and try to not let the monsters ruin what had turned out to be a rather lovely day. The sun had begun to peek through the gloom, although not for very long. She had a feeling that even if they did wash their clothes there, it would take a damn week for everything to dry again.

With the battle behind them, they had nothing else to do but return to the keep and inform all those present that the work was done. The day had gone a little faster than she would have liked, which meant they would likely need to spend another night in the keep before they returned to Edge's Rest.

It meant another night in a keep where the lord might decide he was willing to kill them now that the work they were hired for was completed. Still, it was a lower risk compared to pitching camp at night in the mire that surrounded them. It would take months or even years for the populace to finally regain their confidence and overcome their fear enough to reclaim their land from the monsters that had taken it over. Until then, the wilderness would be treacherous.

The smell of smoke greeted them as they circled and began to ascend the hill toward the keep. This was evidence that there were numerous outlets in the warrens used by the ghouls to come above ground. Hopefully, the smoke would drive any survivors out of the tunnels and into the open where it would be easy to kill them.

Assuming there were survivors. Planning for the worst had begun to feel a little too instinctive on her part. Perhaps now was the time to relax a little.

She patted Strider gently on the neck as they approached the gates. Now that they were clear of the tunnels and had been for a little while, she could smell the remains of their enemies still emanating from their clothes. It was a putrid stench that must unsettle even the horses, although Strider showed no sign that he was uncomfortable with it.

The soldiers appeared to be on alert, likely the result of the smoke that seeped into the region. She could tell they were surprised that they had survived their encounter in the crypts and weren't sure if they were supposed to celebrate or start collecting weapons and armor from the armory.

"The ghouls are dead," Cassandra called and dismounted once they reached the steps. "I would say almost fifty of them and all dead. That putrid smoke you smell is the fire consuming the corpses in the crypts."

"A convenient tale." Selby pushed out from his castle and blinked against the glare of the sun when it shined through the cloud cover here and there. "One that was likely told to many who paid coin to the guild. You would take the coin and leave before any sign of your deceit was discovered."

Perhaps she should have known that he would be this kind of customer—a man so desperately unlikeable that he would attempt to squirm away from coin owed. And he likely thought he would be allowed to get away with it as well. Perhaps he would attempt to arrest the three and hold them until they sent word to the guilds that no coin was owed.

And then kill them, of course.

"You and your men are more than welcome to inspect the crypts yourselves and see the corpses burning. I would rush, however. By nightfall, those bodies will be burned to ash."

"You wish to send us into the pits to see us dead by the monsters you claimed to kill so you could make your escape from here? Your taste for death and inflicting pain knows no bounds."

Cassandra was honestly too tired for this. If it had been the morning after a restful sleep and a filling breakfast, she might have considered taking a more civilized and diplomatic approach. For the moment, however, she smelled and bruises had begun to form where the ghouls had come a little too close to killing her, and she certainly wouldn't deal with this the way he likely hoped she would.

"All right, then," she said and turned to face the man as she climbed the steps. "We'll leave and go to the village to tell the people that while their problem with the ghouls has been resolved, the measly lord who refused to do anything about their issue until the emperor all but commanded it of him refused to pay us our due. The guards already know it and since they have watched your cowardly ass hide instead of doing anything to help, I would say they probably feel the same way."

As those words left her lips, she turned her gaze onto one of the guards who wiped sweat nervously from his hands before he tightened his grasp on his crossbow. He looked like he was no longer sure what to do with it.

"Do you trust me?" she asked and stepped closer to him. "Or more importantly, do you trust him? This threat might be gone but what happens when the next one comes? Or the next? Or the one after that?"

She turned to face Selby and narrowed her eyes. "Do you honestly want your reputation to be that of a lord who doesn't pay those who put life and limb at risk to save yours? I can promise you that those who come to save you next time will take more from you than the coin paid to you by the emperor. It's something to keep in mind, I think."

An inner niggle suggested she was pushing too far and might make things worse for everyone if Selby had so much as a hint of a spine and a modicum of dignity left in him. Still, the fear of facing another monster without being able to call on the guilds for help would probably dig into the back of his mind like a parasite. It would no doubt remind him that he would never be good enough to protect the people he lorded over.

Perhaps it was a little cruel to bring that to his attention while his subjects were present. The soldiers were likely drawn from the village folk and had loved ones among them who would love to hear all about how the Barbarian Princess had dressed him down. In the end, however, he had gotten the work done. Embarrassments among the rich and powerful were quickly forgotten by the local peasantry, given how often they occurred.

Her gaze was fixed on the lord and held him in place until he finally looked away, cleared his throat, and tried to find support among his staff and guards.

"I would say the coin you submitted for the work was not sufficient since you lied about the dangers we faced in that fucking crypt," Cassandra continued coldly. "Investigations have a way of revealing all manner of unsightly secrets that would remain hidden if one merely paid what was owed. I think fifteen gold pieces would suffice."

She looked at the twins, who nodded in agreement.

"Fifteen," Tandir affirmed. "A good, solid number. It won't be questioned."

Selby's eyes narrowed but eventually, he nodded. "You make… sound points. Fifteen gold pieces will be added to the reward."

"Perfect." Cassandra smiled suddenly and clapped the man on the shoulder. "See to it that the coins are delivered to our quarters. For the moment, I think I and my companions are in desperate need of a bath to wash the stench of death away."

CHAPTER SEVEN

She wasn't sure what made her feel so ill at ease.

The keep looked more or less the same, but something was different about it. The sky was more heavily clouded, and Cassandra couldn't bring herself to look farther out. There must be a storm coming, her mind reasoned. It would account for the weight the air had like she was swimming through it.

To help her focus, she drew a deep breath and felt the tick of her heartbeat in her fingertips. Something felt odd as she approached, although it took her a moment to place what had been wrong the whole time.

She was no longer in Massar and had no idea how the detail had slipped her mind. A portal of some kind must have brought her there. Or maybe Theros had transported her in her sleep. It would explain why her brain felt like it had been turned to mush.

Her body froze and she moved her fingers instinctively to the sword at her hip. She snapped around and drew her blade in a single, smooth motion.

Nothing was there. She could have sworn she'd heard something move behind her. A voice had whispered to her.

In the next moment, she realized that she was at Draug's Hill.

Cassandra tilted her head and looked around the ramshackle defenses they had put so much work into rebuilding. Dozens of people should have been out and about to continue the work of establishing their homes, but the streets were deserted.

Yet that still, small voice continued to whisper something in the back of her mind, trying to get her attention but never quite making it clear.

The whispers came from the depths of the fortress. She had no idea how she knew that or why, but she wandered down the steps into the bowels of the old keep.

More voices—perhaps dozens—joined the single one she'd first heard. She drew a deep breath and tried to tell herself this was not real. The voices were not real. None of them were.

A shadow flickered in the corner of her eye but as she spun to face it, it felt like she was wading through mud. Invisible hands grasped her shoulders and hands to hold her down and force her to turn her back on the shadow as it approached. The glint of something cold and sharp flashed in the darkness and arced toward her throat.

In that moment, the bonds were lifted and her whole body lunged from her bed. Her fingers grasped the hand with a dagger at the wrist and stopped the blade mere inches from her flesh.

The strange awareness had been only a fucking dream. The realization was enough to drive the fire through her veins and she growled and forced the hand of the would-be assassin back.

The blade dropped and a second hand caught it and immediately twisted it toward her stomach instead.

Cassandra rolled and her hold on the assassin's wrist dragged them across the bed with her to roll over the edge and onto the cool stone floor.

All she heard from them was a soft grunt of pain as she landed on top and tried to pin them down and force the dagger from their grasp.

Pain hammered into her ribs, and she realized that the

assassin had somehow twisted their body to drive their knee into her ribs to force her off and wrench their wrist free.

She scrambled to her feet and waited for the next attack to come, but the assassin vaulted over the bed in a single leap—an impressive feat—and raced to the door.

"Like hell!" she roared after them, went the long way around the bed, and snatched her sword up on the way. She unsheathed it and the ring of steel on leather echoed out the door—a warning, perhaps, for what awaited the assassin when she finally caught up with them.

Her assailant had already fled the room, but she could hear light footsteps through the hallways to give her at least some sign that she was heading in the right direction. The keep was simple, fortunately, and not the kind of maze that lords tended to make their homes into for whatever reason.

The hallway was winding and it became more difficult to sight the little shit. Cassandra could feel her body still waking up, which slowed her somewhat despite how quickly she'd been woken. It was an annoying feeling and one she truly wished she could do away with by tapping a little magic.

As she turned a corner, a glimmer of movement caught her eye and she whipped around, her sword raised and ready to plunge into the chest of the damn assassin who had fled from her.

What she saw was not one figure, but two. Neither wore the cloak and leathers of an assassin either. They were dressed in nightgowns, the garments a little worn and torn from what she could see through the light from the lamps hanging from sconces on the walls but still comfortable enough to sleep in.

Although one's gown had a hole that looked particularly recent. The woman sank slowly to the floor and clutched the wound on her shoulder as red began to soak down her back. It wasn't a deep wound and certainly not enough to cause any real damage, which was why she couldn't understand why she sagged so dramatically. Her whole body began to shiver uncontrollably.

Poison—it must be. The dagger the assassin had wielded was coated with something that would kill even if it only nicked her. A quick check revealed that there were no cuts she didn't know about before she approached them.

"What happened?" she asked and turned the injured woman on her side.

"We were…well, we were looking for a room," the second bard, a young man, said and looked panicked. "A cloaked figure appeared out of the shadows, stabbed Selene, and rushed away. I didn't even see his face."

"Do you know it was a man?" Cassandra asked.

"No…well, he was a little smaller than I was but quicker than I've ever seen anyone move. Impossibly fast."

Cassandra looked down the hallway again. If she had lagged behind her attacker before, this little pause would mean she would have no chance to catch up. There was the possibility that she could find out who sent the assassin in the first place, but that would be business for later.

She dropped to her knees beside the young woman, who convulsed even harder now. Foam had begun to form in her mouth and made her cough.

"Fucking hells," she whispered, placed her hands on the woman, and closed her eyes. The frothing was merely a symptom of the seizure that the girl was experiencing. The venom that had been on the knife was fast-acting, which told her it was likely taken from some kind of viper.

Although it was stronger than she was generally used to, she could still contain the effects of it and force the body to fight back and neutralize the effects until the venom was safely filtered out. It was what the body would do anyway, provided she lived long enough for it to happen. All she needed to do was help it along while she kept the bard alive.

The easiest way to help someone heal from an attack like this was to allow her body to do what it needed to do and assist it when necessary. She could always implement her will on the body through brute force, but it was a tiring effort and would leave her in pain and exhausted for hours or even days. Letting the body do what it did naturally was much easier, although it took a more delicate touch on her part.

She could hear the young man beside her desperately trying to not make a sound or interrupt her as she worked, but he was anxious. They had looked for a room in which to be alone for a reason, after all, and she assumed it meant the two were close. His worry was genuine, and she could appreciate that he put the effort in to avoid distracting her.

A few minutes later, the convulsions stopped and the frothing at her mouth ceased as well. The woman's breathing returned to normal, and Cassandra began to relax. The hardest part was over, and all she needed to do was ensure that there were no further problems that could return and injure her in the future.

Finally, she leaned back against the wall, sucked in a deep breath, and felt a hint of fatigue in her limbs as she watched the young woman she had been healing open her eyes. She gasped, turned, and touched the injury on her shoulder. The blood was still more or less fresh, but the wound had since sealed and left a mark that was only a little pinker than the skin around it.

"What happened?" she asked and looked at each of them in turn. "The assassin—"

"Escaped," Cassandra whispered and shook her head. "How do you feel?"

"Better... I don't...how did he—"

"The blade was tipped with poison," she answered before the woman could finish her thought. "The venom from a viper, by my guess. Your body was seizing and soon, your lungs would not have been able to fill themselves and you would have died."

"You saved my life?"

"In a manner of speaking. Did I save your life if you were injured by a blade intended for me?"

Neither bard had the answer to that particular question, but it wasn't like she had expected one.

"Thank you," the young man stated. "Are you all right? The effort of healing appears to have drained you."

"It's only temporary. I loaned the use of my energy for her to be able to heal faster than the venom could injure, and it leaves me feeling fatigued. I don't suppose that any of you happen to travel with koffe in your stores?"

"I'm afraid not."

"A pity. It always puts a little fire in the veins after using magic like this."

She drew another deep breath and frowned at the sounds of heavy boots rushing to where they were. All she wanted to do was close her eyes for a while and maybe even go back to sleep, but they needed to start the search for the assassin. Who had put them to their purpose was a question to be answered as well, but it would be easier if they had the man or woman in custody.

"What happened?" one of the guards asked when they arrived at the scene. They noticed the bleeding woman but since there was no wound and Cassandra appeared to have taken the brunt of the damage, she could understand their confusion.

"Raise the alarm," she said and pushed slowly to her feet, using the wall to support her. "There is an assassin inside the walls. They tried to kill me and injured her instead. I only managed to reach and heal her in time."

"An...assassin?"

"Yes. Go, now! Whatever they are, they are quicker than most men on horseback and might already be outside the walls of the keep. But the possibility remains that they might still be plotting their escape and I would not have it made easy for them."

"Right. Raise the alarm! Alarms!"

Two of the guards rushed away and in less than a minute,

bells rang and shouts from around the keep could be heard as guards were woken and word spread that an assassin had made an attempt on the life of the Barbarian Princess.

There was the possibility that Selby might have grown a spine in the night and with a little wine to fortify his bad decisions, he might have called on the skill of a professional to ensure that she did not leave the keep with the coin that was owed. If that were the case, the twins were likely targets as well, but as she hurried to the room they shared, there was no sign that the assassin had tried to attack them.

"You beauties got your sleep, then?" she asked as they stumbled out wearing nothing but their undergarments but still grasping their weapons. "If you had slept through my assassination, my ghost would have pestered you both until the end of time, I swear to all the gods."

"What happened?" Bandir rubbed his eyes and hefted his ax easily with the other hand.

"Someone tried to kill her," Tandir answered and shook his head. "Didn't you hear? Did you manage to catch the fucker?"

"Yes. Yes, I did. That is why I came here—to inform the two of you that the danger is over. They are ringing all the alarm bells to celebrate the fact that the threat has passed."

She paused when both men stared at her, a little confused and their minds still fuzzy from having been woken from a deep slumber.

"I am being sarcastic. The assassin escaped but not before they stabbed a poisoned blade into one of our bard comrades. I had to stop and help her before the venom did its work and by then, I'm not sure where the killer went. They might have already fled the castle for all we know, but the guards will search for him nonetheless."

Tandir scowled ferociously and adjusted his grip on his mace as if ready to use it. "We won't need to search far. I thought the damn lordling couldn't sink any lower but he now sends assassins? And only to keep a little coin from leaving his coffers?"

"I thought the same," Cassandra told him quickly, knowing where the man's mind was going. "And yet I cannot help but think there is something else at play here. From what I saw of the assassin's abilities, speed, and preparedness, I would say that no lord would pay that much coin to avoid losing fifteen gold pieces. For one thing, the services of someone like that would be considerably more than fifteen gold pieces."

"It might be that he was making up for the loss of face you caused him," Tandir suggested. "Then again, given that he tried to fuck you out of the contract fee, he might not have the coin to pay for an assassin."

"That was my thinking." She motioned for them to join her and they hurried down the hallway. The bards were gone, likely to join the rest of their troupe while it was assumed that the assassin was still on the loose. "Suspicions abound, but my instincts tell me that Selby is not responsible for this. We might want to have words with the man, however."

A few of the guards rushed past, likely still searching, but she caught the lead man by the collar of his gambeson and dragged him to a halt.

"Has your lord been woken yet?" she asked. Her tone brokered no negotiation or hesitation regarding the answer.

"He has been woken from his sleep and alerted to the situation," the guard answered as the other three almost collided with him after his sudden and unexpected halt. "You don't think...uh, that he might be responsible, do you?"

There was no need to share her first impressions with the man, and she narrowed her eyes. "That question will be addressed once I've spoken to him. Where can I find him?"

It was the ultimate judge of how they felt about their lord, and two of the men reached for their weapons in case she meant to kill Selby in revenge.

"He was escorted to the throne room," the lead guard announced. "You will find him there provided the bastard hasn't decided to return to his bed."

That answered that question. Cassandra nodded, released her hold on his gambeson, and straightened it as they passed. She looked at the twins.

"I guess we'll meet Selby in the throne room," Bandir muttered and rolled his shoulders as they moved in that direction.

It was a short walk since the simple design of the keep worked in their favor. She pushed the doors to the throne room open. A handful of servants waited on the lord who was still in his night-dress. He looked like he had drunk heavily before he fell asleep and was not pleased to be woken.

She intended to show him that she was even less pleased about the development.

Selby saw her expression immediately, bolted from his seat, and looked around for any sign of guards who might defend him.

There was only a handful and all appeared as exhausted as the man himself. No one jumped immediately into action to protect him.

"I know you have no reason to believe me," Selby said and appeared to seriously consider simply running away. "But you must know that I had no role in this."

Cassandra said nothing as she advanced on the throne. He backed away until he was forced into the seat again and tried to determine what she was thinking as she glared at him.

It was a little sadistic of her, she mused, but he still deserved it. He needed to remember the fear that coursed through his body when he understood what would happen if he chose to act against her.

Finally, she shook her head. "I do not believe you sent the assassin. With that said, the security of your keep is in question. How did they come through in the dead of night?"

The lord looked like the relief would put him to sleep again

MICHAEL ANDERLE

and he motioned for one of the servants to bring him a drink. "Believe me, I am as horrified by this breach of hospitality as you are but for the moment, nothing has been seen of the assassin. I fear my guards were alerted a little too late and by the time they were able to secure the walls, the culprit had already left."

"I can understand that. Whoever they were, they could run like nothing I've ever seen. That added to the fact that I had to stop to save the life of another of your guests means that they would have had more than enough time to escape if they had a mind to."

He frowned like he almost didn't believe that she discussed the attempt with him in a civil manner. Perhaps he expected her to fling accusations and even try to kill him in retaliation.

She drew a deep breath and glanced around the room. As much as she wanted to attack and drive her sword into something, she realized that targeting anything and everything that crossed her path at this point would only serve to make things worse.

The fact that she still grasped her sword had almost slipped her mind. Perhaps that was why the lordling appeared a little more terrified of her than she had intended.

"Well then, as long as I can rely on your guards to maintain their defenses better, I think I will return to bed."

"What?" Tandir snapped and hefted his mace. "No one will be killed?"

"Not unless they catch that son of a whoremonger," Cassandra retorted and motioned both the twins back.

There was nothing more to be done, and she could feel the fatigue of the day they'd had still telling on her body even without the energy spent in healing the bard.

Sunrise could not be more than a few hours away, which left them little time to rest before traveling again.

It wouldn't be enough, but all things considered, she would be more than happy to leave Massar and never return.

Sleep took a while to come and what she did manage was rest-less. Tandir slept with his mace in hand, ready for anything that might make an attempt on their lives, but the night passed uneventfully.

He couldn't tell if he was relieved or disappointed that nothing had come to try to attack them by the time they climbed from their beds and prepared their packs for the journey.

Whoever the assassin was, they were long gone and would likely not be seen again for a while, although he wished he would make an attempt on one of the twins next. He didn't doubt Cassandra's skills, of course, but it was only fair that one of them have their turn with the shite.

From the looks of the rest of their little party, he could tell that they had not found much rest either. The bard who had been wounded the night before appeared to be well and healthy enough to travel, again showing the true skills the barbarian princess could call on when they were needed.

Their horses were being readied and what food could be spared was loaded into saddlebags.

What felt most odd was the silence that filled the whole keep. Nothing needed to be said, but a place like this generally bustled with activity in the morning. It was almost as though someone had died given the lack of sound.

Cassandra looked exhausted as well, but she moved with purpose, clearly determined to leave before the sun crested the walls. The rest of the troupe appeared to detect that in her.

It wasn't like they could disagree. Bandir had already loaded everything and waited for the bards, who moved a little slower and appeared to look around and try to see everything they could. Perhaps they were trying to paint a real picture with their words about what happened when someone tried to kill the Barbarian Princess.

Intentionally tried to kill her, he reminded himself. A human intentionally tried to kill her while she wasn't working or saving someone's life.

Tandir shook his head and tried to not think about it too hard. It was one thing to try to kill her when she had her sword or spear in hand, defending a group of pilgrims or travelers, and another to try to kill her in her bed. He had never thought of himself as the protective type but trying to kill someone he cared about in their sleep was a problem.

Killing them while they were awake was not a problem—or not as much of a problem, at least.

The former paladin had already mounted her horse and muttered something to it as she steadied it. She checked that the rest of the group was ready to leave and gestured for them to mount. He complied hastily since he knew her well enough to see that she wouldn't wait.

"All right, then!" He growled and grasped the reins a little tighter. "Mount up or you'll be left behind!"

They did as they were told and were ready to leave in moments. Nothing more needed to be said and while the people of Massar watched the group ride away, not a word was said in parting.

He chose to take that as a sign of respect from them rather than foreboding.

CHAPTER EIGHT

Given the swamp and mire of Massar, Cassandra missed Edge's Rest. She would always hate the place for that particular feeling but for the moment, she allowed herself to bask in a return to the town that grew more familiar with every passing day.

The welcome that greeted them was a little cooler than it had been the last time around, but she assumed it was only due to the fact that their legend had run its course with the locals and they had moved on to newer and more inspiring things.

Then again, as they rode through the narrow streets of Edge's Rest, she couldn't help a sinking feeling that dropped into the pit of her stomach. Every eye cast her way reminded her of the blade that had been stopped mere inches from her throat. It begged the question of who had wielded it and whose orders had seen it raised in the first place.

Answers would not be provided by riding around the town asking questions, but a keen eye needed to be maintained even as they stabled their horses and returned to the inn to order drinks and food after a hard day of riding.

The twins remained oddly quiet when their mugs of ale were

filled and platters stacked with steaming piles of food were brought to them.

"Is something on your mind?" Cassandra asked and sliced into a chunk of the pork belly that was served as the evening meal. "Neither of you said much on the journey."

"We never thought we would have to deal with assassins, is all." Bandir growled his displeasure. "It's one thing to face an enemy in the field of battle in an honest fight and quite another to be worried about someone stabbing you in the back, slitting your throat in your sleep, or poisoning your…meal."

As the last word escaped him, he looked at his platter, his expression torn while he tried to decide whether he would indulge his hunger or pass on food that could be tainted.

She was already a few mouthfuls in and felt no signs of the poison affecting her body.

"I would take it as a compliment," she answered as the bards prepared themselves to perform for the patrons present. They strummed lutes and hummed tunes before they broke out into a song based on their fight with the ghouls. "No fight with either of you in the field of battle would be considered a fair and honest fight, so your enemies are forced to pursue alternate, villainous methods by which to rid themselves of you."

"The assassins won't come for us," Tandir pointed out and took a tentative sip of his drink before he decided that if he would die, it would not be on an empty stomach. "But it's interesting how you managed to compliment yourself there."

Cassandra winked. "It is a gift."

Her eyes narrowed and she turned to listen a little closer to the song that the patrons now clapped and laughed about as the lyrics described the battle in the crypt.

"My memory might be a tad fuzzy," Bandir said, "but I think we would remember it if she had charged into the fight bare-breasted and bathed in blood, don't you think?"

His brother nodded. "I should say so. A blind man would remember a sight like that."

"You'll have to forgive the artists for taking leave of reality," she answered and shook her head. "I assume it will be what gains them and their song the most attention."

"I doubt they'll ever sing about the two of us fighting barebreasted," Tandir muttered.

"If you had breasts like these, I'm sure more folk would want to hear about them being bare."

She wasn't sure why she was in a good mood. It had been a few long days in a row and the need for sleep already beckoned as her belly filled and the warmth of the ale began to spread. There would be no singing and dancing until late in the night this time, and she had every intention to find a bed and crawl into it for a long night of hopefully relaxing rest before they returned to Langven with news of the completed contract.

The twins looked at their chests at her comment. Tandir nodded in agreement but Bandir looked a little closer.

"I would say the womenfolk have an interest in my chest."

"Did you pay these womenfolk?"

"That is not the point."

Cassandra laughed as the song came to an end and the attention of the patrons settled on them again. Calls for more music and more drinks followed, and some offered to pay for the drinks and food they already ordered.

Her protests about how it wasn't needed fell on deaf ears and they listened to another song about them heading into battle, this time fighting a group of imperial deserters who had taken over a small town.

It hadn't been much more than a skirmish, but if folk believed the tale being told, it was a battle for the ages with the gods coming down to wage war with and against them at various points.

She gave them points for effort but lacked the energy to listen to any more of it. As soon as she could slip out, she headed to the room she'd asked the proprietor to set aside for her. It was simple with only a bed and a candle if it was needed.

It seemed logical to assume it might be the finest room in the establishment given that the mattress was down instead of hay. Before she knew it, she drifted off to sleep—thankfully dreamless, although it felt like she had barely closed her eyes before the sounds from outside woke her.

"I swear to all the gods in all the realms, they did not make the fucking night long enough," Cassandra muttered and squinted at the sunlight already seeping through the cracks in the walls and under the door. From the brightness of it, she could guess that she had slept well into the morning and the sun was already halfway up the sky.

The temptation to lay back again for a little more sleep was hard to resist, but she pulled herself clear of the bed, groaned, and stretched before she collected her things and left the room. She splashed her face with water from a nearby well to wake herself properly.

It was simple to collect the coin owed to them now that the contract was completed and one of Langven's men was quick to point them to the only dwarf blacksmith in the town.

He was outside the walls and near the river next to the docks, where the dwarves had built a water wheel that harnessed the power of the moving water to drive their bellows and reduce the work they had to do themselves.

That in itself was enough for a recommendation for their work. Efficiency was not everything when it came to metalworking, but it accounted for more than most people realized.

Thankfully, waking the twins to get them to work for the day had not taken too much time or effort, which meant that not too many others awaited the services of the dwarves when they arrived.

The patriarch of the family saw her almost immediately and

cleaned his hands on his apron before he hurried to where they stood patiently.

"Well, I think I would know the three of you by reputation alone if I were blind and deaf," he said. He boasted an impressive, grizzled beard that hung to his knees or would have if he didn't have it braided and balled up. His mask covered it as well to ensure that no stray strands were caught by the sparks flying all around the shop. "Anan Stonearm, at your service."

"Cassandra, at yours," she answered and remembered her manners. "These two are Bandir and Tandir of the DrakeHunter clan."

"Aye, I know ye well. Much has been said and heard of your exploits in these parts, and I am most pleased that you would choose to support my shop. How can I help ye, then? Do ye have weapons and armor needing to be forged?"

"We are well-armed and armored," Tandir answered quickly.

"Well enough, anyway," she answered and narrowed her eyes. "But we have weapons that need your keen eye and armor that needs a little repair since both have seen a great deal of service. We also have javelins that will need new hafts if you have wood-workers among you."

"You'll need to speak to Sefast, down that way." Anan pointed down the road to another shop near the river. "Most days, he makes shafts for bows and the like, but he's got a keen mind for spears and javelins. Tell him I sent ye and he'll be sure to provide a good price for good work. Speaking of which, would you mind if we could take a look at yours? It has become a thing of legend."

Cassandra smiled, hefted her spear, and handed it to the dwarf. "It does not need any repairs to it, I don't think. Spells were put on it to keep the haft safe and the edges sharp."

"Aye, keen spellwork is woven into the steel," Anan agreed and inspected the edge carefully. "Runes put into the tang likely do most of the protecting. It's good work although likely human or maybe elf, if I were to venture a guess…aye, definitely elf. They like to use their spears like this. But you are right. It has no need for sharpening or repair."

That was the case with the spear and her armor needed the work of a mage, but her sword had a few nicks in it from the fights that needed to be sanded out. The twins presented theirs, but their armor was not magical and so the gambesons needed to be repaired and the ringed mail had to be worked through.

"How much will all this cost?" Cassandra asked. Dwarves were sound steelworkers, given that their culture was heavily touched by such work, but their prices tended to reflect that. She did not want to be guilty of underpayment, which would result in rushed work that would see them dead in the future, but she was well aware that demanding the best would see the three of them paupers before the day was out.

"I would say thirty gold pieces for all of it," Anan answered and cleaned his hands on his apron again. He did that often, although she decided to not point it out. "I do have another offer if you have a mind to listen."

She tilted her head. "Go on."

"You three have a reputation. Folk admire you in this region and well beyond it too, I would say. If you would be willing to carry our mark on your weapons and armor and if you were to leave yours on our wall over there, I would be willing to pull five pieces from the price."

Cassandra looked at the wall he mentioned and realized that more than a few names and sigils were carved into the stone, likely markers of trust from those who had their weapons and armor repaired by the Stonearm family.

"If folk saw us carrying your mark on our weapons and armor, or saw our mark on your wall, it would be considered an endorsement," she noted and approached the wall. "Those mercenaries, sellswords, and other vagabonds who saw it and survived would know that you were the one who armed and armored us. It would earn you a great deal of business besides."

His eyes narrowed as he tried to understand why she took such a roundabout way to state the obvious.

"I suppose you are right."

"I would say it is worth more to you than five gold coins. I would say at least twelve."

Haggling was a tradition and the dwarf smiled when he realized what she was doing, but it turned quickly into a scowl as he ran his fingers through his beard.

"Six, at the very most."

"Ten and three silvers."

"Eight and five. And I'll throw in the value of a recommendation for a good mage who would be able to have a look at that amulet you use as armor."

"Done." Cassandra retrieved the coins necessary for payment, placed them carefully on the table, and let the dwarf count them. From what she'd heard, they liked to handle the money themselves and generally wore an anti-magic amulet of some kind so that they could avoid being swindled by any skilled illusionists.

He counted them quickly, and when he was finished, swept them smoothly off the table and into a coin purse before he gestured to his people to get to work.

They all understood her efforts, of course, and she doubted that the dwarves expected her to take the generous offer of a discount on their work without some haggling on her part to increase the amount, but she couldn't help feeling a little bad over it. Still, what was owed was owed, and she collected the chisel, moved to the wall, and searched for an empty place where she could leave her name.

She didn't recognize most of the names and marks left there, but one that was easily noticed. It was the largest of those on the wall and was a clear marker for anyone who entered the shop to see.

"It is interesting that the Ebon Pack give you their business," she commented and ran her fingers over the mark of a wolf's fang on a shield that had caught her attention so boldly. "Well, not that interesting, I suppose. Given the good fortune they have enjoyed lately, it makes sense that they would want their men to be equipped by the best in Edge's Rest."

Anan peered at her and grinned as he approached the wall as well. "Ah, yes, Commander Langven made a point to see to it that his men always carry weapons and armor worked on by my hands and those of my clan. And with you and the twins leaving your mark as well, I will have the full set of legends in the making doing their work with my steel. A blacksmith cannot ask for much more."

Casandra made no effort to disagree and instead, pressed the chisel to the stone and marked her name and title carefully. She squeezed it in with the rest of the names and sigils left by others. The question in her mind was whether her name and those of the twins would be as easy to forget as most of those already there. No one could tell what the future held for them and all they could do was survive long enough to see what happened to their legacy.

Or die and let the gods make that decision for them instead.

She turned to the twins and motioned for them to go ahead and leave their names along with their clan name. This would ensure that they would enjoy the same benefits she did if she happened to die before they needed to return there. Both shrugged and took the tool from her hands. Whatever skills they had with the blade while killing people quickly disappeared as they worked to carve their names into the stone wall as well. She assumed that whittling was not a skill lost on them, but they had some difficulty with this task.

"One would think that you had never tried to sign your names before," she quipped.

"This one keeps getting it wrong," Bandir insisted. "I'm only trying to correct his mistakes before he ruins the whole thing."

"I would say that the two of you will ruin the whole thing and destroy the damn wall while you're at it."

"Never fear, milady," Anan interrupted, having watched the twins progress as well while he brought her sword to bear on a bench grinder. "Me cousin and his team built this shop. It would take a great deal more than the antics of these two young lads to undo good dwarven handiwork and bring the whole shop down on our heads."

"Oy, who is he calling a lad?" Tandir snarled and reached for the sword at his side, his gaze directed firmly at the dwarf.

Cassandra stepped in, caught the hand that was on his weapon, and yanked it away firmly.

"Apologies, my friends. I'm old and in the habit of calling everyone I speak to lad. I meant no disrespect by it, I assure ye."

Tandir still looked annoyed by it but she nudged him in the ribs with her elbow to indicate that the dwarf was not the only one who owed an apology.

"And…I did not mean to react that way. It is not a term I enjoy having directed at me."

"No harm, no foul, I say."

"Well, there was harm to the wall," Cassandra pointed out and ran her fingers over the damage done to wipe off the dust that had been cut from it. "But aside from that, no harm. While we are on the topic, I don't suppose that your cousin is still in business in these parts?"

"As it happens, he is." Anan nodded and bound his beard up again as a few sparks spat from the sword being dragged over the grinder. "He was called in to help fix a few holes in the town walls and he finished that work not too long ago. My cousin is obsessed with games of chance, poor devil, so I think he will look rather desperately for more work if you need his services. You will find his shop on the other side of the cliff where he mines his stone."

She nodded. "I think I'll pay him a visit."

The twins looked oddly at her but asked no questions as they left the shop and she looked for signs that would show her where she would find the stoneworkers.

"I can understand why we would need the assistance of a metalsmith and a woodworker," Tandir stated from close behind her. "And yet I cannot understand why we would need the services of a stonemason. We have no weapons or armor made of stone, do we?"

"No, yet I happen to know of those who could use the work of a good dwarf mason. You know, the types who have been working to rebuild a fortress on Draug's Hill, led by a barbarian shit who has absolutely no idea of how to lead his people and yet manages to do his best anyway?"

"You think we could pay for him to help the people of Tors-burch?" Bandir raised an eyebrow. "Dwarf work won't be cheap, but provided that we still have a decent amount of coin left from our job, I suppose we might be able to afford it. We could also afford if it you had a mind to start delving into that dragon's treasure you've been hoarding."

"Between you and me, there isn't much of it left," Cassandra answered and shrugged slightly. "Between helping the folk we've encountered on the roads and trying to build their new home in a way that would allow them all to live well enough, I've spent most of it. Why do you think we waited so long to repair our weapons and armor?"

"Our weapons and armor," Tandir reminded her as they circled to the other side of the cliff.

"You two need not follow me. Keep an eye on your weapons and armor or find a place that serves cool drinks. I'll find you there."

"You don't have to ask us twice. We'll wait until you've spoken to the mason."

She nodded and waved them off before she turned and

followed the path to the other side of the cliff in search of the mason's workshop.

As it turned out, it was easy to locate her destination given that he had dug into the cliffs as far away from the town as could be managed to avoid any accidents that would destroy the settlement on top. This was where he sourced his stone, which was dragged to the shop to be worked on.

The dwarf was very easy to find since he was seated at a rough table and appeared to be studying plans while his workers busied themselves with various tasks. He looked older than Anan and thick streaks of white cut through his dark-brown beard. His light-gray eyes lit up when he saw her approach him.

"Good day." She greeted him with a smile. "I am Cassandra, the—"

"Barbarian Princess," the dwarf interrupted. "I heard a great deal about your adventures last night. I am honored by your presence in my humble shop. I am Sifeas Stonearm at your service."

"And I at yours." She bowed her head slightly. "I come in need of your services."

"Do you?" Sifeas looked surprised, tilted his head, and looked at his shop. "I…didn't think a barbarian princess would have much need for a stonemason's skills."

"I would say a princess needs a castle, but the walls that need your work are not necessarily mine. There is a settlement I am invested in seeing succeed on Draug's Hill. They need materials and skilled work to shore their defenses up."

"I know of the place. I would have assumed it was the kind of settlement that likely couldn't afford my services."

"Luckily for them, I can." Cassandra drew a handful of gold coins from her pouch. "And I have been told that it would be lucky for you as well. Are you interested?"

The dwarf ran his fingers through his beard and considered

the proposition for a moment. "I would need to transport myself, my team, and all the supplies we would need. The cost of that and the work involved would be…I would say thirty-five gold coins all told. It could be more depending on how much work is required."

"And it could be less," she pointed out. "I'll settle on thirty pieces here and now, and we can negotiate further once you've assessed the state of the fortress."

"Done."

She took the man's hand and sealed the agreement for the moment. His quick acceptance, however, made her wonder if she hadn't been cheated. Not that it mattered, though. He needed the coin and she needed him to be on the move to Draug's Hill without dragging his feet.

Everyone knew that contractors tended to drag their feet when they thought they were not being paid a fair price for their labor. Cassandra was more than willing to make sure that he was out there and getting the work done as quickly as possible, even if it meant paying a little more than was necessary.

All things considered, they still had enough coin to last them for a while as long as they didn't throw it around, especially with the bonus handed over by Selby for their good work.

Papers were drafted quickly and signed to ensure that it was known that the dwarf's services were under her employ. Any attempt on his part to cheat her out of what had been paid for would be considered something that would allow her to take action against him for it.

She honestly doubted that it would come to that since all folk in this region lived and died on reputation. No one would deal with a stonemason who was known to do shoddy work and given that they tended to take any law into their own hands, it was the type of action that would end with his throat slit in the middle of the night.

Once all the dues were paid and the paperwork complete, Sifeas shouted at his men to get to work. They said they would be ready to move to Draug's Hill when the sun came up, which left with her little to do other than to find the twins again—and hope they hadn't landed themselves into too much trouble.

From the sounds of it, however, trouble was what they had found. All she needed to do was follow the yelling. She broke into a slow run to where a small group had gathered. Her first impression was that they had assembled to start a fight, but it was immediately corrected when she saw that Tandir held his brother back. Another man was on the ground, being helped up slowly by his comrades, although they needed to push and shove to get to him.

"Stop!" Cassandra snapped but she couldn't hear herself over the shouts that issued from all sides. "Oy! The whole godsbe-dammed lot of you! Shut your fucking holes or I'll slit the throats of those who don't!"

That seemed to work most efficiently. The twins stopped their fighting and looked at her, and the people ceased their yelling and gave her a moment to see what was happening.

The group that appeared to have picked a fight with the twins looked like they had come off a long journey, the kind that was undertaken with the knowledge that not all would see the end of it. They were gaunt, dirty, and looked desperate, although none carried anything more threatening than a knife by way of defense.

"What happened?" she demanded and turned her attention to the twins. "Keep your words short and to the point."

"That one there grabbed me," Bandir snapped and pushed his brother away. "He shouted at me and said we were responsible for their problems and that we owed them. When I tried to push him away, he threw a punch at my face."

"He was only reaching for you," Tandir answered and adjusted his shirt. "He wasn't looking for a fight. It would have to be a special kind of fool to try to throw his fist at a man twice his size looking as ill-fed as they do."

"I know what I saw."

Cassandra turned to the man who had accosted Bandir, narrowed her eyes, and studied the group as she tried to determine why they were so incensed. "You accosted one of my men. I would know the reason why."

The group of twenty or so looked like they hadn't expected to be taken seriously. All appeared to have been under the sun long enough for a hint of madness to creep in, and she wanted to know why it drove them to the twins. Finally, the one who had started it all with Bandir stepped forward. He was a young man with barely a hint of red fuzz on his chin.

His eyes were the oddest color of blue—almost purple at a glance—and what she could see there was more than the desperation she saw in the others. Pure anger radiated from him, even though he was shorter than her and leaner too, almost to the bone.

"You are the Barbarian Princess?" he asked and his bottom lip trembled. "And these two...the DrakeHunter twins who fight with you?"

"You have me at a disadvantage, boy."

"I am Gaelin Uran. My home...our home was plundered by an army that attacked from the northeast. They said they fought under the banner of Grimm the Cruel, drove us from our homes, and harried us until we reached the wastes."

That explained the desperate look about them. But all those who were present were adults with no children among them. It made no sense that children who would generally be among the group were missing, which led her to believe there was a darker story that was not being told by those assembled.

And she imagined there was a good reason for that. Cassandra gritted her teeth when she felt something hot in the pit of her stomach that made it difficult to focus for a moment. She knew the name, of course. The folk were scorched, hungry, homeless, and desperate for vengeance. All they were doing was lashing out at the wrong people.

"Their commander said that the barbarian princess was responsible. That her rising to stop his Herald caused this."

"What happened to you happened to others," she replied in a low tone. The people who had gathered started to move away when they lost interest now that there was no fight. "They killed all who were in their path."

"They didn't only kill." The boy looked down and covered his face with his hands. "I… They burned everything, salted the fields, and made sure that nothing of our home would ever be a home again."

She placed her hand on his shoulder and gave him a moment to compose himself before he looked at her.

"Grimm will pay for what he has done," she whispered and held his gaze firmly. "Justice will be served. But first, you and your people need to be kept safe. It will not happen here. You will rest here for the night and with fresh supplies and provisions, journey to Draug's Hill. You will be safe there."

"It…Draug's Hill? There are dread stories of that place."

"There are dread stories of every place in the world, Edge's Rest included. There you will find roofs over your heads, food, and work, as well as a wall to protect you. Do you understand?"

He nodded. "How will we know the way?"

"You'll travel with us. But…uh, try to not insult the barbarians, all right?"

CHAPTER NINE

There had originally been no plans to begin their journey so soon. Cassandra wasn't sure she liked returning to the road so often but it was important to keep morale up. The twins enjoyed fighting and traveling as much as the next adventurer, but they also needed time to rest and relax, which was what Edge's Rest represented for them.

Still, they made no mention of any complaints, nor did the bards as they also loaded their horses and mules in preparation for another long trip. She had put up token resistance to stop them from coming. It was merely an escort journey to take the twenty or so refugees who needed a refuge to a new home. Too many people in Torsburch had died, which meant they would always welcome new arrivals.

The entertainers were not dissuaded, however.

"Noteworthy adventures have a way of following you around the world," Julian informed her.

If that was what they called falling constantly into trouble with a little help from the divine, maybe they were right. Still, it was better that they traveled in larger numbers and especially since none of them looked like merchants. The bandits had an eye for that kind of thing, and they could guess that someone so unencumbered was either a mercenary or desperate.

Either way, it was not worth the risk, not for so little loot to be gained. The group moved quickly. She patted Strider on the neck, nudged him to move a little faster, and shielded her eyes to scan the horizon. Just because it was unlikely that a foul element would attack didn't mean they wouldn't. There was always the possibility that the folk they encountered were not that intelligent and even worse, were desperate.

They had eventually decided to travel with the dwarves too, although they moved a little slower. Still, by the looks of the crossbows and spears they carried along with their supplies, she assumed they were more than capable of defending themselves against any attackers who might show themselves. She appreciated the fact that they had come with every intention to fight through difficulties.

Any other group like theirs would expect to be protected. She would have had to hand out more coin to hire bodyguards for them.

After a few days of travel, however, Cassandra began to think there would be no skirmishes. By the time the walls on Draug's Hill rose in the distance before them, only partially obscured by the heat radiating from the earth, she decided they would not be attacked after all.

She was almost a little disappointed. Much was said about the power behind the crossbows the dwarves used, although she would have to wait to see them another time.

The gates were already being pulled open as they approached and she was the first one through. She recognized the people and responded to their smiles and waves, all while their hands were on their weapons, ready and waiting to attack anyone who tried to take their new home from them.

Draug's Hill was a good location, perfectly positioned so it had a commanding view of the region. Wells were dug deep into the soil to provide water, and there was only one road, winding and open. This enabled anyone who stood on the walls to rain fire on those who were attacking. The rest of the way was sheer rock face.

With that said, the route was littered with debris and ruins from the battle that had been fought there previously.

The walls themselves had crumbled for years. When Karvahal and his people had arrived, it had been in worse condition than expected but it was still in place and still a home. It was also more defensible than Torsburch was. The move had not been seamless but water and food were available and enabled them to settle.

"You can tell when the bones of a place are well-made," Sifeas commented and ran his rough hands over the walls around the gates. "This one was well-built. It will make rebuilding it a little easier."

"But not cheaper, I imagine?" Cassandra brought Strider to a halt next to the dwarf.

"There is much work to be done but the price holds for the moment. I'll let you know if it changes."

"You do that."

"All right, you festering maggots. We won't be paid to lounge listlessly about this place so let's get to work!"

His voice carried well, she had to admit, and she couldn't help a smile when his workers pulled their horses and mules in and began to unload them. A few set up a camp for them to call home while the work was in progress while others engaged the people of Draug's Hill to find places for them to start working.

There was more than enough to be done, but around the gate-house was where most of the repair was needed.

They appeared to know their business well and didn't need a princess to tell them where they needed to go or why. That left her the task of finding somewhere for their refugees.

"I see you've brought more strays to my doors, hoping I would welcome them. I don't suppose it would do any good to tell you to take them and wander off in the direction you came from?"

Cassandra slid from her saddle and smiled as Karvahal stepped out from the shadows cast by the wall, grinning as widely as he possibly could. He was still the young man who had watched his father be killed by a powerful mage who could handle fire as whips, but there was something a little firmer about him now. Perhaps it was the fact that so many people had entrusted him with their lives and their safety. That kind of thing had a way of maturing folk, even if they didn't want it to.

He stepped closer and she wrapped her arms around him in a tight embrace. She knew he had come to shake her hand, but she assumed they were beyond such concerns by now.

"I knew you would welcome any who are in need," she answered once she decided the hug had lasted long enough. She took a step back, her hands on his shoulders. and scrutinized him as a mother might to ensure that a treasured son was still in one piece. "How have things been here?"

"Rough, but we can manage. I've heard a great deal about you traveling around and making a name for yourself."

"And the name has spread."

"Is that why you brought a group of stonemasons here?"

"The walls need shoring up and I had some coin to pay them for it. But yes, and that is why I brought the refugees as well. They almost started a fight with the twins because someone named Grimm the Cruel took their homes and drove them into the wastes, saying it was the fault of the Barbarian Princess and the DrakeHunter twins."

"Call a boy Grimm and no one is surprised when he turns out to be a bastard shit from a whore." Karvahal spat to emphasize his point. "What are the odds that the very same villagers he drove from their homes found their way to you?"

"Low. Which was why I assumed they were not the only ones.

I would say this Grimm is looking for me specifically and he's burning a path through the lands to find me."

"And so you brought them here?"

"As long as they are out of the fight or at least behind walls, I will be happy to fight the shit on my terms. There is no other reason for him to burn through the northeast. At least when his Herald did it, she left the people alive."

"Escalation was always a possibility. You cannot be surprised by this."

Cassandra shook her head. "Unfortunately, I am not. I think more refugees will arrive in Edge's Rest before long, provided they survive their journeys. There will be little else for us to do other than draw his forces out."

"Do you think he will try to find you himself?"

"The man who sent a Herald out to announce how much of an entitled mule's ass he is? I doubt it. At least at first."

"So what do you want me to do with these refugees?"

She looked to where they had begun to lower their packs. They looked exhausted and on the brink of collapse.

"They'll need a home."

"Are there no children among them?"

"I noticed the same thing. I would assume there is a story to be told about that, but I did not find it in myself to press them for it. They need a place to lay their head. All are farmers, by the looks of them, and if they can be put to work helping your people set up the fields contained by the walls to start planting and growing food, I think the arrangement will benefit all of you."

"And what about the entertainers you brought to me? Will they provide us with food as well?"

Cassandra looked at them and narrowed her eyes. "The truth is that they have followed us ever since we saved their lives from a sand drake that was attacking them."

"A…sand drake?"

"Aye. A big fucker about the size of a draft horse with a club at the end of its tail, armored with rocks, and able to dig itself into the ground and come up to attack almost anywhere."

"Is it…cowardly that I am thankful I was not there to fight it with you?"

"It would have been cowardly if you had been there and ran away. Anyone with a head on their shoulders would have been terrified to face a beast like that."

"Head on their shoulders, eh?" Karvahal chuckled, shook his head, and looked to where the twins stood. Tandir had his arm wrapped around his brother's neck and Bandir exerted the effort to dislodge him. "I suppose that discounts the two who were with you."

"They're brave enough and good fighters. And the only ones crazy enough to journey with me as I do what I do."

"As I said, no heads on their shoulders."

She snapped her fist out and punched the chieftain on the shoulder.

"Why are the bards with you if you already saved their lives?" he asked and rubbed where she had struck.

"They made a song about our fight with the drake. From what I heard, they make good coin on it and are intent on making more. They say watching the events transpire themselves enables a better retelling of those tales in musical form, although I don't understand that much. They don't even follow the events that closely with their music. I'll never make sense of this."

The barbarian chuckled and shook his head. "They've followed you for a while then, have they?"

"Rather recently. They came with us to Massar, a swamp on the border of the empire that had issues with a pack of ghouls that had infected their region. We couldn't allow them to follow us into the crypt where the ghouls were hiding, but after tales of what transpired from the twins, they were sufficiently prepared to mangle the events in the name of producing good entertainment."

Karvahal guided her to where a handful of barrels were propped and poured from one of them into a pair of simple clay cups. He handed the first to her and took the second for himself.

She hadn't expected the wine to be any good but it was cool and refreshing nonetheless Cassandra was almost halfway through it before she paused.

"How long do you plan to remain this time?" he asked once he'd sipped a fair amount of the wine as well. "I cannot imagine that you would be stuck here for too long before the need to travel the world, righting wrongs and saving the innocent, takes you away again."

"A few days at least," she answered, drained her cup, and refilled it from the barrel. "I mean to ensure that work on the walls is progressing and does not need any more coin to be provided. I'll leave you a small purse that should cover what the dwarf might charge, but I think you can trust him to be fair in his dealings."

"And you possess so much coin now?"

"The work with the ghouls was paid for by the emperor himself, and I managed to push a little more out of the lord who oversaw the whole process after he tried to fuck us out of the payment. Then again, there was an attempt made on my life that might have influenced him as well."

"Your ability to bury the most important news is one of the reasons why we so enjoy having you with us. Who made an attempt on your life?"

She scowled and tried to not look too upset by the thought as she took another sip of the wine. "A skilled assassin. Faster than I've ever seen in my life and carrying a dagger poisoned with some kind of snake venom."

"Did you question this assassin? Find out who sent them?"

"He...they got away."

"What?"

"Like I said, they were fast. I was barely able to stop that blade from sinking into me before they escaped and stabbed someone else on their way out in an attempt to slow me. They were never found."

"Well...that will need to be discussed later, I suppose. Is there anything else you need to tell me?"

"Try to keep the refugees away from the bards as best you can," Cassandra answered. "I don't know why, but I have the impression they do not like each other—glances, abrupt statements—the little things but still, there is something there that could turn into a conflagration if not stemmed early."

"You say that as though you are not sure when you will leave."

She shook her head and looked at the walls. "They came from the northeast. I would assume that the Herald came from there as well. I think I should journey there before too long, make a point of finding out how many displaced families are in the region, and try to find a way to stop them."

"They have a fucking army." Karvahal raised an eyebrow and drained his cup as well. "You'll need something of similar size and power to drive them back, assuming you didn't find out how to perform that...darkness spell the Herald was capable of."

"That is dangerous magic. The kind that they no longer teach anywhere. I wouldn't even know where to start."

"But you are considering it."

"Power that can level an entire fortress in one stroke is the kind we need to be alerted to, one way or another."

"In a few days, then? Will you take the bards along with the twins to see if there are more tales to be wrung out of them?"

Cassandra tilted her head. "I'll need to scout on my own. The lutes and flutes stay here and I think they might be a boon to the morale of this place."

"So only you and the twins, then?"

"They will remain as well. I'll need them to keep everyone safe, even if it means they need to get along somehow."

"I take it you have not discussed the matter with them yet?"

"The discussion will be a short one. I'll tell them, they'll complain, I'll threaten to break noses, and they'll decide that a little rest while keeping watch on the wall construction is to their benefit. I have a system for dealing with them and it is very, very effective."

He laughed. "You don't think they'll try to follow once you've left?"

"If they do, I'll drive my boot so far into their groins that they'll chew on their balls for a week. Like I told you, I have a system."

"Indeed." Karvahal covered his groin uncomfortably merely at the thought. "Are you sure it is safe for you to ride out there alone, especially since this...Grimm appears to be looking for you specifically?"

"From what I've gathered, I would say he has no idea what I or the twins look like and has based his search on simple descriptions of me in armored undergarments and barbarian twins who ride alongside me. It is why I will go alone—to ensure that any reputation I might have does not precede me."

"And if it does anyway?"

"I'll have to fight my way out of trouble. It would not be the first time I've done so and I doubt it'll be the last."

"Unless it...well...is the last."

He made a good point. She inclined her head and considered another taste of the wine when the sound of fighting carried over the courtyard. When she turned, she realized that the twins' wrestling had begun to get out of hand.

"It's time to employ that system of yours," Karvahal pointed out.

She raised a finger at him but could think of no good rebuttal and chose instead to turn and deal with the culprits before anything was broken. It was a good system, but the twins would get into trouble no matter what she did. They would be a boon to the defense of Draug's Hill, provided they did not bring the walls down on their own.

CHAPTER TEN

Traveling alone had its benefits. Cassandra remembered dreading the thought when she struck out, only her and Strider, into the wilderness, and there was no denying the downsides. The loneliness was difficult to avoid, which led to many one-sided conversations with her horse as the miles stretched on.

She also dismounted often and walked with him for stretches, telling herself it was because her ass was sore from the saddle and she needed time to stretch. Despite this, as they continued roughly to the northeast of Draug's Hill, she began to relax as the time passed.

Having folk to constantly look after and keep an eye on in order to ensure that they weren't doing anything stupid had a way of draining her. Walking along on her own and not owing answers or responsibility to anyone was a feeling she hadn't realized she missed.

It wouldn't be long before she was desperate for the presence of any being that spoke to her but for the moment, she was determined to enjoy it. She had a feeling there wouldn't be much time for that, not if she came upon what she thought would be waiting for her in the direction in which they traveled.

The further north she journeyed, the more familiar the landscape became. Lusher forests began to grow as thick rivers cut through it, engorged by the snow melting in the mountains in the middle of the summer. The water was cool and refreshing and while the roads were in poor condition, those rivers that didn't have decent bridges had good places to ford.

From what she could see, the region was perfect for expansion. She imagined that if it were only a little closer to the major population hubs, it would have teemed with life as all races and types settled there.

Yet she knew there would be an additional reason for folk to avoid the area if something wasn't done. The type of person she guessed this Grimm was would use scorched-earth tactics to devastate the landscape if the people inhabiting it made things difficult for him.

She nudged Strider into a faster walk as they approached the crest of a gentle hill. The forests were intermittent for the moment and opened a little more into grasslands ahead, and she wanted the opportunity to scan their surroundings while she had the chance to do so. She had pinpointed a town in the distance as her current destination, but she couldn't see the condition of it from this far away. For all she knew, she was looking at a husk left burned, scorched, and destroyed.

The sun was helpful for once and slid to the west and in front of her so she wouldn't be highlighted—a good thing since she realized there were riders on the road ahead of them. She nudged Strider to advance down the hill to where a small thicket would obscure them from view. Moving quickly would only catch their attention and she would be discovered, but if she managed to move nice and slowly, she was still far enough away to make it possible that they wouldn't be seen.

Cassandra realized she was holding her breath as the closest scouting party disappeared from view through the trees and gave her a moment to settle and relax. She should have assumed that scouts would be spread through the region. Any good military commander with enough numbers would ensure that every mile ahead of their army was mapped and scouted to the smallest detail.

Perhaps she had hoped that Grimm was not a good commander of men and would therefore fail to think about the benefits of scouting.

It didn't matter in the end. She was out of sight for now, but she would have to plot her route through the region a little better and with more care for where the parties were.

"I don't suppose you have basic knowledge of the landscape and any paths I could take that these fucking patrols wouldn't happen to be on?" she asked and raised an eyebrow at the horse as she pulled out the map she had of the region. "No? I assumed not but thought I should ask anyway. How well do you suppose they know this land?"

Strider had no answer for her and she rolled her eyes and patted him on the neck before she spread the map to study it. The process would take a fair amount of work since there was only one road for her to follow with a handful of paths branching off it.

The simplicity of it was rather appealing when she considered it. All she had to remember was to stay off the roads and make sure she didn't get lost.

"That should be easy, right?" she muttered and folded the map up again. Strider wouldn't understand her since he couldn't read her mind.

No, he wouldn't be able to understand her because he was a horse and did not speak or understand the common tongue.

Cassandra sighed and patted the beast on the neck again as she tucked the map away and took hold of the reins. If they traveled off the road, she wouldn't risk the horse breaking a leg by stepping into a ditch she hadn't been able to see while astride. It meant she would walk most of the way from that point. They moved into the light tree cover and she kept her eyes on the road.

It was far enough away that she hoped no one on it would see them but close enough that she would be able to follow it without getting lost.

Unfortunately, even that hope was dashed when the sun began to descend behind the mountains to obscure her view even more. It also made it much more dangerous for her to continue over the untamed ground where she had to push through bushes and try to find a path around while watching for the twists and turns of the road.

When the light grew dimmer, there was no point in continuing and she could hear running water ahead of them. She did not want to end up walking into a stream or a river, not only because of the noise it would make but also because the water would be cold. A fire was out of the question if she wanted to avoid being seen by those who patrolled the roads.

Finally, she found a position where she could set up her small camp, even in the darkness, with a thicker patch of trees and bushes to keep her hidden from any eyes that might have searched for her from the road.

Bread, dried meat, and a couple of dried strips of fruit along with a few mouthfuls of water were all she was willing to spare for an evening meal. It was still warm enough that she didn't need blankets, but she wrapped herself up and held her sword in hand as she started to drift off. It had been a long day and she had long since learned the subtle art of sleeping the moment she closed her eyes.

The peace didn't last long, however.

Cassandra's grasp on her weapon tightened at the sounds of boots and hooves nearby. She opened her eyes and made the physical effort to not move when she realized that one of the patrolling scout teams had paused close to her camp. They carried torches and talked amongst themselves, which told her she had not been seen yet. She forced herself to remain utterly still and watched them move through the area.

They were on the road, she realized, and not close enough to attack, but the torches made it seem like they were much closer. She couldn't hear what they were saying, but there was no attempt on their part to delve into the woods. But if they were looking for something, she assumed that if they saw a horse among the trees, it would certainly catch their attention.

She turned her head slowly to look at Strider and mentally begged the beast to not make a sound, not to move, and to do nothing that would cause dozens of armed men to descend on them. There were many places where she imagined herself dying in battle, but in the middle of the night at the hands of a group of soldiers was not among them. How would bards sing about her simply being killed like that?

Not that she cared that much about that kind of thing but still. She couldn't help thinking about the legacy she would leave behind if she were killed there.

Strider made no sound and appeared to still be sleeping. She could have sworn that horses had keener senses than humans, but the beast showed no sign that he was aware that they were seconds away from being discovered.

He remained utterly immobile—no nicker, no whinny, and not even loud breathing—while she tried to find a way to watch both him and the guards.

The beast would not be the death of her. That much was a relief and she twisted slowly but froze when she noticed that the group patrolling had come to a halt. Her heart was in her throat, beating loudly enough that she was sure they would be able to hear it.

She held her breath while the silence stretched on. Finally, the boots and hooves moved away and soon, the lights from the torches disappeared into the night and left her in almost perfect darkness again.

A heavy hoof thudded on the dirt and made her mouth go dry again, but she realized that it was only Strider shifting his weight before he uttered a soft, rumbling nicker.

Any other time would have resulted in an explosion of rage from her, but silence was still required and she knew he would not pay attention to any of the glares she directed at him. She reminded herself that he had maintained his silence while their enemies were nearby and she couldn't complain about that. With a sigh, Cassandra settled into the position she had been comfortable in before but was not surprised when sleep was a while in coming.

She did not feel rested by the time the sun began to rise and the birds made a clamor of noise around her. Anyone who thought the forests were peaceful had not spent much time in them. She growled and pushed slowly from the hard earth she'd slept on. Gone were the days when that would happen without consequences, and she needed a few minutes of groaning and stretching to restore her body to a normal state of function before she began to pack her simple camp and saddle Strider.

Although again, she would not ride him until they had a few decent roads to travel on.

It wasn't long before they reached the river she'd heard the day before, and while the water was ice-cold and fresh enough for her to refill her skins, it was shallow enough to allow her to ford it and only came up to her knees in the deepest parts.

What was more surprising was the bridge she watched the whole way across. Out in the open, she would be easy to see and anyone looking for someone sneaking about would immediately have questions about the person who forded the river rather than crossed the bridge. Fortunately, her luck held and no one appeared while she was exposed.

The most surprising part, however, was the condition of the structure. From a distance, she hadn't been able to tell but up close, it was clear that it was in good condition and the stakes driven into the river to support it had been placed recently.

Cassandra had expected the landscape to be torn apart and left for nature to recover, but the roads were in good condition. There were no doubt many reasons for this but what she saw did not match what she had been told about the areas where Grimm's troops were advancing.

The closer she came to the town, the more she realized that something was amiss with the story she had been told by the refugees. Heavy traffic on the roads forced her to take to them again. So many people would increase her chances of being seen and a woman traveling alone in the forest would attract more attention than one among countless others.

Sure enough, when she mounted Strider and joined the travelers, no suspicious gazes were cast at her. She was merely another person journeying through an area she had expected to be deserted in light of an army that tended to rape, pillage, and burn everywhere they went.

Still, it was better to be safe than sorry, and she shifted a handful of her saddlebags to hide the spear she carried. There was no telling if any of the guards patrolling would recognize her but if they couldn't, she would place coin on a wager that her spear was her most recognizable feature.

Her fears resurfaced slowly as Cassandra approached the town she'd seen from a distance. There were no walls, but a few defenses had been raised against possible attackers—trenches and the like—although the town itself appeared to be bustling. The road had begun to clog with wagons driven by farmers who tilled the area and who were stopped by the guards who guarded the entrance into the town. About a dozen of them were on duty, but they did not appear to charge those entering and merely searched them.

It was an odd job for soldiers, she thought and glanced over her shoulder at the forest she was leaving behind for a moment.

The open fields stretched ahead of her, thick with what appeared to be barley beyond a handful of plots of various vegetables.

This was not a land that had been burned and salted. If anything, it appeared that Grimm's soldiers were merely there to encourage production. It made sense, she supposed, since burned and salted landscapes did little to pay taxes or help feed armies.

But it in no way confirmed the story the refugees had spun when they approached her.

She couldn't turn back now, of course. If she tried to flee, it would attract attention and she had a feeling riders would be dispatched to catch up with her. She could move into the town and if she was unchallenged, she would be able to leave again and return to Draug's Hill to ask some pointed questions of the refugees who now called it home.

For the moment, all she needed to focus on was staying alive and moving past the guards. Each was armed with a mace and a shield and uniformed in black. The lower soldiers' gambesons were worn while the officer among them wore a breastplate and mail beneath, although he had discarded his helm for the moment. The armor was similar to what the Herald's men had worn, but it lacked the red sigil on their chests that those had displayed at the time.

None of them appeared moved when she approached their inspection, still mounted. No one made any mention of the fact that she was armed. Most of the farmers she could see in line were armed with spears, bows, and even the odd club or mace, which made her think there was a problem with bandits in the region. The guards made no attempt to disarm them as they entered the town.

They made a cursory inspection and didn't even search through her saddlebags, although Cassandra had to resist the impulse to reach for her sword when a guard circled behind Strider and returned to the front to nod to his colleagues.

"What's your business in Farrow?" the officer overseeing the group asked in a bored tone.

"I'm looking for work. I was told there were bandits who needed killing in these parts."

The man nodded. "Deserters and remnants of armies that have long since been defeated. If you're looking for bounties, you'll want to speak to the lieutenant at the barracks. Over where you see the palisades."

He waved her through and her pulse thumped through her fingertips as she rode past them and studied the barracks she had been directed to. With the only real defenses in the town, it looked like it had once been a small keep that had been converted into living quarters for the soldiers.

It didn't matter much. She had seen enough to tell her that something was seriously amiss with what the refugees had told her and she simply wouldn't stand for it.

When she was twenty or so paces away from the building, the sound of a galloping horse caught her attention. She looked back at a young man who pushed a horse at full tilt with loose reins as he rushed around those waiting in line. Shouts of protest erupted from those he passed but none were heeded as he finally drew his mount in before he ran the guards down.

Cassandra hated the fact that it had taken her so long to recognize him as the young man who had been among the refugees. He had accosted the twins but now looked considerably less miserable and desperate than he had when she first met him.

He must have followed her. There was no other reason for him to appear and approach the soldiers like a man on a mission. She nudged Strider to move a little faster and tried to not attract any attention. Out of the corner of her eye, she could see the soldiers suddenly look around and try to locate her in the small yet crowded marketplace.

She was the only one mounted, which made her easy enough to see, and the group immediately rushed toward their weapons and horses. The young man was given a sword and shield and he wasted no time in mounting up to race after her as well.

With all need for pretense swept aside, she urged Strider forward with as much speed as he could manage. He neighed loudly, almost as a warning to the people who were ahead and oblivious to the fact that she needed to move out of the town as quickly as possible.

A few did not listen to the warnings and were bowled over as she rode furiously along the street. Alarm bells began to ring from every quarter and the clatter of hooves followed her. There were more of them, which meant they would move slower but given the alarms, she had a feeling that even more would join the pursuit.

The edge of the town loomed and a handful of guards stood alert and looked around as they tried to determine what the alarm was for. They decided soon enough that the woman riding as fast as her horse could go toward them was the one they were looking for. Cassandra pulled her spear from where it was strapped to the saddle and hefted it once as the guards formed up quickly to try to stop her from riding past them.

She pushed herself forward, stood in the stirrups, and stretched as far as she could. The spearhead punched through the throat of the closest man, and Strider didn't so much as slow as he barreled through the ineffective line of the five surviving guards. One of them fell under the horse and was trampled by the hooves before they were through.

There was no time to check but the man was likely dead or severely injured. While she felt a pang of guilt over it as she drew her spear back, covered in the blood of the first man she'd killed, she remembered what happened to the people attacked by the Herald's forces. In this place, they encouraged growth, but that was not the story elsewhere.

On the open road with fewer people to obstruct their path,

Cassandra was able to put Strider through his paces and they increased speed as they galloped toward the tree line.

A warning voice within told her it was too easy. Her escape was going a little too well.

In that moment, she heard the soft twang of a bowstring behind her and not far enough away that she felt comfortable enough to say it was out of range.

She twisted her head in time to see an arrow bury itself into the ground only a few feet from where they were. They had the range but the timing was off. All it would take was one lucky shot. Her armor would hold but if they hit Strider—a significantly larger target and unarmored—she would be unhorsed and they would have a turn to run her down instead.

A new plan was needed. She dragged her mount onto a path that branched away from the road and wound up to a small mill that was still a good distance from the trees. There was not enough to cover her until she reached those trees, but it would give her time to circle to attack her pursuers.

The miller saw what was happening and rushed inside the building, having no desire to involve himself in any fight. She couldn't blame him for it. With a scowl, she ducked when another arrow sailed over her head and thudded into the building's woodwork as she guided Strider behind it and out of sight of the archer.

She twisted her spear and hefted it carefully. It was meant for melee fighting and was a little off-balance for throwing, but it would do in a pinch.

It certainly helped that the archer was ahead of the others and tried to circle ahead of her for a cheeky shot. He was a clever soldier but they seldom lasted very long in the rank and file, and she was there to prove why.

Someone cleverer always came along, anticipated their tricks, and put a halt to them with a spear to the chest.

He screamed, fell from his saddle, and landed in a small bale of hay. She didn't have the time to make sure he was dead, but from the way his bow fell from his hands, she no longer had to worry about him shooting at her.

Cassandra had already drawn her sword when another two soldiers descended on her. Neither expected her to attack, which gave her the advantage if only for a moment. She made the most of it and slashed the throat of the first one to reach her.

The other swung at her with his saber. She swayed to the right, raised her blade to parry, and with a twist of her wrist, sank the blade deep into the man's chest, through his gambeson, and out the other side.

The dwarves had put some of their finest work in, she would give that much to them. Her blade didn't even catch when she drew it out. The man's expression went from shock to blank in the time it took her to wrench her weapon free, which told her she had punched it through his heart and killed him in seconds.

More were coming although in their rush, it looked like they had all forgotten their lances, which made it at least an even fight more or less.

They still outnumbered her three to one but in the end, she would make sure it played to her advantage rather than theirs.

They attacked one at a time. Strider pushed forward, surged into the closest horse, and knocked it over with a cacophony of neighing and snorting, which gave her the time she needed to rush at the other two. Her sword cut directly through the neck of the second man and his head sailed off his shoulders to thunk into the building beside them.

A sword slash caught her and pounded into the amulet's protection, and it heated immediately against her chest. Still, it had done its work and gave her the opportunity to retaliate with a firm strike to the man's shoulder. He screamed and dropped his sword but wouldn't have the opportunity to recover it as she thrust her blade directly through his throat.

There would be no time to celebrate as a pair of hands

grasped her shoulder, dragged her from her saddle, and wrenched her weapon from her hands in the fall.

She landed on top of the man and knocked the breath from his lungs, which afforded her barely a split second to recover before he did.

Cassandra made use of that opportunity, dragged her dagger from its sheath, and pressed it against the soldier's throat.

He didn't wear the uniform of a soldier, however, and looked like a refugee. His clothes were ragged and torn and a young face stared at her as she pressed her dagger in a little deeper, enough to draw blood.

"Why?" she demanded. "Tell me why you are doing this. Don't you know what Grimm is? The kind of monster he is? Why would you help him?"

He leaned forward, gritted his teeth, and forced the blade to dig in a little deeper. "Grimm may be a monster but he is the kind who richly rewards those who please him."

"I gave you a home when you had none. Would he do that for you?"

"You gave me a blanket and a broom in a ghost-haunted ruin. Grimm will give me a palace and all I could ever want when I bring him your head."

The youth shouldn't have warned her like that. It was another weakness in people who thought they were clever—they liked the sound of their voice a little too much for their own good.

Something dug into her side. She looked down at a dagger that pressed through her clothes but was stopped by her amulet's protection. It heated again, and she scowled as she grasped his wrist and squeezed.

The look of triumph remained on his face for a few seconds longer until bones cracked and were quickly followed by a soft scream of pain. It had taken a little magic to weaken the bones where she held him so she could shatter them like twigs.

"You should have considered the disadvantages of crossing me instead of the riches you would win," she pointed out coldly. "You would have lived longer."

As warnings went, she knew it fell on deaf ears. If she let him live, he would simply try again and she was in a foul mood, all things considered.

She pressed her blade down again, hard enough for the blood to flow in more than a trickle, and opened his throat but left the blood vessels around it intact as she stood and cleaned her dagger on his shirt.

He would choke and drown in his blood in minutes—long minutes that would feel like an eternity. She collected her sword and spear from where they had been thrown and moved quickly as she could see horses gathered at the edge of the town, likely the beginning of an all-out hunt for her.

Cassandra had no desire to linger and make their work easy for them.

"Come on, Strider," she muttered, mounted hastily, and checked that their fighting hadn't dislodged any of the bags before she turned toward the road again. There was no need to stick to the path and she cut across the barley fields instead. "It's time to return to Draug's Hill and tell them what we've found."

CHAPTER ELEVEN

The return journey went much faster than the ride out. She knew the paths and roads this time so there was no need to consult the maps to find out where fords, bridges, and the like were. It seemed Strider understood their need for haste as well and maintained a good pace even as night fell. After only a few hours of sleep, she was up before the sun and in the saddle again.

The horse seemed to enjoy going at night more than the daytime, perhaps because it was cooler.

Still, the aches and pains of the constant movement took a toll on her body as they continued the relentless pace and they made it difficult to focus on anything else until the walls atop Draug's Hill met her gaze. She had never been quite so pleased to see it before, but something told her in the back of her mind that not all would be well.

It was confirmed when two riders rode out of the gates as soon as they saw her and pushed their horses to a full gallop to meet her. Cassandra was relieved again to see that the twins had come out and not the refugees who weren't refugees.

They appeared a little worse for wear than when she had left them. Both were tired and didn't look like they had trimmed their beards or braided their hair in a while but simply bound both as well as they could with only moments to spare.

"You have no idea how good it is to see you," Bandir shouted as they approached.

"I wouldn't. I generally only see my own reflection." She knew the attempt at humor would not make much impression on the twins, but it was unsettling to see how badly it was received. Both looked a little confused at first as they approached and reined their horses in. Maybe they hadn't heard her but she wouldn't push her luck on the topic. "Something is the matter. What is it?"

They exchanged looks and tilted their heads. It was annoying how they did it like they were reflections of one another, which made it impossible to tell them apart.

"Everything," Tandir answered finally and shook his head. "Everything is the matter. It all went wrong when you left, to be honest. There isn't much time so we'll explain on the way."

"Yes, you will." Cassandra nudged Strider to walk forward. "I think I might know a thing or two about where the problems started."

"You do?"

"Aye, but carry on."

"Well, like he said, it started when you left," Bandir explained. "The day after, to be precise. The dwarves began to complain about accidents with their equipment and one of the refugees vanished. The bards made considerable noise about that one. I'm not sure why since the accidents were the real problem. They started a fight we had to break up, and two of the displaced people and one of the bards wound up dead before we managed to settle it. Then a scaffold fell with one of the dwarves on it and almost killed him. After a few more of the like, we decided there was sabotage."

She should have guessed that would be the case, but she nodded and didn't want to interrupt.

"A little sleuthing revealed that it was one of the refugees at one point," Tandir continued as they began the winding ascent to the fortress. "And one of the bards at another. Folk started to throw accusations around and we needed to stop them from fighting. The dwarves threatened to leave so we kept everyone segregated and under constant watch."

His brother nodded. "And on top of that, the dwarves had some serious…concerns about what they found in the foundations of the fortress, so they stopped working but still expect to be paid, fed, and housed while they wait for word from the person who hired them about how to approach the situation."

Cassandra tilted her head and looked at one of the twins and then the other, unsure of what to say about that. They wouldn't elaborate on what concerns the dwarves had, and there was no telling how the segregation was. All she could hope for was that no one else had been killed in her absence.

"All that to say," Tandir said, in a tone meant to sum the whole situation up, "we have no fucking clue what we're doing and would appreciate never being left in charge again."

"Aye. The two of us are better at breaking skulls than keeping…well, others from breaking skulls, I guess."

"Wait," she protested. "I didn't leave the two of you in charge. I left Karvahal in charge since he is the chieftain and all that. What the hell happened to him?"

"Oh, he is still in charge, but he decided that dealing with his people, the refugees, and the bards was a little more than he bargained for. Since we brought the second and third parties to Draug's Hill, it was our responsibility to keep them all alive, well, and not destroying the fortress in your absence."

That certainly sounded like how Karvahal would handle the situation, delegating it like any good leader should, but she wondered if maybe he should have been the one to put his mind to the matter instead of the twins.

"Will you tell us, then?" Tandir asked.

"Tell you what?"

"You returned rather soon for a scouting mission—less than a week out. One might say you discovered something and rushed back to share the news. And you did say you knew where the trouble was coming from besides."

She nodded slowly as they approached the gates, which did appear to have benefited from the work of the dwarves and looked rather respectable.

"The refugee who went missing followed me," Cassandra informed them. "As I entered a town, he alerted the guards to my presence and I had to fight to escape. From the looks of everything, I would say our refugees were not entirely truthful. The town I found bustled with activity and Grimm's forces appeared to encourage any and all growth."

"I—" Bandir started to say something but suddenly stopped himself and shook his head. "See, this is why we should never be in charge. Why would you leave us in that kind of situation?"

"On the bright side, if you had traveled with me, Karvahal would have been left to deal with the situation on his own and likely would have removed the newcomers from Draug's Hill. At least this way, we have a way to gauge what the situation is and find a way to prevent it from killing those who have nothing to do with it."

"Do you think there are any refugees who are not spies for Grimm?"

"There could be."

She doubted it but there was no need to make sweeping judgments. If the decision hadn't been made already, of course.

As they walked through the gates, the dwarves all stood quickly when they saw her dismount. Sifeas was the first to approach them and wiped crumbs from his beard before he reached her.

"It's good of you to return, Princess."

"If I had known you would all stop working the moment I

turned my back, I would have stayed," Cassandra answered quickly. "Honestly, at this point, I am starting to feel a little cheated. I should send you back to Edge's Rest and ensure that word is spread that you stop working when it suits you."

"We have our reasons and I waited to discuss them with you when you returned."

"It seems like you could have discussed them with the twins or the chieftain." She turned to face him. "I understand that you and your people have been subject to sabotage by the refugees we traveled with but from what I've heard, the dangers have since dissipated. You can leave or you can stay and continue to work, but do not hope to take me for a fool, Master Stonearm."

"No attempts were made to do that and none have been able to truthfully call me a cheat." The dwarf looked like he tried to control his annoyance, likely not wanting to cause any further problems with their situation. "If the truth be told, we have a problem in the basement, lassie."

"We have a problem above ground as well."

"Kick the beggars out—both sets—and let them settle their differences in the wilderness." Sifeas shook his head. "Your problems would be solved in one stroke that way."

"If only it were that easy. With all respect to my good foreman, is there any way I could wait to manage your crisis until after I finish rooting the vipers from our beds?"

"It's your coin paying for us to stay, lassie, but know that working or no, our rate doesn't change."

"And whose fault is it that you're not working?"

"The fault of whoever built this damned place, is who."

Cassandra rolled her eyes. For the moment, if they wanted, she would see to it that they remained so they could discuss why they weren't working.

"Look for something else to do," she instructed and shook her head. "My coin should buy something other than your fucking sightseeing in the region. See to the crenellations on the walls—

that should keep you far from whatever you're avoiding under the ground."

There was no voice of disagreement from the dwarf and he left her with only the barbarians while a gnawing feeling touched the back of her mind.

Still, she had more important issues to deal with and the twins showed her to the building where the refugees were being kept. A couple who had fought for Torsburch stood guard at the door, although they appeared to be a little lax in their duties. They straightened and grasped their weapons the moment they saw her, however.

She would make a point of berating folk for it another time. For the moment, she shook her head and pushed the door open.

It was a solid stone building by the looks of it, likely meant to be an inn of some kind given how it was organized with the fireplace in the center of the room and a hole through the ceiling to allow the smoke to escape while still covered to keep the elements out.

There was more than enough room to house the refugees, and they had made the best of it, set up around the fireplace, and seemed entirely at home. Still, when they saw her enter the building, every man and woman stood and looked like they weren't sure what they expected her to do next.

Cassandra hated having to make these decisions, but people had expected her to make them even when she had been a paladin.

It was easy enough to sense that they were uncertain, and her mind immediately jumped to the fact that because one of them had been a spy, they were all as culpable. Even if she had no proof of their guilt, it was the simplest decision to make. They would no longer be a problem.

The fact that they were all grown and fairly young further emphasized that they were not a typical group of refugees to begin with. It likely meant that they were all in on the scheme to some degree or another.

After a moment during which she studied their faces, she strode into the center of the room, drew her sword slowly, and pointed it at the man closest to her.

The hostility in his eyes disappeared and he began to inch away, quickly followed by the woman who was behind him. One by one, they backed away under her glare.

"I wish I could enter this building with better news," she stated in a clear voice. "That you are all free to go and this was a misunderstanding from the start. And yet, as I return, I find it is the blood of one of yours that stains my hand. He tried to have me killed and when I look at the rest of you, I would consider each to be equally guilty."

They exchanged glances and while there was division among the group, she took another step forward.

"This will be your one chance to survive this day," she told them in cold, clipped tones. "You will surrender now and tell the truth regarding your intentions. It is an honest gesture of goodwill on my part, but I will not treat wolves as sheep any lon—"

Her words were cut short when one of the spies moved. She'd assumed they had already been searched for weapons, but he had a throwing dagger in his hand and with a running step, he launched it at her with all the power he could manage.

Pure reflex made her raise her sword and deflect the blade away from her. The look of division among the group was gone and instead, all suddenly held weapons and rushed at her.

Cassandra had already moved to retaliate. They likely hadn't anticipated being in this position or they would have come better armed and armored. Or perhaps they knew that if they were searched, it was better to improvise weapons as well as they could while there instead of carrying anything that refugees would most certainly not possess.

Either way, all they could count on was the advantage of

numbers as they wielded clubs made from broken pieces of wood, daggers, and the like. One of them had managed to make an improvised studded mace using chunks from a clay pot.

She would give them points for inventiveness but as she ducked under a strike to her head and opened the bowels of the woman assailant, it was clear that these were not soldiers.

Why they were chosen to fight for a man like Grimm if they had no experience was a mystery, but not one she would delve into at the moment. She bounded back as more of them surged forward and closed the distance quickly.

The twins had not expected the attack—that was what she assumed, at least, given how slow they were to join the fight. They finally did and she was able to put some distance between the group and herself. It was probably best that she hadn't brought her spear, although it might have given her a little more of an air of authority that could have prevented their foolishness in the first place.

But there was no time to consider the possibilities as the dozen or so refugees assailed the three of them.

Two more were killed quickly and another oddity touched her. These were not fighters but instead of trying to escape or even lay their arms down since they were outmatched, they continued their futile attempts to kill her.

Perhaps their inexperience told them they still had the advantage of numbers, which meant they could still win. But Cassandra's coin was on them not caring and being more determined to try to assassinate her, even if it cost their lives.

It would, unfortunately. She stepped forward, drew her dagger, and buried it into the chest of the spy closest to her. Still in motion, she twisted and dropped to one knee to cut the hamstrings of another who had tried to circle and flank the twins.

It was a good thought but not the kind that would work and especially not with him moving as slowly as he was. He needed to be quick and decisive and instead, he had second-guessed himself a few times too many and was punished for it when Tandir swung his mace to crush his skull.

She was on her feet immediately and lunged at the remaining two who decided to shout something and charge at her as well. Before they could act, she sliced her sword across the throat of the first and reversed her stroke to behead the second one.

Death was always unfortunate, but Cassandra couldn't find it in herself to regret these. Certain rules should be followed, even for spies. Pretending to be refugees, priests, doctors, or anything of the kind would always be the lowest of the low since that put the lives of actual refugees, priests, and doctors in danger.

She doubted that Grimm cared much, however. He likely would have encouraged this kind of behavior given his moniker. Cruelty would be the point of all his endeavors.

But there was nothing left now. What was done was done, and she took a moment to clean her blade on the robes of one of the fallen before she turned to the twins.

"Remind me to never put the two of you in charge of searching prisoners for weapons," she muttered and shook her head.

They laughed.

"We didn't search them," Tandir informed her. "I searched the damn bards and Karvahal's men searched these."

She didn't even want to think about what they would do with the bards. The twins had told her that one of them had been involved in the sabotage too, which meant they would have to find out why that had happened as well.

When she pushed the doors open, Karvahal's guards stood with their weapons drawn, and the bards had gathered as well and looked on in confusion.

"What happened in there?" one of the guards asked and stepped forward.

"They were spies for Grimm the Cruel," Cassandra answered,

drew a deep breath, and shook her head. "When I offered them the chance to surrender, they attacked. Good work you did checking them for weapons on a regular basis but in the end, they all died. Why are they out?"

The bards looked at one another and tried to decide who she was talking about until they realized she had focused her attention on them.

"The spies are dead," Julian stated and tilted his head toward the building she had just exited. "The problem is solved. We should be free to go, yes?"

"One of your people was caught sabotaging the dwarves' work. As far as I can tell, all of you are as guilty as those fucking spies."

He nodded. "Ah, well, that is unfortunate."

Cassandra narrowed her eyes and tried to determine what he was talking about when suddenly, something sharp drove hard into her side. She looked down at a dagger that had cut cleanly through her defenses. It had likely been spelled or she might have felt some kind of reaction from her amulet.

She could feel the immediate reaction from her body and the way the impact had struck deeper than the blade. It was a familiar weapon too. She knew she'd seen it before.

CHAPTER TWELVE

The world spun for a moment and Cassandra felt the strength begin to seep from her. A healer mage had once told her that it was a sign that her body was reacting to an attack and so stopped everything else as it focused on the injury.

Of course, that knowledge didn't help her much, but it was still the first thought that came to mind as she turned. The woman who had stabbed her was the same one whose life she'd saved from a remarkably similar stabbing not that long ago. It was odd how the details didn't come to her mind but they would eventually.

"Bitch!"

She wasn't sure why she said that. It had blurted almost on its own as she twisted and hammered her elbow into the woman's nose. She had a name. Everyone had names, but she couldn't remember hers. It was somewhere in the back of her mind but she couldn't find it.

The other bards drew weapons and began to attack. As it turned out, the twins were as bad at searching prisoners as Karvahal's men were, but there was more to it than that. She grasped her sword and willed her body to cooperate.

The world spun and she felt nauseous. It was more than an ordinary kind of sickness. The venom had begun to spread and her body wanted to convulse.

If she had fought more capable foes, she would have been dead already, but as the twins barreled into the fight, the entertainers were disorganized, confused, and not quite sure who to fight and why.

They didn't have the same suicidal bravery as the other spies and it gave her the moment she needed to pull herself together.

Cassandra took hold of what power she could manage, poured it directly into the wound, sealed it, and drove the venom out the way it had come. It was a less efficient way to achieve the healing but she didn't have the time to let her body heal itself.

The venom was out and dribbled from the wound along with a few drops of tainted blood. She could have healed the wound too if she'd had a few minutes.

"Fuck you all!" She growled, grasped her sword grimly, and let the pain fuel the rage that had burned inside her ever since she had killed the disgusting cretin who had followed her. "I'll fucking kill all of you myself!"

A warning like that felt like it was in order and she rushed into the fray. A scream roared out unbidden as she hammered the pommel of her sword into Julian's head and cracked it open. To be sure, she thrust her blade through his chest and left it there as another of the bards attacked her.

She staggered back and stopped another dagger from pushing in before she sidestepped and left a leg extended to flip the man.

He landed awkwardly on the road and she drove her boot into his skull with enough force to shatter it and spew his brains in the dust. She didn't know she was capable of doing it until it happened, but she gave herself no time to consider her choices.

Cassandra spun as the rest of her allies raced forward to join the fight. The twins had a handful of bodies already spread around them. Few of the bards were left and by the looks of it, the only one they had managed to stab was her.

Her ego was not happy with the blow but at least it meant her healing skills would not be needed by any of the others as the last of the entertainers—spies, she reminded herself—were felled with relentless efficiency.

All but one, it seemed. A soft groan drew her attention to the woman who had stabbed her, which was enough to justify killing her outright. Since they finally had one of the cretins alive, however, there were a few questions she wanted her to answer.

Whether she wanted to or not. She kicked the dagger away from the would-be assassin's hands. It was the same as the one that had come so close to opening her throat in Massar, which did answer a few of the questions she had, at least about the attempt on her life. She didn't like thinking about it but thankfully, they had someone to discuss it with.

"It's good of you to return to us," she all but snarled, grasped the woman by the collar, and dragged her to her feet. "I would assume you were the one who tried to kill me in Massar, but I doubt that you stabbed yourself in the shoulder. No doubt all of you were involved."

The woman nodded slowly. "There's no need to be hostile, Princess. We are all professionals here."

"Given that this is not the first time you people have tried to kill me while all I've done was save your life, hostility is required in this case." She had every intention to drag the woman to the top of the walls and throw her down but she paused for a moment and tried to control herself while she considered their situation.

For now, all she did was pound her fist into the assassin's face with enough force to hurl her off her feet and elicit another groan from her as she dragged herself slowly to her feet.

"Who the fuck are you?" Cassandra demanded.

The woman took a moment to stabilize herself and tentatively probed the area where bruising had already begun to appear on her face. Her nose was broken, but there was likely some internal damage as well given how she had dropped after the blow. She peered around as if to judge the odds of her survival if she simply cooperated and appeared to conclude that her best chance lay in not being difficult.

"I and my troupe are—were—a band of assassins, the kind who take such matters seriously and are skilled in executing them. An open bounty on your head was issued some time ago, and we found a way to insinuate ourselves into your ranks, gain your trust, and elevate your legend all at the same time so we could charge Grimm the Cruel more when we collected."

"I like to think that would have ended poorly for you," she commented. "A man known for his cruelty isn't likely to take too kindly when those who work for him haggle for higher pay."

The woman nodded slowly. "Perhaps. Either way, it was Julian's decision, not ours. When he made the call to have you killed in Massar, it could have easily been interpreted as Selby trying to take his revenge on you."

"You know how that turned out."

"Aye. I killed the one who did it, but he managed to nick me with his dagger before I could get back. I barely managed to slip the body out of your sight before you came to save my life. I do owe you for that, at least."

"You owe me much more," Cassandra snapped and the assassin raised her hands. She made a valiant attempt to maintain her composure, but there was a hint of a break in her façade as she took a step away from the barbarian princess.

"Agreed. What is fair is fair. You saved my life and I repaid you by stabbing you in the back. Well, side. I aimed for your liver but your elbow stopped me shy of it. It was a good blow, by the way."

"You should know that flattery will get you nowhere. With that said, thank you."

There was no reason to be rude, after all. If they killed her, it wouldn't matter how she was treated, but she wanted to live with herself after all this was finished.

"But why would two teams be sent to kill me?" she asked and shook her head. "I cannot be that important to anyone and certainly not important enough to gather two teams of assassins and convince them to work together."

"We worked on our own. The Atrans were a separate party and tried to push us from our purpose—which, in fairness, might have saved your life. Unprofessionalism ends up getting you killed in this business as the man who failed his attempt on you discovered so abruptly. But those appeared to be spies sent to keep track of you and were actual subjects of the Cruel One. They were also quite fanatical, from what we were able to determine. Those who were found dead after you left were those we caught trying to leave these walls with the one who did get away. I would expect any who escaped are already racing to Grimm with reports of what took place."

"I…well, at least one of them never made it to his destination. He grew a little greedy and chose to come after me on his own. I would say it is unfortunate, but I would be lying. But why would you try to prevent Grimm from finding out about our location?"

"Well, since we were not working together, you can see how there were different goals in mind. We wanted to kill you, whereas they were readying themselves for the arrival of Grimm and his army, the types who are not likely to take many prisoners, no matter what pretenses had us on opposing sides to the army. It was our objective to kill you quickly and with as little pain and suffering as possible, and see to it that our reward was paid in full."

Cassandra tilted her head. The assassin was right about one thing, of course. The two parties working against each other had likely saved her life and the lives of all those inside the walls, although she could not quite tell how long their lives were saved for.

"How many of the spies left these walls?"

"We did not keep count of the shites. I would say at least a handful managed to escape. Even if you did kill one, others are likely already spreading word of your whereabouts."

Not long, then. She shook her head and turned away for a moment. The walls were impressive but not enough to stand against a real army, even if the dwarves worked night and day to reinforce them.

"Well then." The assassin cleared her throat and put her hands on her hips. "I've told you all I know and I have been perfectly cooperative."

"After you tried to kill me."

"Well, yes, but that is in the past. As of this moment, I have provided you with information that was sorely needed. I don't think I am asking too much to be allowed to flee this place before Grimm the Cruel arrives and turns the hill into a crater. Indiscriminate slaughter and the stopping of it might be your business, but mine happens to be a great deal more precise."

"The only way you'll leave is off the edge of the wall," Tandir interjected before she could answer. "I don't suppose your assassin training ever taught you to fly."

"My training, as you call it, was the kind you gain while actively experiencing the lifestyle, and no, I was never taught to fly."

"Your luck is as terrible as ours, then."

Cassandra could think of no reason to object with the barbarian's reasoning, and she motioned for two of Karvahal's soldiers to take the assassin. They did and bound her quickly, although they again neglected to check her for weapons. She would address that later, but for the moment, she needed to speak to the twins.

"What are you thinking?" Tandir asked once they were out of earshot of the bard-turned-assassin.

She raised an eyebrow, tried to process all she had been told, and regarded them intently. "I would say we might have a little over a week before Grimm's army arrives, provided the rest of the spies moved as quickly as the one I encountered. And they will come to burn Draug's Hill to the ground and kill all those inside. Our decision, therefore, is a simple one. The bastard knows we are here. If we were to move, it would make the march this way for naught and drain his resources. We could have the whole place vacated and on the way to another location in a week. It would be the wiser course."

"It doesn't feel right to run away," Bandir protested and shook his head.

"It wouldn't be running away," his brother corrected him with a shrug. "I think they call that a...tactical retreat?"

"Well, if there are tactics to it—"

"Then again, if we do leave, it would only delay the inevitable," she added and rejoined the conversation. "If we run now, we will still have to fight them eventually, and for every moment we allow them to move through this region, the more entrenched they would become and more difficult to drive out. More people would be killed by them in the meantime. However, if we can stop them here and now, it would demoralize his forces and drive them back to where they came from once and for all."

"Provided we can win."

She nodded. "There is that. I cannot guarantee that we would be able to defeat their army, even if we have the advantage of walls. Then again, I cannot make that guarantee for the future either. We would be slow, and they would likely find the time and means to harass us and slow us even further until their armies can catch up."

"Both scenarios and both tactics have their risks, the kind that will likely claim our lives," Tandir stated when he finally understood. "You think that if we stay, we might prevent the most loss of life. Loss of life...which is bad, as you keep trying to convince us."

"Not quite successfully from the sound of it." She rubbed her temples and tried to consider all the different ways it could all end. None of them were particularly appealing, but they hadn't been when she stood against the Herald either.

Then again, this had begun to feel considerably more dangerous. She had barely survived Belladonna and from the sound of it, they faced the very real possibility of fighting the one she had been too terrified of to resist.

"And in the end, even if we do…relocate, he will continue to send his hounds after us and we will likely spend a good part of our lives being hunted," she continued and met their eyes levelly. "And while we do that, more of the North will be taken until there are no longer any little pockets of civilization like Edge's Rest for us to hide in. It will all have been burned to ash or turned into fortresses from where Grimm can extend his arm a little farther."

The twins exchanged a look and again, it seemed like they were communicating telepathically, which made it difficult for her to tell what they were doing or thinking.

"There isn't much of a choice at all, then," Tandir muttered and scratched his beard.

"No, I didn't think so." Cassandra scratched the side of her face before she realized that was exactly what the twins were doing. She stopped immediately. "Not for people like us, at least. So, what do the two of you say?"

"That we have considerable work to do. Well, the fucking dwarves have considerable work to do and we need to get them to it."

She nodded. "Aye, I'd say the same."

CHAPTER THIRTEEN

The assassin was being annoyingly cooperative. Tandir wasn't sure why but since he had been in charge of searching for weapons among the bards who were assassins, he wouldn't ask any questions.

They had gone through the worst of it too many times already and he wouldn't make a fuss about it, although he made damn sure that she was no longer armed. He didn't even know her name—not the real one, anyway—and he'd already searched a little deeper than he had most lovers.

But she wasn't armed—at least not anywhere he could reach—and she'd seemed quite amused by the whole venture. It left him feeling odd about it as he walked back to his brother and Cassandra. They hadn't made any real decisions about how the hell they would stave off an army led by a sadistic shit, which meant none of them knew what their fate would be.

"How long do you think it would take?" Cassandra asked Bandir as they exited one of the buildings.

"It could be a while, but I wouldn't need to take up the time and energy of the dwarves to do it," his brother answered.

"Gather a few of the villagers, give them all shovels, and start digging."

"Are you building a moat?" Tandir asked as he approached them. "We wouldn't have to do it all around the damn walls. Only in front of the gates and we would have to build a bridge to span it. We couldn't fill it with water so we would have to put stakes in to stop folk from trying to jump in and climb out."

She stared at him for a moment and Bandir shook his head.

"He's the clever one. I'm the fighter. We meld our skills like that."

"I fight well."

"Well, yes, but I'm still better."

Tandir chose not to justify that with an argument. "When do we start?"

"Immediately," Cassandra answered and suddenly looked a little unstable on her feet. "We don't have much time as it is…"

Her voice trailed off and she appeared to have almost fallen asleep, and the twins lunged to catch her before she dropped.

"You're exhausted." Tandir pointed out the obvious and helped his brother to carry her to a nearby seat for her to settle in. "When was the last time you had real rest?"

"I had a little here and there."

"That means you don't remember the last time. And you did that…whatever you had to do to heal yourself too. I've seen you do it enough times to know that it makes quite a drain on your body. Especially when it is your body that needs the healing."

"I might be a little tired," she admitted.

"A little?" Bandir scoffed. "You almost fell asleep while you were talking to us. I know we might not be the most entertaining barbarians on the continent, but that is a sign that you need some rest."

Cassandra nodded. She was stubborn and set in her ways, but she was not a stupid woman. Tandir had grown to respect that in her, and even she would have to admit that she was in desperate need of real rest.

"Only a few hours, mind," she insisted. "We don't have many of those to spare and I'm sure I'll be able to get as much sleep as I'll ever need when I'm dead."

"She's dreary when she's tired, isn't she?" Bandir pointed out as they helped her up and guided the princess to the closest bed where she could sleep comfortably and without being disturbed.

"I think the term is cranky," Tandir answered.

"You two know I can hear you, yes?"

"Good. The exhaustion hasn't dulled her ears. That is a good sign, don't you think?"

"Fuck off." Cassandra growled but she had already curled comfortably as soon as she was settled into a bed.

It wasn't the best she'd ever seen, most likely, but the hay was fresh and it looked comfortable, at least, although Tandir had a feeling she would sleep on rock if it was nice enough to not crack her skull open when she landed on it.

"Do you think she'll only be a couple of hours?" Bandir asked as they closed the door to the room quietly behind them.

"I know that she will murder anyone who attempts to wake her," Tandir answered and shook his head. "And I know that person will not be me. But I am the smart one. Given how skilled a fighter you are, maybe you should try it."

"I might not be the smartest of the two of us but that doesn't make me stupid."

"It might do."

"Fuck yourself."

There was nothing quite like looking through the world like this.

Cassandra knew she was dreaming. She remembered being

dragged to a bed by the twins and told she needed to rest. Waking up would be painful, even though she knew they needed every hand ready to help to prepare their defenses.

They were right, though. She needed the rest and wouldn't do anyone any good if she fell asleep like she almost had with them. If she fell asleep while helping someone with something, she could even cause some damage like drop a hammer or rocks on their head.

Still, she didn't like it. She felt weak, something that she had promised herself she wouldn't feel, not for another minute in her life.

It was interesting that she dreamed of the world around her, a rugged land far to the northeast of Draug's Hill. She wasn't sure how she recognized it but she knew it was on the edges of Grimm's holdings. Riders approached it out of the dark and there was a hope in the back of her mind that they were bandits looking to slay the spies who escaped from the Hill and inadvertently bought her more time.

But it was a fool's hope. They carried the burning sign of Grimm the Cruel and were a far-ranging patrol searching for any sign of where the Barbarian Princess had hidden.

"How did they get so far so fast?" she muttered aloud and felt like it was something she would say even though she was asleep.

"I may not know all futures for a certainty." At the familiar voice, Cassandra knew somehow that even if she turned to look, she wouldn't see the usual grizzled face of an old man and his donkey approaching her. "Living creatures are rather difficult to account for in such a manner. But I felt certain enough of this one to show you."

It wasn't a dream then. She should have assumed as much. Her dreams were generally the kind that would get her into trouble if anyone happened to listen in.

Her attention returned to the situation that unfolded in front of her and her mind seemed to unravel a little as she tried to determine what the hell was happening to her. She was rather new to these kinds of visions.

One of the spies rushed to where the riders were, gasping for air and looking even more ragged than he had been when she had seen him last. It was unsettling to think that she was looking into the future but had no power to stop it even with that knowledge.

Without so much as a word, one of the riders immediately turned and headed back the way they had come, no doubt to relay the information he had received to the people who could act on it.

"The Cruel does seem to have a mind that travels upon the one road," Cassandra said, still speaking to herself for some reason. "I wonder who he'll send this time. I doubt he'll come himself."

As if the vision responded to her, everything twisted and it felt like she had moved somewhere that changed shape and blurred. For a moment, a voice was all she could hear.

"Oh, the son of Karlath is too proud to send an underling to handle his work." Theros' voice echoed through her mind and she realized she was in the sky, looking down at Draug's Hill. "You already killed his favored pet and now, you've been seen in his lands. He'll come for you himself this time, although he might have several hundred friends at his side when he does, merely for the fun of it. One or two thousand if he intends to make a statement of it."

This time, she did turn, although she wasn't sure why she was surprised when nothing visible presented itself along with the voice.

"Thousands," she whispered and shook her head. "If every mercenary beyond the Northeastern Pass appeared before Grimm arrived, we wouldn't be able to meet him in the field."

"No, you couldn't." The lord high god sounded a little troubled, although she thought perhaps she was projecting her thoughts into his mind.

The perspective shifted again, and Cassandra realized that she was drawn to the ground again. She flinched and expected an impact that never came and instead, she wandered through the passages under the fortress in its very foundation.

"But then," Theros continued, "why would you ride out to meet someone who is already coming to you? Wouldn't it be better for you to be ready when they arrive?"

She could feel the vision starting to slip away and something like frustration bubbled within her. "Why in the hells can't any of your messages and visions be a little more informative instead of going around in circles and riddles like this?"

"I can stop giving them to you if you plan to be this ungrateful every time."

She shook her head and felt like something or someone whispered at the very edge of her consciousness. It was impossible to focus as she couldn't hear what the voices were saying, only that they were whispering.

Nothing worked. Her whole body felt like it was set in lead and impossible to move. Something hurt her eyes.

"Fuck…"

The word sounded real. Like it was stated and her ears heard it. It was odd how it wasn't the kind of thing she realized until it was altogether too late, and she pushed up from the hay as the aches and pains returned to her body.

"I did…not miss those," she whispered and groaned softly.

It had been more than a few hours. She'd told the twins to wake her but by the looks of it, the afternoon sun had come, gone, and been replaced by the morning sun. It cut directly through the window that hadn't had any light when she'd gone to sleep but was aglow as the sun began to rise.

"I will kill them." Cassandra dragged herself to her feet and pulled off pieces of straw that had caught on her clothes and hair. "I'll kill both of them and feed their kidneys to the buzzards. There are buzzards here, aren't there? Of course there are. Buzzards and scavengers are everywhere in the world."

As annoyed as she was, she couldn't be too angry at the twins. They likely knew better than she did that she'd needed her sleep and she felt better for it. It made the whole situation a little more acceptable as she stepped out of the small house she had taken over for about half a day and a whole night.

Still, there was work to do and by the sounds of things, many had begun while she had dreamed and had visions or whatever had happened. Although most dreams disappeared from her memory moments after waking, the vision remained.

She wandered to one of the wells the little place was known for. Water had been pulled up already so she had the opportunity to wash before she drew more, this time to take a sip.

"Some koffe," she whispered and spat the foul morning taste from her mouth with some water and drank the rest of it. "My life and all my worldly possessions for some koffe."

"Be careful what you wish for, lassie."

She turned as Sifeas approached the well, likely for water. The dwarves were hard at work at the top of the wall, putting everything in place for the battle that would inevitably take place on them. It was narrow and contained, which meant that this time, they could hold the walls.

"You wouldn't happen to have koffe in your stores, would you?"

"Heavens, no. It's grown deep in the jungles to the south, but I know a man who takes that route regularly. He's a merchant, and he makes a good deal of coin bringing the odd and expensive to them as can afford it. I could drop him a word that someone here would like some koffe and would be willing to pay."

"I suspect you'll want some pay for that as well."

"A favor among friends. The twins told me what you will

likely face on the walls and what you plan to do while you face it. All told, I would say you have quite a task ahead of you."

Cassandra nodded. "I appreciate that. Although I will have to again ask you to delay discussing the matters that made you and your men wait. I do appreciate your patience."

"And I appreciate the coin that you are paying us for work my men would consider some of the easiest they have ever undertaken."

She smiled and patted him on the shoulder. As much as she wanted to deal with the situation as it presented itself, she still had to have a chat with the twins before the sun climbed any higher in the sky.

There wasn't much of anything to say, and she wasn't partial to awkward silences. She moved toward the wall where the twins helped the workers to carry the heavier items that couldn't be lifted with the rope and pulley systems that had been arranged along the length of it.

They appeared to be enjoying the hard labor and laughed and shouted at the dwarves who toiled to draw items up as well.

"You two," Cassandra shouted and motioned for them to join her near the gate as she approached the area where they had built an improvised stable for the horses, mules, donkeys, and beasts of burden they had traveled with. Strider waited for her inside one of those stables, but she would not saddle him. Not yet and not today.

The twins put their loads down and sprinted toward her, looking like overgrown children as they took the steps two at a time. She would never understand where they found all that energy, but there was little else for her to consider for the moment before they finally reached her.

"Do you need us?" Tandir asked, only slightly out of breath.

"Are we going somewhere?" Bandir placed his hand on the stable structure and patted it like he had built it himself.

"We are not," she answered. "The two of you are. I'll need to remain here to oversee the preparations so I'll leave the responsibility with the two of you to head to Edge's Rest. Find Langven and tell him to bring the whole of the Ebon Pack. I assume the bastard can't wait to join a fight like this. Any other mercenaries who are interested should be made most welcome, but… Well, try to not bring any more spies back."

"How the hell are we supposed to know if they're spies?"

"I said try. I trust your judgment and if you think anyone is… suspicious, tell them to remain and that we have enough people. I can't assume there will be too many of them, but there are those there who would like a chance to stand against Grimm the Cruel."

The twins exchanged one of their looks and nodded.

"I guess there will be no point in arguing this with you any further," Tandir stated.

"Well, I would like to go but the last time I left the two of you in charge, the whole place almost came crashing down. This way, at least, should there be any problems, we'll still have the walls to defend us. Hopefully."

They chuckled and nudged each other's shoulders.

"Be safe, the two of you," she said and placed her hands on their chests. "I'll need you alive to fight in this battle, and you'll be damned before you leave me to it all on my own."

"Do you hear that, Bandir? It means she likes us."

"It means she'll miss us."

"I'll do neither if the two of you don't move your asses." She pushed them into the stables. "Go on, and I expect you to be on your way back in no less than three days or there will be hell to pay."

"Yes, Mum."

"Off with you!"

Cassandra shook her head and turned away. There was so much to do and she had planned to get it done the day before.

Plans had changed, she'd slept the whole of the day before, and now, she needed to catch up.

Sifeas was already discussing matters with his masons when she heard horses ride through the gates, carrying the twins to their task while she went about her own.

It was about time that she got around to it, after all.

"Very well, Master Sifeas," she called and caught his attention immediately. "I've kept you and your men waiting long enough."

"I think you were rather justified in that," he answered with a hearty chuckle. "You fought not one, but two groups of assassins and spies after all. It isn't the kind of business my clients generally have on their minds. A few do, however, and when it happens, I find it is best to give them and theirs a little space to deal with their business."

"All while charging them your daily rate, I assume?"

"A dwarf has to make a living. But in the process of making that living, we found something quite odd under the fortress that I think you would want to be aware of."

"Yes, well, before we get into that," Cassandra interrupted, knowing it had to be a severe annoyance to be constantly told to wait and wait and wait some more. "I think it only fair for you to be aware of what you are working to defend. I know the twins might have told you a little, but I would like there to be no secrets and nothing unspoken between us. A good business approach, wouldn't you say?"

He stroked his beard carefully and nodded. "A good business approach indeed."

"Then you should know it is very likely that in a few days, this fortress will be surrounded by the vanguard of an army led by a maniacal tyrant with delusions of grandeur. It is likely that if they were to find out that you helped to fortify this place, they might choose to take revenge on you for it once they take control."

"You sound as though you expect to lose this fight."

"I expect to win, but I am not so arrogant that I cannot see all the other possibilities. It is quite likely that we will all die and Grimm the Cruel will choose to make an example of those who stood with me in this fight, even if you did as little as simply repair the walls."

The dwarf nodded slowly and drew a deep breath. "I do appreciate that, but if I were to run from working when there are those who tend to take their revenge on stonemasons and architects, I would have no work in these parts."

"Not like this. The Herald was a powerful mage who was terrified of the man and refused to surrender even when she was defeated. There is something different in this one, something I cannot quite place. You disregard him at your own peril."

"I wouldn't dare." Sifeas moved over to a nearby table, poured some water from a small jug for himself and her, and offered her a cup. "I am not a fool. Dwarves are well aware of Grimm the Cruel and the atrocities he commits on a regular basis. Rumors and reality are difficult to tell apart in these times, but it would appear that he encourages the spreading of these rumors."

"And you choose to stay?"

"Are you going to be paying me and me lads?" His voice was completely unperturbed and he took a sip of the water.

"Aye." Cassandra narrowed her eyes. "You know what this man is capable of, then?"

"I heard you well, lassie. But if there is still coin to be earned, there is still work to be done." He looked completely unmoved. "I've never left a job unfinished in all my life and I am not about to start now merely because the next despot decided he needs to show the size of his cock to the world."

That was one way to put it, she supposed, although it felt as though there was a little more to it than simply a display of power.

"Now." Sifeas put his cup down and clapped briskly. "Is there more you needed to say, or will we head down to see what the problem is? Perhaps you need one last nap before we get started?"

She smirked and shook her head. "Lead the way, master dwarf."

"Then if you will follow me, we have some business that needs looking at."

CHAPTER FOURTEEN

The fortress was something of a maze. As they descended into the bowels of it, she wondered why she hadn't realized there were so many tunnels below. Her first worry was that there was no integrity. If their enemies decided they wanted to find a way to tunnel into the fortress, they would find most of their work already done for them.

There was no telling if that was the case, of course. It was always more difficult to dig in these rockier areas, at least from what she'd gleaned from a conversation with an engineer who had been a member of a variety of sieges across the continent.

This convoluted maze allowed them to move under the fortress completely undetected, which begged the question of why the area had been built to begin with.

"How long do you think it would have taken to tunnel this much?" Cassandra asked as they continued through the many branches. She was utterly lost by the third turn they took, but the dwarf appeared completely at home and led the way with a torch in his hand. Sconces were carved directly into the walls along the paths with about three or four paces between each one, but she imagined that it would take too much work to keep them lit all the time.

"As far as I can tell, digging the tunnels wouldn't take very long. Well, relatively speaking. Three or four years. Building these tunnels, on the other hand, would take a great deal longer. Some of the intricate stonework all along here, for instance, would take significantly longer. I would need to map the tunnels for a proper guess, but as far as I can tell, it would have had to take at least…ten, maybe twenty years to build."

"I thought Karvahal said that his father built it."

"He might have built the fortress or rebuilt it, but this was constructed long before the lifetime of any human I've ever met. Or their grandparents, for that matter. It is impressive work, I must say, although I could suggest a handful of improvements."

"Improvements?"

"Suggest, merely. I would assume you are not paying me to make modifications to render these tunnels a little less gloomy and feel a little more like home. To a dwarf, at least. Come, it's not far from here."

He was right about the age of it, at least. The rocks that had once been cut cleanly were now marked and pocked with signs of age and exposure to the elements that she had not expected.

It was easy to forget the signs of trouble eating into the back of her mind as she continued to try to remember every twist and turn that brought them deeper into the hill.

"There's considerable work that will need to be done to ensure that the walls stand up to attacks," Sifeas continued, and Cassandra needed to increase her pace to keep up with his. "As far as I can tell, they should hold against the odd field-built catapult and scorpio, but if they happen to have something with a little more power behind it, they could knock the walls down and walk right through. A proper torsion catapult would do the walls in with half a day's work by the engineers who know how to make and work them properly. Of course, you cannot trust a human to put up a solid onager, at least not one that'll last the day without needing to stop for repairs."

She had a feeling that the dwarf could likely go on for hours about how superior dwarf siege engines were to those made by humans, and as interested as she was to hear of his experiences, they had more important things to discuss at the moment.

"Sifeas, if you would—"

"Oh, right. Of course. Anyway, I cannot promise that our work will be up to proper dwarf standards, at least not in only a week. I tell you, some of my kin are able to transform a mountain into a damn city and use the mountain itself as a wall."

"I think I've seen something of the like."

"They are less welcoming to humans than we might like, but one day, there might be an alliance between one of the great dwarf cities and a human kingdom or an empire, maybe to help spread the talents of my kin among your people, but that is the problem with you humans. Dwarves pass their knowledge and skills onto their offspring for dozens and even hundreds of generations, and therein lies the secret to great works like you would find in Yurmun and Igdra. But you would be hard-pressed to find any similar talents spread among humans for three, or even four generations."

This was another topic she felt like he could probably go on about for hours, although she was less interested in hearing about it.

"Sifeas?"

"Right. We, can't turn radishes into rubies is what I mean about this." He grunted, stroked his beard, and frowned deeply. "Still, for a shoddy human habitation, it will be as strong as it ever was, but you'd expect such work will be loud and dirty, which is why what is below is so important."

She nodded and sensed that they had begun to approach the area where she assumed all the trouble was coming from. While she didn't know how to explain it, something about the area had her on edge.

Something seemed to hover in the corner of her eye and at the edge of her mind. She could understand why the dwarves had been unwilling to continue working there.

"This is the place." He grunted and motioned for her to take the lead, and she stepped out in front of him.

The tunnel opened into a domed chamber. It was larger than the little house she had spent the night in. Much larger, she realized as she approached the point where it cut sharply downward. She wasn't sure how she'd missed it.

"Watch it there. My boys put a ladder in to get us to the bottom." Sifeas motioned for her to descend. "You go first and I'll toss the torch down and follow you."

Cassandra nodded. She didn't want to say anything as she feared her voice would break and betray the uncertainty she felt as she began to climb down the rope ladder.

It wasn't only from how much the whole place unsettled her for some reason, but rather because the ladder felt a little unsteady as she moved.

Still, she knew better than to criticize a dwarf's work while she stood on it, and after what felt like an eternity, she was finally at the bottom.

"I'll toss the torch down!"

She did appreciate the warning. Her eyes had been immediately drawn to the rest of the chamber and she almost forgot that it was her task to hold the torch.

It fell quickly and she snatched it out of the air and tried to get a clearer view of what surrounded them.

"It's impressive, yes?"

Cassandra nodded and approached the series of sculptures that lined the chamber. She took a step forward, thinking for a moment that she was looking at a living creature.

"Truly," she whispered and extended her hand almost afraid to touch the statue in front of her. "How would they have been able to make these?"

"How do you mean?"

"Well, this level of detail. It's incredible. They look like… warriors. Different warrior groups. There is a Gendrail Monk from the frock and the staff. A Sevarian Skirmisher—you know, those who were known as the finest horse archers in the world. There are a handful of orc bloodhunters."

"Aye. Over there you will see a handful of dark elf night-walkers."

"And the dwarf shield wall over there too. A Yakul Blade Master on the left. It would appear as though someone put a great deal of time and coin into collecting a sculpture of every famed type of warrior in the world."

"Aye, it would seem that way," Sifeas agreed. "Although you might be interested to know that these are not sculptures."

She turned to face him and her eyes narrowed as he lit another torch to spread a little more light.

"Is there a specialized term for this kind of stonework?"

"I am sure there is, but this was not the work of chisels and hammers. I'm not saying a dwarf could not have done a fine enough job, mind you." He scratched his chin and approached the dwarf shield wall. "But these should have been made to look better—prettier. Folk don't want their imperfections carved into the immortality of stone to expose their lazy eyes and warty knuckles to any who might see it."

"Why not?"

"Well, those who generally pay for the sculpture to be made are usually not those who make the sculptures. The people who are willing to pay for their faces to be made into stone will want them to look like themselves, only much better looking."

Cassandra nodded. "So, you are saying that…these statues were not sculpted because they are too ugly."

"Too ordinary-looking. There is nothing ugly about ordinary

looks."

She supposed that made sense, although she still struggled to understand what point he was trying to make.

Finally, she came to the conclusion that she wasn't sure what he was trying to say.

"How were these statues made, then?" she asked and moved a little closer to the blademaster. His beard alone was enough to tell her that not all was right since she could make out every individual strand of hair.

"I would say it was the work of a gorgon or perhaps a basilisk. Given that they are arranged into groups and in orderly ways, I'd be willing to bet me knuckles against me nuggets that it is the work of a gorgon."

"Gorgon?"

"You know...damn beasts, woman with the lower body of a snake and snakes in her hair, turns any who look her in the eyes to stone."

"Oh. Right." She had heard of them, although the tales she had been told generally seemed like parables, each one with some kind of life lesson. None came to mind, however. "Why a gorgon?"

"They like organizing their kills neatly to make it easy for folk to notice. Gorgons like to be left alone above all."

Her hand had already begun to inch to her sword as she scanned the various openings and entrances into the domed room. If he was right, the damn fortress was built directly above the lair of a creature that could turn folk to stone with a look.

According to legend, anyway.

"From the looks of the armor we see on the dwarves and the others present, I would say it is active in seasons, and the one we might be looking at would be a few decades away."

"The only issue is that you think if we continue the intensive work above, she might be tempted to awaken early to see that we do not disturb her again."

"Well, I assumed she would turn us into the personifications you see before you…" He paused, looked at her, and realized what she meant. "Ah, I see. My mistake."

Cassandra drew a deep breath and studied a handful of the statues in front of her. She wasn't quite sure that she believed it herself, but the evidence before her was difficult to ignore. The more she studied them, the more obvious it became that there was no sign of them being carved by human hands or even dwarf hands. Maybe elves could conjure magic to make the stone look so life-like.

"You understand why my workers are a little afraid of being near this place, yes?"

She nodded. "Provided there is such a monster here, there is much to be afraid of, yes."

"It might slow the project down a little, you see?" He tugged his nose thoughtfully. "And…well, it will cost extra as well, wouldn't you know."

She was only half-listening. The nagging feeling was in her head again, and she had no idea how she could shake it. It was almost as though she could feel and hear the anguish of the people who had been turned to stone in the gorgon's collection and for a moment, the whole place felt a little familiar.

Her thoughts latched onto the vision she'd had the night before. The dream that was not a dream came to her mind again and she began to study the faces. Theros had shown her the vision for a reason, and she knew there was something to be taken from it all—something to be learned and something she could take advantage of.

"I think you need to continue your work at the pace intended before," she told her companion softly and looked around again to be sure that nothing moved beyond the perimeter of her vision.

"Are you sure?"

"Yes."

"And if the monster is in here and you happen to wake it? Don't you fear the dangers you would put your people in, as well as mine?"

"I will stand watch over you if it will ease your nerves. We have a known enemy approaching and I will not have the work slowed because of one we fear might be here."

"Your recklessness is something I would have expected from the twins." Sifeas did not sound pleased by what she'd said. "Putting lives at risk merely because you would see the work completed will end poorly for you."

"Recklessness has been what has kept me alive until this point," Cassandra countered and motioned for them to leave. "I have consistently faced all manner of dangers that always possessed some kind of advantage, and the only one I could possibly claim is that they will never be able to anticipate what I will do next."

"And you think your enemies will not anticipate that you are willing to wake a monster like a gorgon in order to ensure that the walls are completed and ready to stand against them."

She began to climb the ladder and held the torch carefully in hand. As much as she felt confident about her decision, she did not want to be alone in the dark, not in this place.

It was not a risk the dwarf would take. He put his torch out before he clambered up after her.

"This is the only reason you are still alive?" he asked once he was at the top with her again.

"Aye."

"And how long do you expect to be alive for if you use tactics like these?"

It was a surprisingly good question and one she needed to think about before she replied.

"Not long."

"Interesting."

CHAPTER FIFTEEN

"I still don't understand how she managed to find herself in so much trouble so quickly."

Tandir looked to where Langven approached him at the head of their troop.

"How do you mean?" the barbarian asked.

"Well, I am aware that the trouble you are facing now is related to the battle we had with the fucking Herald and her horde. Yet you would think that this Grimm fellow would have taken the time to gather himself, collect his armies, and decide that hunting her wouldn't be worth the effort."

"I cannot speak for the mindset of a man who chooses a moniker like 'the Cruel,'" Tandir answered and raised an eyebrow. "But I would say it has something to do with his pride. She defeated him—or beat his Herald at least—and that means he wants her to pay. More importantly, he would want the world to know that she paid for defying him."

"A show of force?"

"Most likely."

"But committing...how many were they again?" Langven frowned.

"We don't know yet, but the assumption is several hundred, at least."

"Well, committing that many men must be the kind of idiocy that prompted him to send a Herald out to announce his plans to the world in the first place. I would say that if he is willing to throw so many men away merely to kill Cassandra, he is not the type who should be in charge anyway."

"I find that is the case with most who are in a position of power."

Langven paused and used his hand to shield his eyes from the glare as he studied the fortress they approached. "I would say he would have to be willing to lose a lot of men to take that fucking place. He is a godsbedammed moron."

"You will hear no arguments from me."

The commander had been surprisingly willing to help. Given the degree of stink he'd raised over helping on a lower fee the last time, it would have been in his character to ask for an exorbitant amount of coin for the aid of the Ebon Pack or even to simply decline outright. It wasn't like they were short of coin, not since the battle with the Herald.

But he'd agreed, gathered his men, and ensured that all the mercenaries he trusted in the city were with them as well when they began their march.

He had grown as a person. Or maybe he felt a little guilty that he was growing fat in his new position while Cassandra and the twins were out there, fighting for the common folk and earning almost nothing for it. Since she had played a major role in the reputation the Pack now enjoyed, perhaps he felt he owed it to her.

Either way, Tandir was glad for the help. It was desperately needed and it had taken them almost a week to travel to Edge's Rest, gather the men, and ride out. It could not be long before the vanguard of the Cruel One's forces began to arrive, prepare their camps, and take action to seal the region off for a siege.

He had never been in one himself, at least not one with actual armies. Most of his fighting experience came from the kinds of battles that would never make it into bard tales— or those written by bards who weren't assassins, at least.

"What kind of forces are we looking at in there?" Langven asked as they started up the winding path to the gate.

"There are the fighters Karvahal had on his side—those who survived the fighting at least," Bandir told him as he brought his horse to the front as well. "Cassandra, the two of us, and those you have with you. Oh, and there might still be a few of the dwarves we brought to shore the walls up, although I'm not sure how much of a fight they intend to put up."

From the way Langven's eyes narrowed, he could tell that not all was well. He studied the walls and the barbarian could almost see his mind going over a dozen considerations and calculations as they approached the gate. Finally, he tilted his head and nodded.

He might as well have said that what they were doing was possible, especially when they reached the moat they had begun to dig.

Cassandra hadn't come out to greet them like they had her, although he assumed it was because she was busy running everything inside.

Sure enough, she scrambled down the ladder from the wall as they came through the gate.

She looked tired but certainly glad to see them as the troops followed their commander into the fortress. It appeared that living quarters had already been set up for the new arrivals, and they had been stockpiling food and supplies. Bandir's idea had been to bring as much as they could carry as well, which meant they had enough to see them through for a while, at least.

It depended on how many fighters they had among them and how many were still alive as the days passed.

"It's nice to see that the two of you didn't dawdle in Edge's

Rest for longer than necessary," she said and laughed as they slid from their saddles.

"I told you she would miss us." Bandir chuckled as she moved forward to wrap them both in a warm embrace.

"You look like you've been through it. Has there been much action while we were away?"

Cassandra shook her head. "Not in the way that you might think. Merely considerable work that needed doing and the dwarves refused to do it unless I protected them."

"Sifeas told you about the medusa they have down there, yes?" Bandir asked with another chuckle.

"A gorgon, and yes."

"You don't believe him, do you?" Tandir started guiding his horse into the stables, which had also been enlarged to accommodate the horses of those that were coming to their aid.

"I...am not sure what to believe yet." She ran her fingers through her hair. "But it does not matter what I believe. The dwarves believe it. We need them to finish the work on the walls so I am doing what I can to ensure that they do it with sound minds."

"Well, given the luck the three of you have, I would say there is most certainly a half-reptile beast in the bowels of this fortress, ready to turn any and all who look upon it into stone with a single glance." Langven laughed.

They turned as he approached, his hands tucked casually into his belt.

Cassandra grinned, took his extended hand at the wrist, and shook it firmly.

"Thank you for coming, my friend."

"When presented with the opportunity to join you in yet another impossible battle against odds heavily weighted against you, how could I say no?"

"I would say the Ebon Pack could probably name their price for any kind of work after this is done."

"It is difficult to do from the afterlife, but I will take note of it."

She smiled. "It hasn't been so long that I can't see how much you've changed. But I do have to ask why you came back to die with us."

"You gave me two things I wasn't ever sure I'd have again," he answered with a chuckle. "A reason to be proud and a fresh start. I couldn't very well waste those by leaving you to die on your own, now could I?"

"Some would say you are wasting your fresh start."

"And those are the people who will appreciate it if one was ever offered to them."

Tandir tilted his head. They still grasped the other's hands, and it had lasted a while as well. Both looked into the other's eyes. He couldn't quite understand what was happening, but before he could apply his mind to the oddity, they parted and Langven cleared his throat loudly.

"I'll see that my men are situated," he stated roughly. "Once that is done, we can discuss tactical assessments and shifts so my men can join in the others to keep wa—."

Before he finished the last sentence, a cry came from the top of the wall.

"Dust!" one of Karvahal's men shouted from the tower over the gate. "Dust on the horizon! A huge cloud of it too!"

It seemed impossible that their arrival had been immediately before that of Grimm's forces, but it was practically perfect. There would be no time for them to sit and stew, waiting for the enemy to make an appearance.

Then again, whatever preparations they had in place already were about all they would get. It was time to see what it had all been for, and the twins rushed to the top of the wall to see what all the fuss was about.

They were not the only ones. A dozen or so members of the Pack, Langven, Cassandra, Karvahal, and a few of his men ascended hastily and tried to avoid the glare of the sun as they looked across the landscape spread in front of them.

The scout was right, and the cloud of dust spoke of a decent force already advancing. All were on horseback by the looks of it and moved at a good pace despite the heat that beat down on them

In a soberingly short time, they halted their approach a little beyond bow range and orders were shouted. Tandir couldn't make them out given the distance, but the group immediately broke ranks and showed all the signs of a well-coordinated, experienced, and disciplined group of soldiers.

"They're merely the advance troops," Cassandra stated firmly and shook her head. "The vanguard, here to prepare the ground for the rest of the army."

"They also outnumber our forces," Karvahal answered and studied the enemy assessingly. "Two men to our one, by my estimate."

"It doesn't matter," Langven snapped. "With walls like these, they would have to outnumber us more than ten to our one to even hold a hope of breaching the walls. They'll come at us like the sea, crash on the walls, and wash away."

They were inspiring words and a few of the Pack and the Torsburch people cheered when they heard them. Still, the grim look on Cassandra's face told a different story. She didn't say anything but she didn't need to.

The horsemen divided into three teams. The first remained stationed where they were and scanned the surrounding landscape, while the other two moved out in either direction and raised clouds of dust as they circled the fortress.

It took them a while as they were careful to remain outside the range of a powerful bow. The riders studied the outside of the keep, looking for weaknesses to exploit.

From the way they circled to where the first group waited, Tandir assumed they had found no openings to attack through.

They had also likely determined that there was only one way in for them to guard and to attack from.

Cassandra leaned in a little closer to Langven and spoke in hushed tones.

"If I recall correctly from my days as a paladin, Sulla Mar's War Manual stated that a wall provided each man inside the castle the ability to outlast five attacking from without."

The commander shrugged. "I do not recall. It was far too much boring reading to do."

That explained her grim look, at least. Still, if they could kill five men for every one they lost, Tandir knew they would make a good show in the battle.

He fully intended to make sure that at least ten died before he was taken. That seemed like a nice, even number. Plus another ten for his brother, and they could leave a neat dent in their enemies that Cassandra would have little trouble dealing with on her own.

"Is that the banner they fly?" Langven asked as the group began to raise their banners to indicate who they fought for. Instead of the horned skull, it was one in red flames but still in the center of a black field.

"I would say so." Cassandra hissed a breath and stepped forward. She looked like she was intent on attacking the bastards on her own.

Before the barbarian could reach her, the banner was lowered quickly and a white flag was raised in its place as one of the riders moved up the road toward the gate.

"It's a little early for them to surrender, isn't it?" Bandir asked. "Not that I don't appreciate it."

"The white flag also indicates a truce or the intent to parley," Langven explained. "I assume that one has a mind to talk our ears off before the fighting starts."

Cassandra nodded and motioned to one of the Pack who had his bow strung and ready to use.

"Remind our approaching guest that he had better not come too close, even under the banner of parley," she ordered. "A warning arrow, I think."

The archer nodded, drew an arrow and nocked it, and after a quick adjustment to ensure that it did not bury itself in the emissary's chest, let loose.

The projectile flew in an arc, descended quickly, and clattered on the road ahead of the rider, who dragged his horse to a halt. It neighed loudly as it reared on its hind legs.

Once the noise had abated, Cassandra took a step forward. When she spoke, her voice was louder than Tandir expected it to be. Perhaps she used magic to make it carry without having to strain it.

"Speak your piece, emissary, then kindly fuck off."

A smattering of laughter issued from the men and women on the walls.

The emissary needed a moment to regain his composure but he straightened his back and looked up at them.

"Grimm the Cruel, son of Karthelon and Master of the North, bids those within those walls to consider his terms." His voice was strong as well, although likely unaided by magic. "Before the last light of the day flees this valley, any of you may leave the fortress and return to Edge's Rest with no ill will from the one who has laid claim to these lands. If you have not fled before the last light is gone, your life is forfeit and you will die with the rebel known as the Barbarian Princess and her attack dogs."

The word of warning made those inside exchange glances. Tandir knew they considered taking the man's offer, although he couldn't understand why. It wasn't like they could trust him to be true to his word.

Still, the idea of leaving the fortress must be an appealing offer.

Langven took a step forward and his powerful gaze immediately captured the attention of the Pack and those who were with them.

"What do you think they plan for Edge's Rest when they're finished here?" he all but snarled. "If the end is to come, I say let it come here and now with stout stone beneath my feet and strong hearts holding the walls beside me!"

That drew the kind of reaction they were looking for, although the cheers were not quite as enthusiastic as Tandir had hoped that they would be. Still, they didn't have to be excited about the battle to come. All he needed from them was that they stand their ground and fight their hardest when it started.

Even so, a half-dozen or so of the mercenaries made their decision. Having seen the condition of the fortress and the numbers of the invaders, they had no interest in what appeared to be certain defeat and death.

They mounted quickly and the gate was opened for them to ride out.

"Well, the numbers have skewed a little more to their side," Bandir muttered. "But it's for the best. If they were going to leave, it's better that they do it now. There is nothing worse than idiots who get others killed in this kind of fight."

"And it leaves more fuckers for us to kill as well," Tandir agreed as the others turned their attention to the mercenaries, who raced past the emissary at breakneck speed.

True to their word, the vanguard made no attempt to intercept those who chose to leave, likely hoping more would follow. They wouldn't want anyone to think they would be killed the moment they left the walls.

Loud yells behind them caught his attention and he turned to where the bard assassin tried to reach the walls.

"Let me go!" she shouted and pushed those who attempted to restrain her away. "I heard the offer and I don't want to die here with you fools."

The light had already begun to fade, and Tandir looked out to where the mercenaries galloped down the road.

"She won't be able to get clear of the walls before the time is gone," Bandir noted. "I say let her try anyw—"

Rough cries from outside shattered the tension as the vanguard suddenly heeled their horses ahead. They had their bows out and howled war cries as they loosed arrows on the mercenaries, who tried to increase speed and escape.

Their horses were cut down and those men who survived were surrounded and hacked to pieces in moments.

The assassin heard the indignant protests of the defenders and her pleas to be allowed to leave with the rest quieted quickly as a look of realization slid across her face. She no doubt had the same thought that occurred to all of them at this moment—the battle had begun.

"Do you still want to leave?" Tandir asked and placed a hand on her shoulder. "I'll be happy to pitch you over the wall if you're still interested."

She pushed his arm off angrily, even with her hands still bound, but the point remained.

"Cut her free." Cassandra's voice was grim as she nodded to the man who still tried to keep hold of the woman.

"Are you sure?" Tandir took a step forward. "Not a week ago, she tried to kill you, after all."

"She won't leave here, not until the Cruel One's forces are rebuffed," she answered as the assassin's bonds were cut. "None of us will."

CHAPTER SIXTEEN

It was an unsettling sight. Cassandra wasn't sure what she'd expected of the advance troops but this was so much more than she had expected.

Perhaps the darkness of the night made their campfires look more numerous and their tents appear larger from a distance.

Even so, they had quickly begun work on something that was covered by a pavilion. Wondering about it now would do her no good. They would see it all too close and all too clearly before long. And perhaps too often, she reasoned since pavilions began to appear all over their camp.

She drew a deep breath and tried to let the cooler evening air calm her mind. They faced danger from without, the kind that would not hesitate to murder them in their sleep if it could be managed. And there was a danger from below. She still wasn't sure if she believed that a gorgon lurked under Draug's Hill, but it was not the kind of danger she could simply ignore, even if she wanted to.

"A fucking gorgon," she whispered and scowled into the darkness. "How in the hells would something like that end up in a place like this?"

And at a time like this, no less. Theros had warned her about it, although he'd never quite addressed it as such in so many words. But how a gorgon would aid them was still beyond her. He had hinted at it, but she knew better than to expect a straight answer from the lord high god at this point.

The dwarves had finished their work on the foundations and there had been no sign of the serpent-haired monster ready to strike. That left them little to consider aside from the frame they had found.

It was a trebuchet frame, no less. Questions about what it had been doing there were never answered, but the dwarves had assured her they could repair it. While this was good news— about the best that they'd had since Langven arrived with his men— Cassandra couldn't help feeling a little disappointed.

Night had fallen, the armies had arrived, and there was no sign of the gorgon. Theros had hinted that something would come to their aid beneath the fortress, but she could think of nothing else besides the gorgon.

As she stared out over the enemy forces and studied them a little closer, she wondered if her scowl would leave permanent creases on her face. It had been a few days since the fortress had been cut off from the rest of the world.

All they could do was wait for the attack to come but for now, the army was preparing and had set up more tents and pavilions where she could see and hear the work happening.

"Siege towers."

She looked around as Langven climbed to the top of the wall, stopped beside the crenellations, and rested his arm on them.

"What?"

"Golds to coppers, they're building siege towers in those fucking pavilions."

"Have you had much practice in besieging strongholds?" Cassandra asked and a wry grin touched her lips. "It seems a little too much like real work for a mercenary."

He chuckled and scratched his chin, which had begun to show signs of a beard. There was simply no time for him to put a sharp blade to his cheeks.

"Since becoming an up-and-coming commander, I've been reading, which I know is also very unlike a mercenary. But I was trying to make good use of our expanding numbers and equipment and so studied military science. It seemed like a reasonable thing to invest my free time in."

"I would have thought you would spend more of your time with Verda," she answered and tucked a few errant strands of hair behind her ear. "The pretty young girl from Torsburch."

It was a mistake to bring that up and she understood it immediately. He winced at the mention of her name and she cringed at the reaction.

"I'm sorry, I didn't mean to…"

"No," he said as her voice trailed off. "You have nothing to apologize for. It's merely that…well, it did not work out between us. There's nothing else to say aside from that."

Cassandra nodded and wished desperately that she hadn't brought it up. Thankfully, so did he and so was ready to change the subject.

Langven cleared his throat loudly and pointed at the pavilions again. "They have far superior numbers, no question about that—ten to every fighter we have among us. But they will need to get those forces up here. The fortress walls are too high for ladders to be anything more than a death sentence, especially since they have to find a way to get the ladders up the narrow road to the keep. It will be even more difficult to accomplish given that we have enough men to man the walls and shoot at them from the tower."

A few solutions existed for that, and one of them was siege towers that would protect those moving up the road as well as climbing to the top of the walls. If he was right, that was almost certainly what was being built under those pavilions.

She sighed and folded her arms across her chest. "So they build siege towers to give their men a clear way to the walls. We could probably make them pay every step."

"But once the tower reaches the walls, they will pour men into the fortress."

"What about the trebuchet the dwarves rebuilt?"

"It would give them pause but not much. We would not be able to hit all the towers before they reach the walls, and that is assuming we can use it properly and have enough ammunition to keep it fed. As soon as one or two of them reach the wall, the battle will be all but over."

Her eyes narrowed. A handful of answers came to mind, but each seemed as tenuous as the last, although none of them could be tested until the fighting started. This meant that if she made the call on one and it ended up being a waste of resources that killed them all, it would be too late to change her mind.

Still, a decision had to be made. That was why they had put her at the head of their defense.

The sound of blaring horns dragged their attention away from the wall and to the army that had begun to assemble. Men rushed from their tents, retrieved their weapons, and began to form up. All signs pointed to the Cruel's armies about to start their assault.

"Raise the alarm," Cassandra ordered and moved to where she had placed her weapons ready for an attack that they knew could come at any moment.

Langven nodded and bounded down the steps to reach the bell that had been put in place for them to alert the rest of the fortress when the attack was imminent.

The sounds of their men starting to gather weapons and prepare to defend the fortress mingled with those of the enemy while the horns continued to blare below. A small column moved to the front of the invaders' ranks and for a moment, she couldn't tell what was happening. The beating of drums joined the horns, and she could finally make out what appeared to be a draco-suchus of some kind.

Massive horns protruded from all over its back and each one gleamed with an odd bluish light. Its jaw was elongated to about three or four feet long and lined with teeth the size of daggers along the edges to give it a feral, angry look. The scarred beast moved heavily and overall, it was about twice the length of a horse, although maybe two-thirds as tall as a warhorse. Something resembling a throne was mounted on its back and held in place by being fitted to the longer horns there.

A surprisingly young-looking man was seated on the throne and held a staff with an amethyst at the top. His crown signified his authority over the soldiers and his strong, lithe body was draped in rich robes of red, black, and purple. Something disquieting emanated from him, even from a distance, and she accessed her magic quietly to enable a far-seeing spell for a few moments. It wasn't something she used often but she felt this occasion called for it.

Cassandra still wasn't sure how to explain his malevolent presence. An appropriately cold sneer seemed to be plastered permanently onto his face, and his eyes glowed oddly with a terrible light that had no real place on such a fair and youthful visage.

The beast carried him forward and the troops around him all fell to their knees in veneration as he passed them. There was no telling if the reason was merely their fanatical support or absolute fear, but whatever it was, it seemed to have a hold on them that would not let go.

She hoped something could be done about that. Perhaps there was a way to break their spirits and destroy the hold the man she assumed was Grimm the Cruel had over them. Maybe then the fight wouldn't be so terrible after all.

It was well-known that if the head of the snake was severed, the rest of the body would flounder. If they could kill the leader, the army would lose their will to fight.

Hopefully, she amended cynically. There was always the threat that some were true believers who would fight for the cause even if their leader was dead. Some could even believe there was no way he could die and would somehow be reborn in another form, ready to lead them to victory again.

There would be no easy way out of this. Killing the bastard would be next to impossible, she assumed, since he would not be at the front lines and his monstrous mount was easily the equivalent of dozens of bodyguards.

He rode to the front of the army and raised his scepter to bring the soldiers back to their feet. They cheered loudly, both as a way to drive their spirits higher and to intimidate those inside the fortress.

"Hear!" the youth roared. His voice carried unnaturally over the valley and was heard easily by those who had already gathered on the walls. "The death of those who stand against me is something you know all too well!"

His words were greeted with cheers, the rattling of spears, or weapons banged against their shields.

"But these have the blood of my servants on their hands!" he continued. "My Herald, felled by their treachery, and my spies as well, given no chance when they were slaughtered without weapons and their bodies discarded as though common carrion. This cannot stand unavenged!"

More cheers followed and grew in intensity and it looked as though his words were intended to have an unnatural and almost hypnotic effect over those who heard it. A few of the defenders shifted uncomfortably as if the idea of running away had entered their minds.

The men on the ground were experienced fighters, those who had been on the front lines for the Cruel's forces and would have witnessed many of the acts that had earned him his name. They would not be turned away easily.

Cassandra drew a deep breath and shook off the feeling that had settled over her as the sun began to rise behind the forces that now advanced slowly on them.

"They have drunk the blood of my servants," Grimm continued, rose from his throne, and somehow made his voice more powerful. His troops lifted their weapons, worked up into a frenzy. "And the flagstones will drink of theirs so there is no doubt of the hand that rules the North!"

The cheers for him grew louder while the soldiers stamped their feet and banged their weapons on their shields to generate the kind of noise she knew was effective in diminishing the morale of those they were fighting against.

She lifted her spear and without thinking, pounded it onto the wall at her feet. The strike produced a ringing sound that was clean and clear. She'd had no idea that it had any such ability, but it was enough to settle the fluttering in the bottom of her stomach. When she looked around, a few of those who had been affected by the chanting and the speech from below somehow snapped free of its effects and grasped their weapons firmly, and their expressions said they were there to fight to the end.

Running would earn them nothing but a cowardly death in the end.

It appeared to have no effect on those below, however, and Grimm raised his scepter and leveled it toward the castle. A bright flash from the gem at the top lit the ground like a second sun for a moment.

As orders went, it was about as clear as they would ever get and the troops surged forward. In that moment, the pavilions were pulled away.

It was an interesting maneuver and she had no idea how it was performed. Perhaps it was magic or merely another of their tricks intended to keep their enemies on their toes. She was surprised to see that not all of them had covered siege engines.

They were pushed forward by the engineers and she could distinguish two onagers and a handful of ballistae. As soon as they were within range, they loosed their ordnance at the walls.

While massive rocks and bolts were being lobbed at the defenders, it was difficult to feel better about the fact that only four siege towers were being dragged forward.

"Take cover!"

At Langven's shout, the men ducked hastily and a handful of stones hammered into the wall, likely the opening salvo of a sustained attempt to knock it down. The ballistae, however, fired their bolts over, hoping to keep the men and women on the walls down and possibly even kill a handful of them in the process.

None were felled, although a bolt streaked into one of the crenellations, which sustained a little damage when it drove into it with enough force to bury itself between the slabs of stone. Debris scattered across the wall and injured a few of those close to it.

While nothing serious, it was certainly something to keep in mind.

"Trebuchet, ready!" Cassandra called over the din of the battle and looked over her shoulder to where the dwarves had positioned themselves. They had chosen to not be at the front lines, although she knew that with those crossbows, they would be able to punch a handful of bolts through the shields of those advancing toward the wall on foot.

Sifeas had insisted, though, and she was only too glad to have him with them in the fight at all. She would not complain about where they chose to be.

"Ready!" the dwarf shouted, and one of his men lifted a maul and swung it down to release the catapult's mechanism.

The rope at the bottom was dragged with increasing speed to

gather the stone it had been armed with. The projectile sailed over the walls at a surprising speed and gained momentum as it began to drop.

It struck to the left of the tower in the lead but pounded into one of the front lines that marched behind. The strike was powerful and the boulder even rolled through four or five of the lines to kill, maim, and push them back to a loud cheer from those on the walls.

While drawing first blood in the fight was always good, they had hoped to catch the lead tower before it moved up the hill.

"Three degrees to the left!" Langven shouted and motioned for the archers to start choosing their targets as the troops approached their range. There was some advantage to raining arrows blindly on them to slow their progress, but it was more important to be wise about it or they would run out at an inopportune time.

Of course, Cassandra planned for a future they likely wouldn't have. The odds favored them losing the wall and the fortress long before they had a chance to run out of arrows.

It was a delicate balancing game.

They all had to duck again as another volley from the enemy onagers and ballistae hammered home. While she could feel the impacts below her feet, the walls held and showed no sign that the projectiles had inflicted any noticeable damage. The work done by Sifeas and his masons remained strong, although whether it would stand for long remained to be seen.

The dwarves worked quickly and adjusted the aim on the trebuchet. It had not been used in decades so there would be growing pains, they had no doubt about that. The fact that it worked at all was something to be thankful for.

Before long, it was ready to fire again, and with the sound of straining wood and ropes, another stone hurtled out and arced with a little more purpose. Whatever alterations had been made to the machine while it was being repositioned appeared to add a little more speed to the boulder's flight.

This one flew true and the defenders cheered with a little more enthusiasm when the lead siege tower took the hit. There was enough force behind it to shear the top off completely, which left it seven or eight feet short of the top of the wall. A dozen or so men fell from inside and brought the whole army's advance to a sudden halt.

"Now that's what I call an engine!" Langven roared, laughed loudly, and waved his sword to the archers for them to target those who hurried forward to try to repair the tower.

It would not be accomplished quickly, if at all, and the enemy soon came to that conclusion as well-placed arrows caught the engineers who attempted to see what could be done.

For the moment, the invaders were stalled but it counted as a small victory for those in the keep. Cassandra wished it hadn't come at such a cost, but as she turned, she noticed that pieces had fallen from the trebuchet. Whatever had been done to make it launch the rock faster must have damaged the structure, and the dwarves scrambled to repair it again. Whether they could do so in time remained to be seen.

They worked at a decent pace, but the enemy had decided to shunt the lead engine to the side and push the rest up. Those soldiers in the front lines were already creating a shield wall for the group to work behind without having to worry about the arrows that had already killed a dozen or so of them.

This probably was not the triumphant start to the battle Grimm had envisioned, but it would only serve to make his men that much more bloodthirsty once the battle lines finally engaged in earnest.

"Cassandra!"

She looked away from the two towers that advanced again and peered over the wall to where Sifeas waved desperately, trying to get her attention.

Another loud crack was followed by a shudder as more stones and bolts were hurled into the wall. It still held for the moment, but she had no idea how long even the finest stonework could withstand the steady barrage.

He shouted her name and something else too, but she couldn't make out what it was. They had some time before the towers were in range to pose any danger and she had begun to feel like she was taking up space.

She gestured for the twins to take their positions as it wouldn't be long until their enemies would be within range of the javelins they could throw with deadly purpose. Besides, it was probably best for Langven to direct his men since the Pack was less likely to listen to her orders.

Cassandra wanted to be there when the fighting started, but that would take a little more time.

Once she was assured that the defense would continue without her, she descended the wall using one of the nearby ladders instead of the stairs and moved to where Sifeas tried to get her attention and direct his men to continue repairing the trebuchet.

It was interesting to see the dwarf startled when he turned and saw her almost on top of him. He took a hasty step back and reached for the falchion he carried at his hip.

The easiest assumption was that he thought the Cruel One's forces were already taking the walls and he needed to fight, but there was a haunted look about him that she hadn't noticed from the wall.

"How soon until the trebuchet can fire again?" she asked as the dwarves snatched up the timber that had come loose and hammered it into place in a hurry. "That shot bought us some time but they are moving again already."

"Not long. My boys will have it working again without delay. I noticed the section that was weaker when we built it and we will ensure that it does not break again."

"Is that why you called me here?"

He shook his head and she realized that it was him catching himself before he started on another tangent as he tended to.

"No. What I called you about is the matter of other problems we have on the horizon."

"More soldiers?"

"I wish."

That didn't bode well, she thought as he jerked his thumb in the direction of the entrance to the tunnels.

"Please, no," she whispered. "Not right fucking now."

The damn gorgon could have woken at any other time and she could have dealt with it.

"This bombardment has raised a ruckus all around us, knocked buildings over, and likely caused more damage than we can see with the naked eye. But the ruckus is not restricted to what is happening above ground."

"Fuck!" Cassandra growled and hefted her spear. "Take your orders from Langven on where to aim the trebuchet. I'll see if the trouble cannot be dealt with before the walls are overrun."

"So I continue what I was doing before, then?"

"Shut it!" She raised her finger at him in warning, even though she knew he must be joking. They could use a little levity, true, but her mood did not allow for it.

Thankfully, the dwarf only laughed as he turned his gaze on his people.

"Move your rumps, you load of fly maggots! My dead grand-mother could work faster than you, and she was so big she could roll around the tunnels of our fucking homeland!"

He was in a cheerful mood, which she assured herself was probably a good thing. She wished she could share the humor, but she had been dreading the fact that she would have to head into the tunnels to face what she assumed was the greater threat.

And if Theros could be believed, it was also the least likely source of hope she had ever relied on. She maintained a firm hold on her spear as she sprinted toward the entrance, her mouth suddenly dry.

All they had to do was hold the fucking wall until she returned.

CHAPTER SEVENTEEN

There was no mistaking it. Even underground as she was, she could still feel the sheer power of the Cruel's war machines beating on their walls. Her worries about their condition and whether they could endure this punishment for long were best considered by the dwarves, not by her.

Cassandra had many skills but masonry was not among them. She hefted her spear and tried to not focus on the thunderous barrage that continued above her.

The defenders would deal with it. The most interesting part was that it was likely to stop when the towers were close enough that they would risk killing their own men. This meant she would have a clear indication when the battle started in earnest.

Not that there was much she could do about it if she was stuck underground, looking for a possibly mythical creature that happened to make its home under their fortress.

She didn't like leaving the bulk of the fighting to others while she wandered the tunnels. While she had made a point of learning the twists and turns so she could avoid getting lost when she needed to not be, she couldn't help losing all sense of direction and had to rely purely on her memory to guide her.

"Right turn…twenty paces," she whispered and grimaced when her voice echoed through the tunnels. It was difficult to not turn with each heavy rumble from above ground, but she forced herself to listen for something coming from within. "Left turn, follow… And all the way to…yes!"

Her voice echoed again but this time, into the domed chamber they had visited before. The dozens of statues still looked eerily life-like, as though she could expect them to jump into action at any moment and leave her for dead.

It was not a pleasant thought and she was not comfortable enough to turn her back on them to climb carefully down the ladder. Instead, she braced herself and jumped and landed with a hard thud that made her whole body ache for a moment. A quick check revealed nothing broken or anything that needed immediate attention.

That was good news, at least. Her nervous fear had not resulted in a debilitating injury that she would have to waste time and energy healing.

Foolishly, she still could not tear her gaze from the statues. She had only come through the area with company and entering alone made her feel like she was going crazy. The flickering of the torches made the statues look like they were moving. Not those in front that were clearly visible but the ones behind and almost out of sight.

"Get a grip on yourself woman," Cassandra whispered and drew a deep breath. "You will find what you are here for and—"

Her voice was cut off when a low rumble made the cave shudder around her. It was a testimony to the hands that built it that even with the bombardment above, there was still no sign of weakness in the walls or the ceiling, not even a shower of dust and loose rocks.

But the last tremor had not come from above. It felt like it came from ground level, almost, although she had needed to go deep inside the caves to notice it.

The dwarf had recognized it right away from above. Maybe there was truth to a few of the stereotypes surrounding them.

It took effort, but she managed to steady herself as the rumbling continued a little longer than what would be expected from battering rocks with rocks. It felt like something was moving—or struggling to move, she wasn't quite sure which.

She realized that the tremor came from inside the chamber. With a long, slow breath, she grasped her spear a little tighter and tried to determine where exactly it was coming from.

The ground under her shuddered.

"Oh, fuck me," she whispered, spun, and rushed toward the ladder. All her fears about the statues vanished as she tried to get out of the pit before whatever was buried there emerged.

Unfortunately, she didn't make it. The ground bucked under her and she was thrown into the wall with enough force to knock the breath from her lungs as the whole room filled with dust and falling rocks.

The creature was moving now, clearly not restrained by the stone and dirt, and she had only a moment to gather herself. Thankfully, none of her weapons were lost in the mess, and she used her spear to help her to stand slowly.

When the dust began to settle, she realized that the sconces all around the room that had been empty before now suddenly glowed with an eerie green light. There was something magical about the way it was designed to allow the whole cave to activate the moment its inhabitant awoke. For some reason, she knew it was not powered by the monster's magic.

It was unlike anything she had ever seen. Most of the body appeared to be that of a snake, thick, scaled, and sinuous, and it writhed incessantly like it attempted to wake itself up and shake away the stones and dust that collected on its skin. The scales were breathtaking and gleamed in the green light to reveal alternating green and silver diamonds up the thick body that was otherwise mostly brown or red.

But the top was the most interesting and likely the most sinister. After eight feet of what appeared to be a snake, a human's body began to form, although similarly covered in scales and gleaming with the same green and silver as the diamonds in its pattern. The scales grew smaller the higher they went, and it seemed to be covered in regular human skin beyond the ribs.

The eyes glowed with the same green as the lights in the room and scanned the pit quickly as its hands—similar to that of a human's but longer and with talons on each finger—reached into the earth to withdraw what appeared to be a giant spear. It planted this on the ground and used it to keep itself up as it looked around the room, clearly suspicious of what had been bold enough to wake her.

It looked like a woman from a distance, although what appeared to be long hair draped from her skull to about her shoulders writhed and wriggled of its own accord. Dozens of snakes took the place of strands, and Cassandra couldn't help but wonder if they had minds of their own, even though they were connected to a much larger creature.

These were questions for another time and another place. She knew that despite every instinct in her body telling her to get the hell out, it was her task to kill the creature and ensure that it could not strike them in the back. Despite whatever hints Theros had given her about any help it might provide, the priority was to ensure that there was no threat to the defense.

The creature slithered around quickly and she knew that it was only a matter of time until it caught sight of her. As she had no intention of being turned into a little statue, she took the idea to heart. If it couldn't see her, it wouldn't turn her to stone.

She slipped between the statues and huddled close to them as the gorgon slithered forward and spun slowly as it tried to gain its bearings. Its movement seemed more than a little odd, possibly a sign that it was still waking and by the looks of it, had been woken too soon.

Her first opening appeared and she darted forward, any noise she made masked by the thunderous sounds of the attacks above ground. She thrust her spear deftly to open a wound in the monster's tail. The blood that seeped out of it was green, but she noticed something very odd about the skin and the way it began to peel away.

In the next moment, the reality dawned on her. It was shedding its skin. This was a long, arduous process for most reptiles, although those tended to be smaller and did not like doing it when predators were around.

Perhaps it was something she could take advantage of. Cassandra slid between the statues again as the creature hissed in pain. Although she'd inflicted little more than a flesh wound, it appeared to be confirming the fact that it had been attacked, even in its lair, and it needed to deal with the intruder.

It hissed loudly again and the sound reverberated through the chamber, almost to the point where it made her ears hurt, She realized almost too late that it used the sound like a bat to locate her.

Some larger bats in the world used the same manner of locating things in the air or so she had heard. There were books on the subject, and she had always wondered as a child about how that was even possible. She had even tried to master it herself a few times when the training chamber was empty and she'd yelled herself hoarse until she concluded that her hearing was not capable of detecting where the sand jars were when she was blindfolded.

The gorgon had no such issues. Its tail whipped through the room and Cassandra dropped onto her stomach and grimaced as it narrowly missed her. A low, droning rattle issued from the end of the appendage as it swept over her.

"Shit." She gasped, tried to stop the dust from filling her eyes, and rolled onto her feet. Without hesitation, she surged forward and swiped her spear to slash another narrow gash in its back as she vaulted over it.

The beast swung viciously and tried to catch her with the spear, then lashed it into the area around her and made it difficult to navigate the maze of statues. She circled away and attempted to stay clear of the gaze that would turn her to stone.

While she had drawn blood, she could not afford to try to kill the beast with a thousand cuts. She would have to make an attempt on the heart and from there, she would be easy to see, easy to kill, and easy to add to the collection of stone warriors around her.

As it whirled to look at her, she ducked behind the dwarf shield wall, remained low, and moved as quickly as she could to the other side. If the monster followed her around it, she would be able to attack it from behind while it sought her out.

Her spear was already moving in a heavy, powerful thrust as she came to the other side but felt a jarring impact on her arm when it was deflected. The weapon was pushed down into the rocks again and almost knocked out of her hands.

The gorgon had anticipated her movements and Cassandra came to a dead halt. Her gaze shifted to its face as it looked down at her. The snake part of its body had lifted it to almost seven feet tall and the spear moved deftly in its hands to deflect her second attempt.

Something cold dropped into the pit of her stomach and the beast's gaze seemed to drag her inexorably in until she stared into the green orbs with nothing but terror seeping through her limbs. She didn't want to die. No one wanted to die, of course, but this was something else, something different and somehow worse.

Her mind recoiled at the thought of being trapped in stone for the rest of eternity. Voices spoke in the back of her mind and made her feel like she was going mad. She somehow knew that the warriors in this monster's lair reached out to anything and anyone to tell them of their anguish.

Its eyes gleamed and the green glow intensified until it felt like it was taking over the entire room. Her mouth was dry and her whole body seemed to still like she had already been turned to stone. The gorgon leaned closer and the glow suddenly focused fully on her.

In that moment, Cassandra knew she was finished.

Something pushed through her feelings of helplessness and despair. Her spear heated in her hand and the amulet did too. Neither reached the point where they caused her physical pain and it was almost like both worked together to ward off the magic being used against her.

It was impossible, but she couldn't help an almost manic grin. She was supposed to be dead and now, she was not.

Her sense of satisfaction grew when she stared at the beast and the triumph in its face turned to frustration. The gleam began to increase like it tried to turn her to stone again.

"Do you have a little problem there?" she asked as her spear and amulet warmed again. "Is something wrong with the magic you've used all this time and don't know how to live without?"

She couldn't tell if the beast could understand her, but the look of frustration grew into sheer rage and it lashed out at her with the spear in an attempt to kill her in a more traditional fashion. Reflexively, she ducked under it and the strike came close enough that it brushed a few strands of her hair on the way.

Still, it wasn't close enough.

Cassandra dove to the right and felt a renewed vigor. She wasn't sure how but the spear and amulet both protected her somehow, although the former had never shown any signs of it in the past. Perhaps it was meant to act as a shield and a weapon but had to be used properly to fend off magical attacks of a particular nature.

The weapon might even be meant to combat gorgons specifically.

Not that it mattered. It worked and she would use it to her advantage.

The tail whipped toward her again and she rushed toward it, timed her strike, and vaulted over it while she drove the spear into the beast's body. It hissed again, this time in pain, and when she wrenched the weapon free, pieces of the creature's skin stuck to the spearhead and pulled away from the gorgon's body but broke off easily.

Very likely, the monster was not used to folk hunting it in its lair. Added to the fact that it had been woken years earlier than it should have been, it probably needed to shed its skin before it could be the real menace it no doubt was.

It would not be given the chance.

The barbarian princess pushed into motion and slashed her spear into the gorgon's body at every opportunity to cut as deep as she could without committing to a killing blow. She had a few advantages, but the moment she underestimated the monster was the moment she would be killed by it.

She would not be the one to fall this day—at least not to a gorgon. The battle still raged above and if death was in her future, it would happen there, not in the bowels of the keep.

But she couldn't afford to be distracted by such thoughts. Cassandra darted to the side and ducked under another sweep of the beast's spear. The way it was used spoke of experience, but it seemed to be directed toward defense as the beast no doubt preferred to turn her prey to stone instead of killing them outright.

As cruel as it was, she found it difficult to feel anything but disdain for the monster as she circled slowly to the front and parried a few sloppy thrusts.

"I would deliver a couple of cutting remarks to drive the point home before I kill you, but I have a feeling you would not understand me," she told it and straightened her back. "You do seem intelligent, though. Maybe you've merely been asleep so long that you don't understand the language I'm speaking?"

The creature paid no attention to her and its spear arced toward her head again. With a hiss, the gorgon leaned forward and exposed fangs that dripped with venom. She sidestepped the strike and as the creature lunged to bite, she thrust her spear forward through the mouth and out the other side.

It writhed convulsively and almost yanked the spear from her hands as the light in its eyes faded slowly. The green lights in the sconces remained, but she knew they would disappear soon as well and leave the monster's lair as nothing but an empty chamber, full of the stone memories of the horrors that had been committed within.

But as the beast fell, Cassandra felt the voices surge again. The pain was still there but something powerful and jubilant was woven through it. It was as if the statues had watched the battle and were glad to see the monster finally felled.

She dragged in a deep breath and flicked the blood off her spear as she looked at the creature. Maybe Theros had been wrong about this place. In all honesty, it would not have been the first time. Perhaps he thought she could find a way to communicate with the gorgon and convince it to fight alongside them.

If that were the case, the god had been seriously mistaken. Cassandra shook her head and registered the thunderous sounds of the catapults above. Perhaps the dwarves had managed to repair the damn trebuchet and the defenders had slowed their attackers even further. It was only a matter of time until they broke through but at least they could say they had made a decent fight.

One of the lights went out and she turned to look at it and narrowed her eyes. It was only a matter of time, she supposed, but something else had taken its place. She scowled when she realized that the light still illuminated the room even though the source was gone.

It moved toward her. She felt something like a chill when it took on a form as it glided smoothly across the ground and looked almost human in size and shape.

Even more alarming, she realized that more of the lights now stepped away from their sconces and moved to where she stood. She raised her spear, ready to be attacked, but the first light stopped short a few paces in front of her. The other shades of light did the same until they had all gathered in front of her like they were waiting for her to do something.

Finally, the first one lowered slightly and it took her a little longer than she liked to admit to see that it now knelt before her. Like a wave, the rest followed suit, dropped to one knee, and lowered the heads.

Cassandra took a step forward, her eyebrows knitted together. "What...who are you? And for fuck's sake, get up. I might be a princess but I'm not a stickler for rules."

The shades appeared to hear her and rose slowly. Their voices seemed to merge and all spoke the same thing. She realized that the beings were spread across the entire chamber and even deeper into the tunnels.

Had each sconce over the entire area held one of these?

Finally, the voices became coherent and echoed inside her head. They weren't quite as uncomfortable as they had been before. It was like they tried to speak to her but not break her mind.

"We are the fallen, those souls captured by the gorgon," the voices said and merged again to all speak as one. "Some came to fight the beast and were vanquished. Others were taken unawares as the beast arose and attacked the unsuspecting. We were all brought here in service to her as she slept and kept in the darkness as the only light she needed or wanted."

It was an appalling existence. No wonder they had reached

out to anyone who passed to try to find a way out of the particularly horrifying hell that they had been trapped in.

"Well…you're free now," Cassandra said and drew a deep breath. Spirits, as interesting as they could be, would be little use to her in the battle. Now that the gorgon was slain, she needed to return to take her place alongside the others.

"We are not."

She had turned away, intending to hurry through the tunnels to the surface, but stopped in mid-step. "Yes. Yes, you are. The monster is dead. It will not return to bother you."

"She was slain by you. We are bound to you now. All we can ask is that you be a better master than your predecessor."

They began to kneel again and she growled in exasperation.

"Oy, stand the fuck up," she muttered. "I'm not the mistress of anything. But, if you have a mind to earn your freedom, an army is trying to rip this place apart and kill all those within. After one more battle, you can all simply move on. What say you all? One last battle?"

The spirits were all silent for a moment and she wasn't sure what was happening. They moved around and appeared to discuss the matter between themselves.

One by one, each light began to disappear from view. She had told them that they were free to leave and could understand if they had no intention to join her in one more fight, no matter who for.

In moments, the lights vanished until she stood alone in the darkness of the room with nothing to bring to the battle.

The silence was deafening and said more than she thought it would.

It spoke of how the battle above was progressing.

"Son of a whore." Cassandra growled and looked around for her torch that had fallen in the fight. She could use a simple spell to light it and forget this exercise in futility when she returned to take her place among the defenders.

Suddenly, a new light source filled the room. She turned and heard the grating sound of stone grinding on stone. A green light similar to the one that had been in the sconces before came from the eyes of one of the statues. It moved to where she stooped to try to find her torch.

More lights appeared and all burned brighter than they had as torches. Dozens of the statues began to move. They collected weapons, marched toward the entrance, and carved a staircase for them to use to escape the pit.

The first one approached her, its eyes burning a little brighter than the rest.

"At your command," it growled and sounded like water washing over pebbles, "we march. One last time."

An army of stony voices rose in response.

Cassandra nodded and brandished her spear. "I look forward to seeing what you can do."

There was no telling what they could do, but the statues moved as though they were a horde of soldiers marching as one —humans, elves, dwarves, and many others surged toward the tunnels.

She was almost lost in the moment until she realized that she still needed their lights to show her the way out.

"I guess I should join the battle too," she muttered, broke into a run, and heard them behind her. "I wouldn't be much of a commander if I didn't, right?"

The statues didn't answer but perhaps they didn't understand her.

They did seem keen to join in the fight, though.

CHAPTER EIGHTEEN

"I got three!"

Tandir scowled and looked at his brother. "Did not! I watched the whole time!"

"Then you didn't pay attention. One of the fucking engineers slipped around the shields and I killed him."

His brother was right. He hadn't paid attention. Grimm's army was an experienced foe and they knew better than to rush at the wall without the protection of their shields. The archers harassed them every step of the way, slowed the advance, and ensured that they had to remain behind those shields. This meant it was the twins' responsibility to eliminate those who stepped out of cover.

Normally, the javelins would be better used to drag the shields down, but after a few attempts, it was clear this would not be successful as the barriers were replaced quickly and all they seemed to accomplish was to waste their weapons.

As much as the others likely hated the thought, Tandir hoped and wished that the towers would finally reach the walls. They had started with four of them, all being pushed up the difficult path to reach the keep. Now they were down to three and the dwarves worked feverishly to put their trebuchet back into the business of knocking a few more down.

Langven had said that the battle would be almost over when the towers reached them, and he could understand why. Still, it would mean a good honest fight unlike the duck and chuck that they had engaged in thus far.

A group of Grimm's forces advanced in front of the towers and positioned their shields to form a wall as archers came in behind to try to make things a little more difficult for the defenders.

The first of the arrows streaked from the ground and up to the walls, and one of Karvahal's men was caught as he tried to hurl a rock onto the shields. It did not cut deep but he cried out, leaned back, and looked at where the arrow was buried in his shoulder. Fortunately, it wasn't a lethal wound and if Cassandra had been there, she could have drawn the arrow and healed the man quickly and he would return to the fight in no time.

She had been summoned by the dwarves and rushed off to deal with another problem in the tunnels. He'd heard the stories of what Sifeas assumed was down there and if he was right, she was likely facing the fight of her life as well.

Tandir was more than happy to fight a horde of regular humans on his own instead of a monster that was able to turn men to stone with only one glance. Somehow, that seemed worse than being killed outright.

He hefted one of his spears, tilted his head, and watched as the archers leaned clear of the shields to get their arrows out. After a moment of careful scrutiny, he made his judgment, tossed his javelin, and caught one of the shields to force it away to expose three men. One fell with a javelin to the chest and the other two to arrows shot by Karvahal and one of the Pack's archers.

"Another one!" Bandir shouted.

"Because I cleared the shield for you!" he retorted.

"It still counts!"

His brother was right. It still did count even if he helped. The shields were raised again and they were more careful about how the fighters on the walls would be able to expose them. So far, they had taken most of the deaths and injuries but they were mere drops in the bucket. Even if the defenders managed to destroy all the towers, they could simply pull back and rebuild them. All the while, the onagers and ballistae would continue to batter the wall until something gave.

In all honesty, it would be of little benefit and would only prolong the battle. Tandir held his last javelin and looked for any sign of an opening but was distracted when he heard the dwarves shout behind him. The trebuchet was working again, but the towers were already at a point in the road where they did not need to be in single file. There was enough space to allow them to continue toward the wall, which meant that even if the trebuchet managed to strike one of them, the others would be able to circle and continue their attack.

The battle lines would finally be joined and about damn time, he thought. He would be able to hold off at least one, push them back, and let the archers in the tower take full advantage of the exposed position. Bandir could likely hold the other.

He heard the sounds of wood and ropes straining and a second later, a stone streaked over the wall at a decent speed, missed the lead tower, and clipped the corner of the second. It broke a chunk from the edge but the structure itself remained intact although it swayed and began to tip to the side from the impact. Yells issued from the enemy ranks and a group moved forward to try to manually push it back. Those men were unprotected and a few were caught by arrows before they simply let it fall.

No serious damage had been inflicted and Tandir knew that

they could probably push it up and it would be on the move again, but the other two were close now. The wall would protect them from being struck by the trebuchet although the dwarves would likely still launch rocks into the road to slow the approach of the troops or catch and kill them when they moved ahead to climb the towers.

As they approached, the onagers and ballistae stopped their barrage to avoid hitting the towers. He had much to say about dwarves that mostly came from stories passed down from family to family in their clan, but their work on the walls had been something special to see. When they first arrived at Draug's Hill, the walls looked like they would crumble with a strong gust of wind. They had now taken barrage after barrage from powerful siege engines and were still standing and showed no sign of damage aside from superficial chips and dents here and there.

Tandir hefted his mace and moved to the closest of the towers. He held his shield up as the archers at the top now attempted to pick off those defenders they could. Langven shouted for his men to form up into an organized defense and put the two barbarians and Karvahal at the front.

He'd never fought against men on siege towers, but it looked simple enough. The enemy would start to push through while arrows came from the top of the tower. As he saw it, though, the archers would have to contend with those who were in the tower over the gate as well.

There was no telling how it would go, but Tandir was committed to seeing at least ten of their enemies to their deaths before he died himself, which meant not being killed by the arrows. To accomplish this, he would have to hold a shield and swing his mace with only one hand.

It would be an interesting challenge and hopefully not his last.

The first tower approached the wall and a handful of men gathered around the bottom and positioned a few wooden wedges to stop the structure from rolling too close or too far.

The bridge between it and the wall was lowered and crashed into the crenellations to shatter them and enable them to rush across on an even plane. Men were already streaming from the platform across the bridge.

If there was any honor in being the first one across, that man did not survive to enjoy it as he was met with a mace swung into his face. Even though he wore a helm, the weapon crushed his skull and he fell off the bridge and plummeted earthward.

Tandir shifted his position slightly as a few arrows thudded into his shield and he shoved it out to knock the next man who came across over the side of the bridge as well. Perhaps it wasn't the most honorable way to push his numbers up, but they attacked with vastly superior numbers. The only honor was in surviving and making them pay for every step they took into the fortress.

More strikes thunked into his shield and pushed him back a step. He leaned forward again, determined to prevent them from gaining the wall, and pushed forward to thrust with the spike at the end of his mace. It impacted a shield, which told him that they were organizing to drive him back.

"Do you need a little help there?"

He didn't turn, but Langven drove forward with him to present a unified front of shields to push them back. The maneuver cleared the space for him to step in, swing his mace low, and break the knees of one of the fighters who attempted to press forward a little too far. It was enough to knock a couple more of the men back. One fell over the edge immediately but flailed and caught hold of the other. Both plummeted from the height of the tower and their shrieks stopped abruptly on impact.

They had made a good start in the fight to prevent the wall from being taken, but the second tower was now in position. Bandir waited for the bridge to lower and while it was not heavy enough to crush the crenellations this time, the men began to stream across it.

The barbarian caught the first one and almost decapitated him with a single stroke before he chopped the ankles of the next one who attempted to leap down as well.

More of them poured in with hundreds behind. Eventually, something would go wrong, someone would die, and the line would break but for the moment, they held their own. Tandir formed up with the rest of Langven's Pack to stop Grimm's fighters from gaining the walls.

Arrows streaked above them and fighters on both sides shouted, yelled, grunted, and growled as they fought for every inch. It was a press, the kind he remembered from the handful of battles he had been in and where individual skills and fighting prowess meant little. He put his mace down, drew his sword instead, and used it to hack, chop, and stab at any opening that appeared in the shields in front of them.

He had intended to keep count of his kills to compare it with his brother later, but there was no real way to do so. All he could do was push as hard as he could and remain behind the shield as more arrows hammered into it.

The dwarves below began to fire their crossbows, which had three or four times the impact power of regular bows. The invaders' shields split from the impact when their shots struck home.

Tandir sucked in a deep breath, locked his knees, and drove forward again to stab his sword at a helm that appeared on the other side of the line. A few strikes caught his shield as well before a spear slipped past and opened a gash in his leg. All he did was grasp it and yank it forward and one of the men opposite them tumbled from his perch on the tower.

"Fucking shits!" Langven roared, swung his sword, and sliced the throat of one of those who was caught off-guard by the man's fall, although the lines formed up again quickly. "Did they send the weakest of you into the front line to tire us out?"

There was no response from Grimm's men. Perhaps they

didn't hear him, although Tandir laughed and lunged forward into another strike. His blade found nothing but a shield at the end.

In a moment, the stalemate was broken. An arrow from above cut through and he heard a scream from behind him. One of the Pack was felled and staggered back with an arrow jutting from his chest. It was coupled by an added rush from the front, and Tandir began to lose his position at the edge of the wall as he was pushed back by those who came from the tower.

It wasn't quite how he saw it ending and he roared and tried to push back with a thrust into the chest of the man closest to him. His sword caught in the man's ribs and was dragged from his hands, which left him with nothing else to do but snatch the dagger at his hip and slash a throat open. He didn't even know who but lashed out at anyone close enough to him. The barbarian screamed although he wasn't sure why and stabbed and swung at anything that came close to him before he realized that none of the Pack were nearby.

He'd promised himself at least ten and had killed more than that. He wondered if there was a way for him to take a handful more, even if it cost him his life.

One of the soldiers rushed closer to attack him from the side but stopped and his whole body froze as he looked at his stomach where his guts had begun to spill out and a wound suddenly appeared. A dagger glinted in the sunlight before it slashed his throat open.

Tandir glanced at the assassin who stood beside him holding a buckler and the dagger he remembered her carrying. It wasn't quite the weapons he would have chosen but seemed to be what she was comfortable with.

"I didn't expect to see you here," he told her.

"It was fight or die. I generally prefer to run but I can fight when needed." She ducked under a spear thrust aimed at her throat and pounded the attacker with her buckler.

"Do not think this makes you innocent."

"Innocent? I fear the term will never apply to me."

He grinned, sliced an invader from gut to groin, and lunged forward to thrust his shield into a couple more. Something akin to rage bubbled within him. His dagger left his hands, slick with blood and lost in the body of one of their enemies, but Tandir did not pause as he drove his fist into the face of one of the enemy soldiers.

The odd sense of fury swept over him and he continued to punch even though his hand struck the helm a few times. He lifted the man and flung him over the edge of the wall, swept his mace up, and barely noticed that his hand was covered in his blood mixed with his enemy's as he crushed the skull of another and the man behind.

When he swung it wildly a third time, he realized here were no bodies or shields to take the impact. He swung again and his strike came away empty.

Grimm's forces no longer pushed forward. There were no enemies within his reach and Tandir used the moment to steady himself as the wall's stones were slick with blood. He turned his gaze to the men on the tower and wondered why they had halted their advance. This was their opportunity to attack. They had the opening and the ability to take the wall since the defenses were crumbling, and he was determined to take as many of them with him as he could.

Inexplicably, they made no attempt to attack.

"Come on!" he roared and pointed his mace at the nearest man as he tried to understand why they did not press their advantage. "Who else wants to die at the hand of Tandir DrakeHunter?"

None of them answered but simply watched him in confusion and something like horror. It was odd since they were experienced, trained warriors who had likely faced a berserker before.

He could think of no logical reason why he would now give them pause.

After a moment, he realized that they weren't looking at him but at something behind him. The barbarian didn't want to risk looking back at first and expected the group to rush forward as soon as he turned his back. When they simply ignored him, however, he took the risk and looked over his shoulder.

One glance did not fully explain what he had seen and he looked again but this time, turned in the certainty that his face wore the same look of confusion and even a little horror at what unfolded before him.

The statues were moving. It didn't feel right to say they had come alive since they were still the statues he had seen before when the dwarves showed them to him when they took him into the domed chamber.

His mind resisted the unequivocal truth that they had moved and continued to do so. They marched like they had somehow turned into a real army that lined up on the wall. It felt as though they had politely waited for his rampage to end before they interfered.

Everything about them was still the stone he remembered but their eyes glowed. It was hard to tell what color with the morning light falling directly on them, but it looked like a brilliant green.

Tandir had no clue what to say or even think. Would they attack? Did he have to fight them as well? Had Grimm somehow brought the creatures to life to fight alongside his men?

From the looks on their faces, however, he could guess this was not the case, but the Cruel One did not seem the kind of commander who would tell his people about all he had planned. It seemed like something that he would want to spring on them, perhaps as further proof of how powerful he was and how much they needed to worship him for it.

Something told him that was not the case, though. He eased his grasp on his weapon as the rage in his body began to seep away, and the aches and pains he had earned when he thought he was moments away from dying took its place. From what his brother and Karvahal looked like, they had done the same until they realized that their enemies were no longer fighting.

Langven had been pushed to the ground, although bodies around him indicated that he was not yet done, and the rest of the Pack regrouped and organized again, ready to fight either the newcomers or Grimm's forces, whichever proved to be the greater threat.

The statues carried weapons and looked like they intended to join the battle. What appeared to be a dwarf shield wall began to move forward around the defenders and directly toward Grimm's men.

"Do you know what is happening?" Langven asked as Tandir offered him a hand to help him up.

"Those are statues that were in the depths of the fortress," he answered. "They…uh…"

"Came to life?"

"Started moving."

All questions were answered when the statues moved forward, raised their weapons, and began to cross the bridges between the walls and the towers. Their blades and spears were wielded with lethal efficiency. The invaders seemed as shocked as anyone else and although they fought back, their weapons dealt no damage to the hard stone the statues were made from.

"Forward you bastards!" came a ghostly cry. "One last charge!"

It was haunting to watch and in that moment, the enemy forces began to break and pulled back and away from the ghostly statues that appeared out of nowhere to help the defenders.

"Stand your ground! Stand your ground!"

Grimm's officers yelled for their men to remain where they were, but those who followed those orders were cut down quickly and soon, the officers joined the ranks of the dead and were pushed aside as the onslaught continued.

The onagers and ballistae began to fire again but this time, targeted the towers directly, crushed them against the walls, and killed all who were inside, statues and their own men alike. It was interesting to see that the statues could be killed—or stopped, or whatever happened to statues that could move and had glowing eyes—but it took the force of a siege engine to crumble them.

Whoever had made the call had been thinking about the rest of the troops who were quickly being ordered to retreat. The statues were undeterred. They merely jumped from the wall, landed heavily on the bodies below to cushion their fall, and pressed forward. While they moved a little slower than a human might, they made up for it by being practically indestructible.

Those of Grimm's forces who were ordered to stay and slow the supernatural creatures were immediately set upon and torn to pieces. Tandir laughed as one of the statues was struck by a bolt from the ballistae and while it took the right arm off, the creature was unperturbed and moved forward with only the left arm hacking at the enemy soldiers with an ax.

"Open the gates," Tandir shouted, cleaned the blood from himself, and rushed to the steps.

"What? Are you, mad?" Langven protested.

"Perhaps, but I won't have the glory of this victory left entirely to an army of rocks," he answered. "I'll head out there and help them kill every last one of the shits. I have no idea how long this spell on the statues will last and I won't waste one second of it."

He was interrupted when a massive cloud of dust kicked up from the valley below, enveloped the siege engines quickly, and put an end to their barrage immediately. Tandir realized that the engines were falling into the earth, and more of the statues erupted from the holes that developed to show that others were coming from under the ground.

One of the figures below was not a statue. It was a woman with golden hair who carried a spear and used it to fell the engineers and soldiers as they crossed her path.

"Well, that decides it," Bandir stated. "Cassandra is down there and we'll be damned if we let her fight alone."

"She does have an army of statues alongside her," Karvahal pointed out but he motioned for the gates to be opened.

"Do you honestly trust her safety to a pile of rocks?" Tandir shook his head. "For shame. For shame."

"Fuck yourselves. Open the gates and take the fight to them, but enough men will be left behind to hold the wall as well."

He didn't much care about that. Maybe Langven and his pack would stick to the walls just in case they still needed to be defended, but the twins hurried to where the fighting had begun to heat up. The gates were pulled open and they were surprised when the commander of the Ebon Pack joined them, as well as a dozen or so others who hadn't had their fill of the fight yet.

The forces led by Cassandra were still on the move. They destroyed the enemy encampment and killed all those who remained within before they turned their attention to the troops who were retreating.

It was difficult to tell which was the hammer and which was the anvil, but Tandir couldn't have cared less. The rage he had felt before was replaced by something a little more manic, and both he and his brother laughed as they rushed into the battle and joined the statues to attack the rest of the army.

Grimm's soldiers still left pockets of resistance behind but these did little else other than slow the statues somewhat while the main force tried to escape—although perhaps they hadn't seen those coming to attack them from behind.

His army was in disarray, torn between the necessity to fight and a desire to stay away from the statues that were almost impossible to destroy.

There was nothing to stop them, not with the engines disabled and buried in the caved-in earth they had left behind.

"Five silvers I kill more of them than you do by the end!"

Bandir shouted over the sounds of battle and dragged a man's helm off before he cleaved his head in two with his ax.

"I'll look forward to you paying me, then!" Tandir shouted and hammered his mace into the chest of another. She staggered back, spitting blood.

This was certainly a good way to spend the rest of the day, he had to say.

CHAPTER NINETEEN

This was madness.

Complete, utter, and absolute madness. The North was his. His forces were consolidating what had been conquered, which allowed him to press forward with those he trusted and knew would not only perform the task he wanted them to but do it well. They had been with him the longest.

Now, however, something was happening that he never intended to see when he set about conquering his birthright. He doubted that all would be as easy as it had been when he started, but he had never imagined that he'd watch his troops be torn to pieces by this army of stone. He'd not seen the like before and it seemed impossible that the Barbarian Princess had such power. Why was she only calling on it now? Why hadn't it happened before?

Those were questions for later. At the moment, his army was being demolished. It would be remembered, of course, but there would be no mention of the army of stone men. Tales would be all about the plucky heroes who stood their ground against the demigod and his forces.

He had seen enough of the world's history books and the

bard's tales to know how history would remember this defeat.

"It is not a defeat." He hissed his outrage and stood from his throne as his forces were crushed with every second that he remained where he was. "Not yet! Not fucking yet!"

He gathered the power in him, took in the death and destruction all around him, and felt the darkness begin to seep through his body. There had been a time when he feared what the darkness could do if he could not control it within him. As it turned out, whatever the darkness was, it did not like how tainted his body had become and only rose when summoned because he always had something else to feed into it.

It lashed out at the world around him, sucked the light from the air, and attacked everything and anything in its path. Although a few of his men were in the way, it struck where the statues were at their thickest. It was their fault for not winning the battle when they had the upper hand.

The power attacked the statues but to his horror, the damage done was minimal. One or two were dismembered and a few others crumbled to pieces, but overall, their assault on his troops continued without so much as a pause.

"Fucking shits!"

The first of the statues reached him and his beast was ready for the attack. It lowered its head and lunged forward to shatter the first few with the horns that protruded from its skull. Powerful jaws clamped on a second and crushed it easily. His power was infused into it and allowed it to move forward to attack these new enemies and tear them to pieces. He lashed out as well and used the power contained in his staff.

Still, it was frustrating to see that whatever empowered these statues to action somehow helped them to absorb his power. Or perhaps it was because they were pure stone, not living creatures. He hated them and the fact that they had appeared in his moment of triumph.

The hatred and anger that coursed through his body only

added to the power he wielded and he let it seep through him and fill him with a righteous rage. Deep, disconcerting laughter rushed from his body. He had long since ceased trying to understand it and only knew that he reached for any powerful emotion he could and fed it to the flames of power he now had control over.

It would not be enough. Even if he managed to destroy these shits single-handedly, by the time he was finished, they were likely to have killed all his men and left him with an undefeated fortress and nothing to show for the time and effort he'd committed.

They had to retreat. These were his best and most experienced warriors and without them, he would have to see that the rest were properly trained and ready to fight in the coming invasion.

"Pull back!" he roared and pushed his beast forward to cut short the advance of those from the fortress.

His beast was covered in the kind of armor that would protect it against most damage from a battlefield and he had charged it into battle many times, although never at the front of a retreat. His men needed no convincing to obey, although they knew better than to make it a full rout.

He turned his mount and stopped those statues that came in from behind to strike at his troops, drawing their attention as he blasted at them with every ounce of power in him. Something about being on the front lines again was liberating and he relished the opportunity to dirty his hands with the blood of his enemies.

Although perhaps stone and dust were the words for it. It had been a long time since he had fought his own battles, although he still remembered the sheer rush that came from it as he watched the destruction, chaos, maiming, death, and destruction all around him. It was difficult to put the feelings into words, but they were the kind one could become addicted to.

But he could no longer indulge them. As his father was so fond of reminding him, he was a leader first, which meant he left the work to the minions and had to keep himself apart from it. This wasn't only because he needed to stay away from the dangers of the battlefield but because it was the kind of façade that should be projected to the people who served him.

In the end, he sometimes needed to be in the thick of it too and he was interested to discover the limits of what he was capable of. The madness was touching him and the worry was the danger that he would be lost to it. Still, his father always told him that the madness was merely his human body accepting the god half of it.

And what a glorious feeling it was. He tightened his grasp reflexively on his staff when his body surged with something new. It wasn't quite fear but it was the closest approximation, and he stared at the barbarian princess who stood across the field from him. The sun caught her eyes and the blade in her hand.

She wore the oddest armor, the likes of which he had never seen. He wasn't even sure if it could be called armor since it appeared to be only the undergarments, although made out of pure ring mail. With that said, magical power radiated from her that even he could feel, and she wore a protective amulet of some kind, which he assumed was why she had not been struck by his attacks thus far.

His gaze settled on the spear she carried. He had seen it before, almost like a dream or a warning that hung in his mind and made him wonder if there was something magical about it as well.

She stood coated by the blood of her enemies and in that moment, Grimm felt something he had not felt in a very long time—a very human fear that he thought had been purged from his body. He knew this was not the day that he would battle her.

Another time, perhaps. Once he knew what that fucking spear was and why it struck such fear in his chest. He gritted his teeth and turned his beast. His men were being slaughtered but the situation could still be rectified if he could escape the field of battle. This meant he would drive forward hard into the rest of the troop.

Thankfully, those from the keep had considerably fewer of the statues fighting on their side, although the humans who had them had been powerful fighters in their own right and had held the fortress until their stony reinforcements arrived.

He had a certain amount of respect for them. They were not demigods but simple humans who had stood their ground. They must surely have known that there was no way victory would be theirs but still, they fought.

Or maybe they hadn't known. Either way, true courage was required—the kind he had not felt in many years although he had earned his god-like nature. His father had many children over the centuries, and only he had stood firm to claim what was owed him by birth.

Two of the humans rushed toward him. They were clearly twins and wore light armor. One swung a mace and the other an ax, although both had bags on their back that they filled with javelins and they now threw them at him.

Not at him, he realized, but at his beast. These must be the barbarian twins the princess was known to travel with and since they were known as the DrakeHunter twins, perhaps that was why their interest lay in the creature that carried him. It was a drake of some kind, although twisted by the magic he'd infused into its body over almost ten years. Perhaps it was its own kind of creature by this point.

It didn't matter. He raised his staff with the intention to kill the twins before they could attack when something dug into his arm.

He looked down and narrowed his eyes at a dagger embedded in it. It startled him that he hadn't even seen the attack coming. He turned and looked into the eyes of a young woman with thick, curly black hair who wore a garb that made her look like a bard of some kind.

The poison on the blade was what hurt him so much. He had provided those assassins with a venom that would kill almost any creature on earth, although she had to be mad to think he would give her a weapon that was capable of killing him.

He was about to drag the dagger out—he intended to use it on her to see what kind of reaction her body would have when exposed to his blood—when his beast bucked and roared. Without warning, he was flung from its back and the throne fell with him.

"Sons of whores," he whispered, caught himself as he was about to hit the ground, and landed smoothly on his feet. He scowled when he realized that the twins had thrown two of their javelins into his beast. It was not enough to kill but it was enough to injure and make it buck its rider off.

The damn thing had been on dozens of battlefields, and this was when it decided it would be terrified. He shook his head and decided it was time to find something new to ride. It had been years since he'd used a horse, although the idea of riding a troll into battle had begun to appeal to him. Besides, the rocks trolls had in their skin would be better conductors for the magic he carried and would make them a more powerful conduit.

He drew the dagger from his arm and forced the venom out of the wound before he sealed it. The twins jerked forward and then away to avoid the strikes from the beast with the practiced, deft movements of those who had done this kind of thing before.

Maybe he would find a barbarian to ride into battle next. They were known to have the kind of stamina he needed, although there were no rocks or harder surfaces in their skin.

A little magic could fix that, however.

The assassin attacked with them again. She found a spear that had been discarded by one of his men and thrust it hard between the armor plates of the beast. It uttered a thunderous roar as it twisted and tried to catch her first with its tail and then with its teeth. She was a shifty character, however, and immediately leapt out of the way as two more javelins dug into its skin.

The twins appeared to know what they were doing, and each of their strikes was unerring. They slowed his creature and limited its movements under the armor, which forced it to move more and tire itself in its efforts to catch any of the three who attacked it.

None of its strikes landed and before too long, Grimm scowled as the creature moved even more sluggishly and tried to snap its jaws around the skull of one of the barbarians. He jerked out of the way and his brother stepped in to drive his ax through the beast's neck, deep enough to cut into a blood vessel which immediately began to pour the creature's lifeblood. The liquid was purple and gleamed beautifully as it has been infused with his magic for so long that it showed in every facet of the beast's existence.

All he felt was disappointment. He'd thought he'd chosen his mount better.

"It still only counts as one, of course," one of them said as the other with the ax wrenched his weapon free. "We should split the glory for a creature like this."

"Three ways," the assassin shouted and drove her spear in again to make sure that the beast was dead. "The glory for killing the monster goes three ways."

"And it still doesn't make up for what you did."

Grimm could only assume that they held her attempt on the princess' life against her, although the reason why she had given up on that particular task did not occur to him.

"Aye," he shouted, took a step forward, and immediately drew their attention to the greatest threat on the field. "A great glory, to be sure. It is a pity, then, that you will not be able to own it."

The barbarians hefted their weapons and scowled. They looked like they intended to fight him and he couldn't help but feel a swell of respect for the poor devils. Surely they must know that they would not stand a single chance, yet they stood their ground, ready for a fight. He wanted men like them in his military one day. Perhaps his next task would be to unite the barbarian clans by force, make them join his army, and show the world their might under his rule.

There would be time for that later, of course. He raised his staff again and an inkling of fear touched their eyes, although to their credit, they remained steadfast. Or perhaps they didn't understand the danger they were in. They had no way to know that he was royally angry and would take absolute pleasure in flaying the skin from their bodies before he forced them to wander into the wilderness to cook in the sun.

"What?" He growled in annoyance and looked at his shoulder. An arrow protruded from it. How had it hit him?

As Grimm turned, he felt the impact of a handful more arrows and they forced him to take a step back. These were not coated by his venom and so did not hurt as much, but it was still a nuisance and broke his concentration each time.

"If you fucks don't mind..." He hissed when the arrows burned out of his skin, "I'll get around to the rest of you in a minute."

He supposed he should have been a little angrier that they were ruining his robes. They were some of his favorites. Or perhaps he was so unbelievably enraged that it had all come full circle and he was in complete control again.

The arrows continued and as he raised a shield to block them, three came through anyway and punched him in the chest again, and another flitted close to trace a light scrape across his cheek.

"Would you stop that?" he roared and lashed his power out at them. A few were caught in it but the rest was absorbed by the statues. They crumbled but it took far too much power to do it. That did not help as his anger rushed to the surface again and he launched another attack at the archers, who realized they could take cover behind their statue comrades and darted in and out of sight to fire their arrows.

It was infuriating. They were like a pack of wolves nipping at the heels of an elk that tried to escape and never quite committed to any injuries that would kill him. The fact was that they were pestering and annoying him and kept him too busy to escape.

As a tactical decision went, it was wise but he hated them for it all the same. Arrows penetrated his shields and struck him, and he had a difficult time retaliating since they came at him from all sides. The rage in his body built like a flame and he took hold of that image, closed his eyes, and dropped his shields for a moment. The accumulated fire left his mind and fought for release into the world around him.

The heat and the pain of it arced through his body and he couldn't help a manic grin as he embraced the agony and let it fuel his flames even more. He continued to direct the blaze to his enemies until the arrows ceased and he looked around. Dozens of the statues were shattered and five or six bodies were still burning.

But she remained unscathed.

The princess was in front of him and advanced slowly and carefully, although she didn't display the same care as her comrades. In fairness, the statues they had used to protect themselves were mostly gone, although others would join the battle soon.

"I'll admit that I never thought you would come this far," Grimm told her coldly and held his staff a little tighter. "Congratulations are owed. You have enraged me beyond anything I have ever felt or likely ever will after this. I will look back on this day and know that you were the last nuisance that would ever have the chance to anger me."

The woman shrugged, her demeanor calm and purposeful. "I have that effect on people. Especially those like you."

"There are no people like me."

"You would be surprised. There are many entitled pricks who need to take their self-loathing out on the world."

He grinned and gritted his teeth as he took control of his power again. It was like reining a wild horse in and would take constant work and dedication. The moment he lost his focus, it would all crumble. But as he maintained control, he felt his confidence grow. The vision be damned. He would see this princess dead and destroy the rest of her army himself.

Let the bards sing of that.

He lashed out and sent a tongue of flame out to catch her, but she was quicker than he gave her credit for. She dove forward, rolled under the attack, and thrust her spear at him while still in a kneeling position.

Grimm lowered his scepter to block it and as they made impact, a bright flash and a flurry of sparks forced them both back a few steps.

She was not deterred, however, and feinted to the right. As another tongue of flame whipped out at her, she stepped forward, spun on her back foot, and swung her damned spear in an arc that could have severed his head cleanly if he hadn't ducked under it. He fed the darkness in his body and let it join the fire's next attempt to catch her.

This time, she had to dive over a pile of rocks to escape and he felt the manic cackle rise within him again.

The princess regained her feet quickly and showed her speed again as she attacked, thrust the spear toward his stomach, and whipped it around to force him back. She was an impressive fighter and he almost felt bad that he had to relieve the world of such skill.

Perhaps like the twins, there were others like her he could tap for their abilities. He looked around and noticed that the army had come to a halt. They watched the two combatants like they weren't sure if they would be a help or a hindrance if they decided to join her.

Which meant his army was dead or gone by now. It truly was a pity as it would take him years to elevate the rest of his troops to the same standard. Or maybe not if they joined him in battle more often than the others had done.

There would be enough time for them to learn. He lifted his scepter and smiled when the gemstone at the tip began to glow as he lashed his power at her again. If they wanted to watch him kill their beloved princess, it would be a spectacle to remember. A defeat to remember. If there were any survivors, all they would speak of was how terrible it was to anger him.

Blasts kicked the earth up as she jumped away to avoid his attacks. She moved fast but was still mostly on the defensive. There was no need to finish her quickly, however. Let them all see what a mistake they had made. Once she was dead, he would deal with the others at his leisure.

She twisted to the left and lifted her spear and the last blast, aimed at her chest, was pushed to the side when it impacted with the weapon.

The damn spear had thwarted him again. He scowled while his scepter heated in his hand and noticed that she looked as surprised as he had been. With a low growl, he directed another attack at her. No matter what she tried to defend herself with, he intended to kill her. The time for games was over.

He'd no sooner made the decision when she suddenly spun, stopped her retreat, and readied herself to attack him.

That was not how it was supposed to go. He lashed out with another attack, this time to punish her by taking her head off.

The spear spun and deflected the blast into the dirt without her so much as missing a step. Another attack was similarly dealt with and Grimm took a step back when her weapon arced toward him.

He brought his scepter up to stop it and flinched when another flash blinded him and the sparks stung his face.

Pain seized him and he froze. It was odd how such a human

response felt so unfamiliar. It had been so long since he'd felt something like it although it had once been what his existence revolved around. Breathing was difficult and something was happening in his body that made him want to fall and curl into himself.

Grimm looked down. She had feinted with her spear again and driven it deep into his stomach. The pain almost overwhelmed him. He groaned softly and tried to lean on the scepter.

It did not help.

"Gods..." He gasped and stared at the spear. Anything else he intended to say was cut off as he coughed and tasted blood in his mouth.

She stared at him as he dropped to his knees, the weapon still buried in his abdomen. He had been told that shock was supposed to take the pain away, but it didn't. It was worse, somehow.

The princess said nothing as she twisted the spear and drew another groan of agony from him when she yanked it out.

It felt like his body had suddenly voided itself and he stared as his innards slipped out through the gaping hole she'd left. Pain wracked him, so intense that he couldn't put it into words.

All he could do was watch from his knees as she took a step back and lifted her weapon again. The scepter was still in his hands and the power was in his fingertips. If he could only raise it to stop the attack.

She flinched as another shock traveled up the spear when her weapon struck the crown on his head to split it and the skull behind it. The light in his eyes suddenly went out, quickly followed by that in his scepter as he toppled with a soft thud.

It felt almost anti-climactic—like she had expected more from this man who so many feared and adored.

Her people cheered, and Cassandra approached the fallen body, pried the broken crown from his ruined head, and lifted it, bloodied and all, for those of his army still alive to see.

There weren't many, but like the rest of the defenders and even the statues, they had stopped to watch her battle him.

"Your king is dead!" she roared and hurled the crown toward them. "Leave these lands or join him in the afterlife."

That seemed like enough of a threat and they rushed away. Less than fifty of the two or three thousand were left, and when they reached their camp where a few of the horses still remained, they gathered what they could and left immediately in the direction from which they had come.

The sun had begun to set and her body ached for rest. It had been a long day and as the heat of the battle raged, she had been able to push it aside.

She sat carefully on a nearby boulder after she'd made sure it was not one of the bodies turned to stone. Somehow, that felt like it would be disrespectful.

The whole troop began to celebrate their victory and the twins laughed as they approached her.

"You have a way of making the impossible happen," Tandir told her and inspected his mace. "I think we should stick close to your side, especially now that you have an army of living statues at your command."

She could see that a few of those statues stood nearby and watched her carefully. They expected her to go back on her word. The whispers said as much.

"I will not," Cassandra answered tiredly. "I promised them that they would be free to move on to whatever awaits them in the afterlife if they fought for us this one time. I have no intention of breaking that promise."

"There are likely to be more threats," Bandir reminded her. "Even with the shit dead, his army will be hungry and looking to get paid. They will start raiding soon."

"And we will find another way to defeat them," she answered immediately and turned to the nearest statue. "They've been trapped in stone, some of them for hundreds of years. It's about time they found peace."

"As you say."

She glared at the statue watching her. "Right then, how does this work? Is some kind of ritual needed to release you or something?"

The statue didn't answer but the light faded from its eyes almost immediately. The rest began to do the same. In moments, the whispers disappeared from her mind as well. Some thanked her and some sounded like they were weeping. It was difficult to tell what they said and it wasn't long before they all fell silent.

"That's that, then," Tandir muttered and sat beside her. "I didn't think we'd see this sunset but damned if it isn't the most impressive one I've ever laid eyes on."

"The ones we don't expect to see always are," Cassandra whispered and placed a hand on his shoulder. "We'll celebrate tonight. I'll see to it that the dwarves give these statues a proper burial tomorrow. It seems like the least we can do after they helped us."

"Aye." Bandir sat cross-legged on the ground and stared into the setting sun as well. "But that's for another time."

CHAPTER TWENTY

It took a few days to finally see the dead to proper burials. There was no reason to bury Grimm's forces, so they were treated the same as their king and the shared pyre joined them all in death.

Cassandra thought it was fitting. The kind of thing that Grimm never would have agreed to if he'd had any voice in the matter.

The statues were also buried with honor and that took a little longer to perform, even with most of the defenders to help. The grave had no name, but the headstone marked them as the honored dead and the saviors of Draug's Hill.

Again, it was fitting.

Cassandra smiled and traced her fingers over the work. Sifeas would make a comment about how it wasn't real dwarf work, but it was impressive in its own way and a monument to what happened. It would also be a warning to those who had been in Grimm's army to never return to these parts again.

They would, but she hoped not as an army.

"We're off then." She turned to where Langven stood behind her, his arms folded.

"I don't know how to thank you for all this," she replied. "Well,

I suppose the glory and reputation of having been a part of the force that drove Grimm the Cruel from these lands will see your profits grow tenfold before the moon is out again."

"There is that. And considerable loot besides. Those bastards who ran off didn't have the time to gather all their belongings before they slunk away with their tails between their legs."

He offered his hand to her but she approached him instead and wrapped her arms around him in a warm embrace. Although he seemed surprised by the gesture, he returned it after a few seconds and squeezed her gently before he pulled away.

The commander cleared his throat. "Right then. I'm off with my pack. If you're ever in Edge's Rest, feel free to drop in. I'm sure we will have a drink and reminisce about this before too long."

"We will."

She smiled and waved as he mounted and heeled his horse into a gallop so he could catch up with the rest of the Ebon Pack. Even those mercenaries who hadn't been a part of it before could now claim a place among them if they wanted to, and Cassandra couldn't think of a single good reason why they wouldn't.

A mercenary company with a real commander would have to work hard to turn the wrong way.

She realized that another figure approached. It was odd that she could see him coming as Cassandra was generally used to Theros springing himself on her without any warning.

This time, however, he walked slowly, followed by his trusty donkey, down the road to where she stood still examining the monument.

"Well, that was something to behold," Theros said as he came into earshot, "and there's no doubt about it. A barbarian princess could not ask for more excitement than you've enjoyed."

She shrugged. "It's odd, that. I seem to run head-first into dangers that most princesses can only dream about. I would imagine there is some godly influence involved."

"Thankfully, there is some godly influence to help you out of the trouble as well," Theros answered. He looked around and gestured at the earth and in a few moments, a boulder rose to provide him with a seat. It was weathered and covered with moss and looked like it had been there for ages.

The god groaned as he sat and looked and sounded suspiciously like he had arthritis in his knees. She would never understand why a being as powerful as he was would take on a form that had arthritis.

Theros studied the Pack as Langven rejoined them.

"I would not dare say that you have a type," he muttered and patted his donkey absently, "but I can say that I am beginning to see a pattern."

Cassandra narrowed her eyes and folded her arms. While she could not say she was happy to see him again, mixed feelings were involved. She wondered if there was something else he wanted her to do before she'd had real rest and time to recover from the battle. The god did not say anything else, however, and still watched the Pack as they started on their way to Edge's Rest.

"I guess I do owe you thanks," she said finally and watched the retreating horsemen as well. "I would have appreciated a warning about the fucking gorgon, but the direction proved invaluable."

"There was a better than good chance that you would have arrived at the same conclusion on your own," he answered with a soft chuckle and a wave of his hand. "Regardless, as much as you owe me your service to help those who need it, I owe you anything I can do to help you, aside from intervening outright."

She rolled her eyes. "Warping the world and all that. I don't suppose you'll ever explain what that means?"

"Honestly, I have no idea as to repercussions. Only that they are dire."

That didn't answer anything and all she could do was sigh.

"Still," Theros added, "I merely wanted to make sure you knew."

"Regardless, you do have my thanks."

"You did not have to release the stone army, you know," he said after a few moments of silence had passed. "I would even go so far as to say that they did not even expect you to release them. They were yours to command as you pleased. You could have forged a kingdom of your own and directed the world according to your designs if you wished it. You could even consider calling yourself the Barbarian Queen instead of princess."

Cassandra looked at the old man, her eyes narrowed. "If you have to ask me why I did what I did, you do not know me well at all."

He laughed again. "Well, I do appreciate your integrity. Bringing honor to the title of princess does not hurt either, although you will raise that particular bar well above what others will be able to reach. Even at your personal cost."

That sounded ominous—like a warning—and she could see that his features darkened a little and his grizzled and bushy eyebrows hung low over his eyes.

"If you have something to say, I would suggest that you say it. You might be immortal but I am bound by this life like any other human."

Theros glanced at her, snapped from his reverie. "There will be repercussions to Grimm's death. Killing him was the best thing for the world, but it might prove to be troublesome for you. The power he wielded was not natural to any human and even high elves would be burned by it after only a taste. I assumed all his talk of being the son of Karthelon was the kind of shite his kind tends to profess to gain the loyalty of their subjects, but I fear he might not have been lying about that. The fact that you managed to kill a true demigod in all his glory is more impressive than you know."

"Karthelon?" Cassandra shook her head. "I've never heard of him."

"He's not the kind who has many followers, at least not in

temples and the like. He's a vile bastard who has searched for a worthy heir for as long as I can remember and does not care where they come from as long as the woman who carried them is killed by the child they bore. The process he puts those children through twists them into beings that suit his purposes better, although I've…that's all I've heard of him."

Cassandra scratched at her chin. "And now I've killed the son who survived whatever gauntlet of horrors he's perfected over hundreds of years."

"Indeed. And he will feel a strong desire to punish you for the death of his son. I doubt it would be over any familial bond he might feel toward Grimm but rather because you managed to thwart whatever plans he might have had for the boy. In the end, it won't matter. You'll need to be careful and never be afraid to ask for a helping hand. The wrath of a god is nothing to scoff at."

"Are you talking about yours or his?"

Theros smiled and pushed from his seat. "I guess we'll have to see about that. Until then, Barbarian Princess, I will continue to follow your ever-progressing career with great interest."

She watched him as he wandered to the road again and followed the pack although at a much slower pace. There was much about how the god chose to present himself that she didn't understand, and perhaps she was in no position to ask questions either.

She shrugged, drew a deep breath, and smiled as in the blink of an eye, the old man and his donkey were nowhere to be seen.

It was odd for a shade to enjoy the sunlight. Perhaps he merely missed how it warmed his face. The promise was that one day, he would feel it again. One day soon, he would know what it was to feel the elements on his cheek again.

Of course, he would need a cheek for that and a body to

attach it to. Yes, he could take on a physical form and even take over the bodies of others and feel everything through them, but it wasn't the same.

His eyes were closed and he imagined what it would feel like as he pushed the dark thoughts to the side for a while. In this moment, all he wanted was for his mind to be silent so he could simply enjoy it.

Something touched him.

He opened his eyes again and he looked up to where a cloud had begun to obscure his view of the sun. Of course, if he had a body of his own, he wouldn't be able to look at the orb like this without risking going blind, but it was worth it for the few moments of peace.

These were inevitably interrupted. Karthelon reached toward the face—or what passed for one in the form the shade was in— and brought what had touched him up to his view.

The sunlight glowed directly through his fingers and allowed him to inspect the speck of ash that had fallen on him. He realized that more were falling like an unseasonal snowfall, but it was localized to the highest tower on Grimm's fortress. It was as if it was seeking him out for some reason.

And there was only one reason for it to act that way. Although he knew what he was touching in that moment, it was necessary to confirm it. He was called obsessive by some but ensuring that everything he did was correct down to the last detail was the only reason he was still alive.

Or whatever a shade was. His eyes closed again and his fingers trapped the speck inside his palm to crush it more than any human hand would be able to before he breathed it in slowly.

He knew whose ashes they were but confirmation brought something he hadn't felt in a long time. A terrible rage swelled in the pit of his consciousness like a storm that made the sea roil, consume all in its path, and spit out naught but driftwood and the occasional body.

There would be more than the occasional body in this case. Karthelon gritted his teeth and tried to contain himself. In this state, he could level the fortress, and while it would feel excellent for a moment, it would put his work of centuries to waste.

Fortunately, he was better than that. He repeated those words continually in a gentle, hypnotic trance that finally brought the fury under his control. Rage was a useful tool for those who knew how to use it properly. In the white-hot form it tended to take, it would burn all in its path and while that did have some uses, the deadliest form it could take was the deepest, darkest ice of the tallest mountain.

This was the kind of lesson that so many of his children ignored until it killed them. Only one had truly listened and had understood his words when he spoke to them to show the wisdom of a god as well as the power. Yes, he did have his human moments, but that was because it was half of him.

Now, all that was left was ash carried by the wind to his father.

The sun was gone. In its place, clouds thickened overhead and arcs of incandescent lightning flickered across them, immediately followed by the ominous boom of thunder. It welled but remained contained like him.

His son was dead. He needed to find out how it had happened and why.

Again, he knew already, but confirmation was required. His hand caught another fleck of ash and he crushed it again and inhaled it slowly. He let the shade tell him all he needed to know about it while his mind was unclouded by the need to seek out those responsible and avenge his son's death.

Karthelon felt the burning power of another god in the action. He'd known that Grimm had gone to deal with the famed Barbarian Princess himself when his assassins and spies had failed to do so. He'd suggested it himself. Revealing to the world what he was capable of was the first step to establishing his place.

And yet all had gone wrong. A blade of power had cut Grimm down, ended his life in pain and suffering, and doomed him to endure the same in the afterlife. As close as he had been to success, he was still a failure like so many others before him and would meet the same fate as the rest.

But the time had come for Theros to stop interfering in his machinations. The lord high gods had ordered things their way for too long and it would end by his hand.

He released the speck of ash and let it drift to the ground. The shade moved and left a gentle wind in his wake as he traveled over the exposed tower and down the steps to where the guards were waiting for him.

With a flicker of his hand, he motioned for them to follow him down the winding steps of the tower and into the bowels of the fortress. His destination was far from the sunlight he craved so.

That would have to wait. For now, there was work to be done.

The Silent Ones followed him into the throne room, empty now as it would be until a worthy heir presented himself again.

"Your king is dead," the shadow hissed to the soldiers who stood guard over his throne. "He failed in his quest and will suffer dearly for it."

The Silent Ones turned to him and their eyes asked the questions they could no longer give voice to themselves.

"Another will rise in his place, never fear." The shade raised a hand to assuage their fears. "But until then, there is work to do. No longer can we allow this woman to continue to disrupt my plans. No, we must dispose of Theros' little whore once and for all."

The eyes continued to watch and ask questions. Maybe they didn't believe him when he said Grimm was dead. No matter. In the absence of a king, his shade would take power until another rose. There were a few candidates and some showed promise, but they were still in the early stages of proving themselves.

He turned his back on them, approached the empty throne, and considered the glittering souls who filled the amethysts around it. There was work to be done. The shade fell back into its position next to the throne and Karthelon left his form there for the moment. He needed to see what had happened himself. The shade could not wander far from the fortress, not while its power grounded it in this realm, but in the others, he could travel and find the others who told him what truly happened, how his son failed, and how this little bitch managed to succeed in killing a demigod.

The rage chilled him, a pleasant feeling. The bitch was not to be underestimated, but he was patient. He would find her weakness and everything that there was to know about her, and when the time was right, he would destroy her. Everything that had stood in defiance to Grimm would be gone, he decided.

It was the only way. With the lord high gods still holding their positions jealously, paths would need to be cleared and openings found.

Karthelon was patient. The rage burned cold in his heart as he looked over Draug's Hill and watched the brilliance of Theros disappear. The bastard had likely come to congratulate his champion on a battle well-fought.

And from what he could see, it was. The bitch was resourceful, a proven fighter who found unconventional means to win a battle that was Grimm's to lose.

His consciousness draped down and flitted like the wind. A gorgon…interesting. An army of the dead had been brought up. Of course, when a necromancer did it, all hands were raised to stop them but when Theros did it, songs were sung and heroics spoken of.

There would be songs. So many songs. He knew it. Theros did so love to hear the names of his people praised. He thought he was humble, traipsing around the world in the form of a frail old man, but his ego needed to be continuously stroked through hearing of the deeds of those who fought in his name.

Ego would be the downfall of all the gods. It was only a matter of time before death claimed them all.

But the bitch would die first.

AUTHOR NOTES - MICHAEL ANDERLE
NOVEMBER 16TH, 2021

Thank you for not only reading this series but these author notes here in the back as well.

So these author notes will be a bit of a bi#ch session on packing a medium SUV to travel 25 hours.

As many of you know, some years ago, my wife and I started the process of purchasing a home down in Cabo San Lucas, Mexico, a process that ended with a closing a few weeks ago. Cabo is about a 25 hours drive (probably a 40 hour trip with stops and sleep etc.) from where we live in Las Vegas, Nevada.

This trip will be my first time driving across the border. I hope I don't screw up any laws.

The reason is that we need to move some of our stuff from this house to the house down in Cabo. While we tried to purchase local – not everything we want is down there.

One easy example is chili powder. Making chili isn't a thing down there, and apparently, neither are the type of towels my wife likes. I mistakenly figured that it would be a few towels, and we would be good.

I was so mistaken. *Oh Gawd, I was mistaken.*

I didn't think about the fact we have a pool and four showers inside the house. For those who (like me) can't do the math, it means we need approximately four god-zillion towels, hand towels and washcloths.

And of course, they need to be in a rainbow of colors matching the beautiful blues, teals and greens of the house.

I don't have a massive cargo box truck to haul the four god-zillion towels.

Clever me, I purchased those bags where you can suck the air out of the plastic bags, so things like towels get smaller as you pack them.

Idiot me bought the box of plastic bags complete with a *hand suction pump*. I think my arms are about to fall off now.

I'm looking at everything I must pack. I have about 97 cubic feet of stuff and 65 cubic feet of storage space.

I'm so screwed.

I hope you have a great rest of your week or weekend and look forward to chatting with you at the end of the next book!

Ad Aeternitatem,

Michael Anderle

CONNECT WITH THE AUTHOR

Connect with Michael Anderle

Website: http://lmbpn.com

Email List: http://lmbpn.com/email/

https://www.facebook.com/LMBPNPublishing

https://twitter.com/MichaelAnderle

https://www.instagram.com/lmbpn_publishing/

https://www.bookbub.com/authors/michael-anderle